Midnight Blue

LOVE IN COLOR SERIES

SUZIE WALTNER

Suzie Waltner
Ps 98:1

Anaiah Press
BOOKS THAT INSPIRE

ANAIAH FROM THE HEART
An imprint of Anaiah Press, LLC

Edited by Candee Pick
Cover design by Eden Plantz
Book design by Anaiah Press, LLC

For Tina Jackson. Your positive attitude, quiet strength, and bright smile encourage and inspire so many people. I am blessed to call you friend.

One

Where had that girl gotten off to?

Scarlett Sykes glanced through the bank of kitchen windows to her left in search of any sign of the eight-going-on-nine-year-old on the large deck or in the sprawling backyard.

When she and her cousin had returned through the butler's pantry after putting the food out in the formal dining room, the high-backed barstool Harmony had been sitting on while they worked was empty.

"She's not in here." Cassidy stood in the opening to the mudroom that ran between the garage and the kitchen.

"She's not outside either."

Laughter, the clinking of plates and glasses, snippets of conversations, and soft country music filtered from the party. Surely, the girl hadn't gone in there. No, while Harmony might wander—the temptation to snoop around a large, fancy home too tempting for a grade-schooler—she'd avoid the guests. Which left Scarlett with more than half the estate to search. *If* the girl had stayed inside.

"Harmony?" Scarlett whisper-shouted as she hurried past the sunshine-lit breakfast nook toward the hallway that ran behind the formal living room and opened into a family room with a large blue sectional. A quick glance to her right confirmed no one from the party noticed her as she entered the passageway lined with evenly spaced framed photos. "Where are you?"

A soft *woof* came from ahead, and she rushed past two closed doors toward the dog while straining her ears for any inkling of her daughter.

"Hi, pretty girl." Harmony's voice came from inside the next room.

Scarlett's heart rate slowed with her pace. The kid had scared her half to death with her disappearing act.

"Who did you find here, boy?"

The male voice stopped Scarlett's forward motion, bolting her to the floor four feet from the door. From her vantage point in the hall, she could see a wall lined with walnut shelves filled with books and trophies.

"You're Jake Turnquist!"

Harmony's excitement stole the breath from Scarlett's lungs. Of course her daughter would consider meeting the country music sensation the highlight of her year. Maybe even her entire young life. Despite her cousin's assurances they wouldn't cross paths with any of the band members, Scarlett second guessed her willingness to assist today.

Please no. Not now, Lord. He'll break her heart.

"I sure am, and this is Trigger," he said. "And who are you, young lady?"

A lump formed in Scarlett's throat. Could it be the same dog? The one who had walked right up to her and licked her fingers when Jake's mom took her to see the litter of puppies and asked which one she thought he'd like best for his sixteenth birthday?

"My name's Harmony. Harmony Sykes."

"Harmony, huh? A pretty name for a pretty girl." His smooth voice invited more conversation.

She rested a shoulder against the wall and listened. He'd always been easy to talk to, putting strangers at ease with a word or two.

"Do you like to sing?"

"Yeah, and I play guitar. My mom says I'm better than my daddy."

Oh, Harmony. How she wished she could give the girl what she deserved most.

"Does she now?" Amusement coated the question. He was probably used to young fans fawning over him. "And you have your own guitar?"

"It's old, but I want a new one for my birthday."

"And what else do you want for your birthday?"

"A puppy, a horse, and a da—"

Scarlett straightened from her position. "There you are, Harmony." She burst into the room and cut off Harmony's wish list just in time. How could she know the daddy she so desperately wanted stood in front of her?

Jake stood with his back to the door, one hand resting on the girl's head. A black lab with graying fur around his nose, muzzle, and above one eye stretched on the floor under a table-style desk with his head resting on his paws. A fist squeezed Scarlett's heart.

"Mom!" Harmony's bright, blue-eyed gaze landed on her. "Look who's here!"

The man spun to face her. The polite expression on his face morphed into wide-eyed and open-mouthed shock. "Scarlett?"

"Hi, Jake." She kept her tone flat despite the awareness zipping through her. The magazines and social media posts didn't do him justice. With his chocolate brown hair peeking out from beneath his trademark hat, studious gray eyes, and well-defined shoulders under his green and white plaid shirt, women of all ages crushed on the famous musician.

His gaze darted from her to Harmony and back. Would he say something? Finally acknowledge his child? *Please not here. If you hurt her, Jacob Turnquist, I'll strangle you myself.*

"Wow, it's been a while."

That was all he had to say after almost ten years of silence?

Her nails dug into her palms as she choked back a sarcastic retort and a long-overdue dressing down.

"There you are, Jakey." A brunette with big hair, a pound of makeup, and a figure-hugging shirt brushed Scarlett's shoulder as she squeezed into the study and sidled up to him. She grabbed his biceps like she was drowning and he was the life preserver.

Gritting her teeth, Scarlett held a hand out toward her daughter. "Let's go, Harmony. Mr. Turnquist's got a party to get back to." She hated the cattiness in her tone.

The girl chattered nonstop as Scarlett dragged her back to the kitchen where Cassidy washed dishes at the island's sink.

"I see you found our little wanderer." Cass winked at her niece and wiped her hands dry on the towel resting on the granite countertop beside her. "Did you find anything interesting?"

Harmony pounced on her. "Guess who I just talked to, Aunt Cass? Jake Turnquist! He's even cuter in person. And he has a dog!" Her red curls bounced with every word.

Cassidy's brown eyes lost some of the sparkle when she raised one eyebrow.

Scarlett gave an almost imperceptible nod. "Give me a minute?"

"Of course. Harmony and I have everything under control here."

The Tennessee spring sunshine warmed Scarlett as she walked to the back corner of the kitchen and slipped into the stone tiled mudroom. The back door they'd used to haul supplies from the car stood to her right and the garage door ahead of her. She turned left and walked past a large cabinet with a built-in bench and coat hooks before stepping into the bathroom.

Once inside with the door locked, she rested her hands on each side of the white pedestal sink and stared at herself in the mirror.

Seeing Jake Turnquist again beat at her emotions like a toddler with a toy drum. What was he thinking after finding her at his party? Did he wonder if she'd gone back on her promise? That she wanted something from him now?

She wanted nothing from the man who had broken her heart a decade ago.

~

To give himself a few more seconds of peace before returning to the center of attention, Jake shook his date loose and led Trigger to the large round dog bed behind the desk while wishing those too-short minutes with Scarlett had stretched longer. He'd needed a break from the crowd invading his house but hadn't expected to find a little girl hunched beside his dog. The animal, a big softy when it came to anyone willing to pet him, had laid on his side and soaked up the attention from the child who was probably thirty pounds lighter than him.

When he stood, the newest groupie—what was her name again? Right. Daphne—gripped his arm again, her long fingernails digging into his skin.

"Come on." She tugged at him. "Everyone's waiting for you."

She continued to cling to him as he closed the door to the office and headed back to the party. Her heels clicked on the hardwood with every miniscule step while his mind remained on Scarlett. She'd grown from cute to pretty over the years—filled out in all the right places while retaining her athletic build. Her blue eyes still the most hauntingly beautiful he'd seen on a person. Her red hair with blonde highlights, now styled at the bottom of her shoulder blades instead of down to her waist as she'd worn it in her youth, suited her as a mother.

Scarlett Sykes. The only woman who'd ever held his heart. Judging from the age of her daughter—a tiny version of Scarlett with her blue eyes, red hair, and a smile that lit up the room—she'd gotten over him soon after high school. The girl mentioned a dad, but also said her last name was Sykes. Had Scarlett kept her maiden name?

They reached the opening end of the hallway, and a brunette with short hair caught his attention as she worked at the far counter in the kitchen. She turned her head toward the door to the pantry. "Yes, right there is fine."

Before he could get a better view of the woman's face, Daphne dragged him past the floating staircase in the foyer. Someone had opened the frosted-paned double doors to the right where a table laden with food awaited. He turned left into the formal living room where some of the thirtyish invited industry and media folks squished onto the matching cream couch, love seat, and armchair arranged in front of the extra-wide stone fireplace. Others clustered next to the white built-in double bookcases on either side.

"Ladies and gentlemen, the man of the hour." The band's manager, Cameron Becker, or Becker as he preferred, held court in the center of the crowd. He smoothed his tie with one hand while extending his other. "Jake Turnquist."

Applause filled the room as Jake touched two fingers to the brim of his favorite black cowboy hat, wanting nothing more than for the crowd to disappear so he could climb those stairs behind him and spend the afternoon in the music room.

He extricated his arm from Daphne's clutches. "Thank you. I'm thrilled 'Favored' made it to number one this week. After three records, we're blessed the fans keep listening to us." He forced a smile as he surveyed the mixture of his band members in jeans and boots alongside the media and industry execs garbed in an array of slacks, dress shirts, and floral print dresses. "Thank you all for coming to celebrate with us this beautiful May afternoon. Please, get some food if you haven't already."

As the applause faded to the hum of conversation, he scanned the room in search of anyone with red hair with golden highlights and a white shirt. Why was Scarlett here? Had she come with someone? Was she visiting family or back for good?

"Great job as always." The sunlight shone off Becker's bald head as he approached and hooked an arm around Jake's neck. He turned to Daphne, who hadn't left Jake's side. "Will you excuse us a minute?" Once the woman with the big curls and a too-tight bedazzled pink top stepped away and intercepted another band member, Becker tightened his hold. "Now you can concentrate on the last leg of the tour, then the next album. You're working on the new stuff, right?"

"Sure." His life had become a whirlwind he couldn't escape. Weeks spent on the road, trying to remember what time zone he was in, not a moment to himself between his bandmates, fans, and the media. How was he supposed to write with all the noise surrounding him?

Jake eyed the crowd now gathered around the rectangular walnut dining table as they loaded clear plastic plates and caught sight of designer jeans and long, sleek blonde hair. "Excuse me, Becker. I need to talk to Andi." He made his escape and eased in beside his lead backup vocalist and bass player.

"Have you seen a woman with reddish blonde hair and a little girl who looks like her around here?"

Her perfectly shaped eyebrows lifted as she inclined her head. "Hello to you, too. I'm enjoying the party. Thank you for asking." She picked up a stuffed mushroom, took a small bite, and moaned in appreciation. "This is amazing. Who did Becker hire for food today?"

"I have no idea."

"Really, Jake? You're okay with not knowing anything about the help that comes into your home?"

He shrugged. "I trust Becker." A glint of irritation flashed in her aquamarine eyes, but before she could expound, he pressed on. "Sorry, Andi. The woman? It's important."

"There are a few redheads here, but no children. What's she wearing?"

"White blouse and black slacks." Which emphasized her feminine curves.

"Sounds like the caterer." Andi pursed her lips. "But she's got

7

brown hair. I can go check and see if she's got someone else with her."

Jake frowned. The woman he'd seen in the kitchen fit that description. Was Scarlett working with her? Why would she bring a child with her, though? "I'd appreciate it."

"Want me to pass along a message if I find her?"

"Um." What excuse could he give? One that didn't pique Andi's curiosity. "Nah, just let me know where she is."

With a wink, Andi edged around the table and made her way to the kitchen via the walk-through butler's pantry, stopping to talk to a few guests along the way.

Jake could count on his bandmates having his back. While Andi, Levi, Seth, and he had been friends since grade school, they'd played together for twelve years now. Mia had occasionally joined them while she finished high school, then became a permanent member of the band. Through lean times as well as success, they'd made a pact to stick together. And Jake planned to honor that, despite Becker's repeated attempts to convince him otherwise.

As if reading Jake's thoughts, the man left the group of record label execs visiting in the foyer and jumped back into manager mode. "You've got until the end of June here in Tennessee before you're back on the road. Use these six weeks to work on the new album, and don't get distracted."

The muscle in Jake's jaw twitched as he ground his molars together. "Got it." He trusted the guy, but why did Becker insist on micromanaging every area of his life?

"Excellent. Now, go mingle." He nudged Jake toward a group of people getting drinks at the buffet console along the far wall.

As Jake answered their questions about the upcoming tour and the future album, he kept one eye on the door.

When he caught up with two more bandmates at the bottom of the stairs in the foyer, Mia tilted her head to one side, and the teal tips of her ebony hair brushed her shoulder as she studied him. "Who's got you so distracted tonight?" She bumped his shoulder and inclined her head at two women seated on the couch facing them. "Your arranged date or her eye-fluttering friend?"

"He's preferential to blondes." Levi folded his arms in front of his chest.

Jake winced at becoming the center of speculation along with the memories of his last girlfriend and her obsession with social media fame.

Andi returned, and he turned toward her. "What'd you find out?"

"Kitchen." She smirked with a knowing look in her eye.

"I wanted to surprise you." His brain worked double-time to formulate an excuse to visit.

"She's with the caterer Becker hired, who *also* happens to be someone we all know." Andi crossed her arms.

"Really? Who?"

"Her bossy cousin." One of her eyebrows rose.

Of course Cassidy wouldn't be far from Scarlett's side. What would Seth think of this turn of events? Jake scanned the room until he found his friend engaged in conversation with their producer and one of the marketing assistants from the record label. Now, how could Jake slip away from the party without drawing Becker's attention?

Andi jerked a thumb over her shoulder. "Go. We'll cover for you."

Mia smiled at the comment. "Especially if it means we can mess with Cameron." She refused to call the man Becker no matter how many times their manager corrected her.

He pressed his palms together in front of his chest and mouthed a thank you before making his escape.

Two

"What are you doing?" Scarlett dropped the biscuits for dessert on a tray. The knocking of cabinet doors accompanied her as her cousin opened and closed them along the wall behind her.

"I'm in love." Cassidy moved to the refrigerator on Scarlett's left and opened the double doors.

From her stool-top perch on the other side of the island, Harmony giggled. Scarlett slid the biscuits into the oven and shook her head at her cousin's antics while silently agreeing. She missed living in the country with wide open spaces all around. While she could never afford a home like this in Franklin, she'd be satisfied with a small cottage on a few acres away from the busyness of the city.

Cass shut the stainless steel refrigerator doors and slid open the freezer drawer at the bottom before moving to the corner where she peeked into the front entryway. "Too bad the guests are out there. I'd love to take those stairs and sneak a peek at the rest of the house. What do you think the master bath looks like?"

"I can give you a tour."

Scarlett stiffened and glanced at Cassidy, whose eyes were as large as hers must be. Heat warmed her cheeks as she lifted her gaze above Harmony's head to collide with Jake's.

"Hey, Cass." However, his gray eyes remained on her. "Been a while."

"How do you know her name?" Confusion filled Harmony's voice, drawing Scarlett's attention as the girl spun around toward the man she had not yet stopped gushing over.

"Your mom, Cassidy, and I grew up together." Jake took another step forward. "We were friends."

It was impossible not to compare the father and daughter in front of her. Their snub noses with the slightest upturn at the tip, square chins, even the set to their shoulders proclaimed the legitimacy of Harmony's parentage.

Scarlett attempted to pull moisture into her mouth. She'd follow Jake's lead and pretend she didn't have any kind of connection with him, but Harmony would interrogate them for the next hour about their former friendship with Jake if she didn't put a stop to this conversation. "A long time ago. Before he got too famous for us little people."

He reared back as if she'd slapped him.

Cassidy moved beside her. "Did you need something, Jake? We've got work to do, and I doubt the owners of this place would appreciate you showing their home to the help, even if you are the star of the show."

"He won't mind." Jake pulled out the stool next to Harmony's and settled onto it. "Trigger would love someone to play with him outside."

Fighting the urge to yank her daughter behind her and out of Jake's reach, Scarlett rested her hands on her hips. "Harmony will stay in the house and do her math worksheets and finish her science picture."

"Mom—"

She pointed to the abandoned backpack on the island. "Remember our deal? You promised to do your work if I got you out of school early."

Yes, she'd bribed her daughter with the promise of a new book, but it was the easiest way to keep her from wandering off. Something she'd already done once. "You shot a hole in our bargain as it is. Do you really want to make it worse?"

"Another time then." Jake shrugged his broad shoulders. "Trigger and I like to hang out here whenever I'm in town."

Why had Jake brought his dog to a party? And who would let him shut the animal up in their home?

"Didn't I read somewhere you're heading out for the second half of your tour soon?" Cassidy pulled a platter from the fridge and shoved the pinwheels into Scarlett's hands, then pointed toward the dining room before returning for a bowl of fruit. "Hold that thought. We really are working and need to put the last of this out before finishing up dessert."

Bless Cassidy. Scarlett could hug her cousin, but with her hands full, she instead turned toward the dining room, then paused. "Harmony, why don't you come with me?"

"Aw, Mom. I wanna talk to Jake."

She lifted an eyebrow at the familiar address.

"I mean Mr. Turnquist." The girl corrected herself.

"Go ahead." Jake pulled out the stool beside Harmony and sat as if he had all the time in the world and this crowd wasn't here for him. "I've got this."

What in the world was the man doing? Now, after not acknowledging her existence for years, he wanted to spend time with his daughter?

"We'll be back in a hot minute." Cassidy nudged her forward. "If you want to make yourself useful, you can pull the biscuits from the oven if the timer goes off." The moment the two women stepped inside the walk-through butler's pantry, she rested her free hand on the back of Scarlett's shoulder and lowered her voice. "You doing okay?"

No. Not at all. Seeing Jake again after all these years had shaken her. After what he'd done to her and their daughter, she thought she was over him. Indifferent at least. Despite Harmony's infatuation with the country musician, Scarlett had fought to forget the boy she once loved.

"Scarlett?" Lines creased her cousin's forehead.

"Sorry. Yeah, I'm fine. Let's set these out and get back. I don't want Harmony bothering him with her incessant questions." And the sooner they could leave this beautiful house with its pristine furnishings and glamorous people, the better. She didn't belong to this world like Jake now did.

"I'm praying for you."

Cass was a prayer warrior, and the best kind of ally to have in her corner. Those prayers, along with family and friends, had carried her through worse times than this. Times when she questioned whether God cared. "I appreciate it."

They squeezed in between guests crowding the table, excusing themselves while replacing the depleted trays of food with fresh ones. As they returned to the kitchen, Harmony's voice reached them as she listed every song Jake had recorded over the past seven years. The situation could've been worse.

"At least she's not asking about how he knows us anymore." Cassidy echoed her thoughts.

"But for how long? I hope you're prepared for a cross-examination on the drive home."

"Want to hear the song my daddy wrote?"

Cassidy gasped, and Scarlett rushed through the entrance. "Harmony, why don't we let Jake go back to his party? He's not here to entertain us."

"No, you ladies are a pleasant distraction from all the schmoozing and shoulder rubbing." His eyes remained fixed on Harmony. "I'd love to hear your song."

"Okay." Harmony straightened and took a deep breath, ready to belt out the tune.

"You know what?" Cassidy squeezed Scarlett's elbow in solidarity. "I bet Jake would get a kick out of hearing you sing one of his songs. What about 'Midnight Blue'?"

"Oh, that's an excellent idea." Scarlett caught on, and despite the pain the song caused whenever she heard it, she welcomed it now. "That's your favorite."

Harmony's entire face brightened, and she stood. After another deep inhale, she sang. "Somewhere deep in the night lies the color that assures me everything's alright. As one day closes and another begins, my world is shaded through a colored lens." Her sweet voice always warmed Scarlett's mother's heart.

"From where I stand, there's no better view as I count the stars with you." As he sang along, his smoke-colored gaze darted to Scarlett before he focused on the girl beside him. "The days are short, the hours too few whenever I'm with my midnight blue."

Scarlett's chest squeezed. Him sitting here, singing with their daughter, was so much harder to bear than listening to Harmony sing along with the radio.

Before they finished, someone cleared his throat. She lifted her gaze to find a tall man in a suit with his arms crossed, looming behind the duo.

"Hey, Becker." Jake didn't turn around.

The man rubbed his bald head and scanned the room before his gaze rested on Jake. "Did you forget about your guests?"

Her head whipped back to Jake. Was this the same Becker he'd talked about when he broke things off with her? The potential manager who promised big things for the band? If so, the man still must have a lot of sway where Jake was concerned.

A sheepish smile filled his face. "Guilty."

"Wait. Is this your house?" Cassidy's voice raised an octave.

"Yep." Jake winked at her cousin, and Scarlett swallowed the envy threatening to make an appearance an instant before his attention returned to her. "If you ladies will excuse me, duty calls." As he stood to leave, he squeezed Harmony's shoulder. "Thank you for the song. Your momma's right. You have a beautiful voice."

The girl grabbed his hand and peered up at him. "Who'd you write it for?"

"Harmony Rayne Sykes!" The moment the girl's full name left her mouth, Scarlett wanted to reel them back in.

J ake paused and swallowed the bitter taste in his mouth. Anything to keep from looking at Scarlett. If singing the song he'd written with her in mind while she stood in the room hadn't already punched him in the gut, hearing her daughter's middle name knocked the wind clean out of him. She'd given her daughter their name. The one in the song he'd written when they were teenagers dreaming about their future.

He risked a peek at the now-bashful girl who had simply asked the question countless others had before. No matter how many reporters and fans had asked, he'd never revealed the inspiration behind 'Midnight Blue.' But surely, Scarlett had figured it out.

They had something special back in high school, something he'd not found since. Apparently, Scarlett didn't remember him in the same way. Not if she and Harmony's father had chosen *that* name.

"Come on, Jake." Becker's annoyance jerked him back to the present. "People have noticed your absence." He nodded at the women. "You can bring dessert out anytime, then start cleaning up."

Jake refused to glance Scarlett's way. The raw pain in his heart would reflect in his eyes. *Give it a break, Turnquist. She's moved on. Time for you to do the same.*

Becker clamped a hand on his shoulder and steered him from the room.

Before they reached the hallway, Jake spun around and focused on Cassidy. "If you stick around a while, I'll give you that tour."

When his manager's fingers pinched the nerves between his neck and shoulder, Jake ducked away.

"Didn't I just tell you no distractions?" Becker scowled. "And why are you slumming with the hired help?"

He didn't appreciate the guy's tone. "They're old friends."

"Old is right. The mother's got to be at least thirty-five."

Twenty-six. But he wouldn't get into it. This wasn't the place. Besides, the sooner he forgot about Scarlett Sykes, the better.

They returned to the front room, and once his polished black loafers landed on the gray-and-white rug, Becker raised his voice. "Why don't you play something new for us, Jake?"

Murmurs of agreement filled the room, punctuated with a squeal of excitement from Daphne, who had perched herself on the arm of the couch next to Andi.

His insides heated as he frowned at the other man. This wasn't the plan. He'd already told Becker he didn't have anything new. Was his manager trying to force Jake to deliver something to appease the label, or was this simply Becker's attempt to entice him away from the kitchen?

Jake's gaze landed on the tallest person in the room. Levi shrugged his wiry shoulders from where he stood in front of the far bookcase, and Jake inclined his head in acceptance. With the continued buzz around the room, Becker had put him in a position where compliance was his only choice.

"Want me to grab your guitar?" Seth approached from the foyer with a clear plastic glass filled with ice water.

"Yeah, that would be great. I'll grab a stool from the kitchen."

Becker scowled at the pronouncement. "You stay here. I'll get the stool."

He raised his voice to address everyone. "Give us a few minutes to get set up, folks."

As the guests returned to their conversations, Jake scoured his mind for something to play. One song hovered. A tune he'd written more than a decade ago when life was simpler. When he had only a dream of music and the love of a girl. Did he dare play it here, with Scarlett only two rooms away?

Becker plopped a black stool in front of him, drawing attention their way again.

"Just waiting on my guitar." He took a seat.

"Right here." Seth handed the acoustic over before setting the instrument's stand in the closest corner.

Jake strummed the opening chords before he lost himself in memories. His voice teetered on reverent as he sang the first song he'd written for Scarlett. The one with the same name she'd given her daughter. Rain.

A hush fell over the room as the final note faded. He opened his eyes to a mixture of teary smiles and awe. A couple people lowered their phones. The moment his fingers lifted from the strings, applause erupted.

"Will that be on your new album?" a giddy female voice near the back of the room called out.

"You bet it will." Becker moved from where he stood to Jake's right and stepped in front of him. "That ballad is a hit if I've ever heard one."

The unmistakable tone of victory in his manager's words and the straightening of his shoulders tightened an invisible vice around Jake's chest. He didn't want the song on the next album. Or any for that matter. If he had to sing it at every show, hear it over the radio, talk about it in interviews, he'd break. Someone would find out about his relationship with Scarlett. She had a life —a daughter—and he refused to involve them in that kind of a media circus.

Over the course of his rise to popularity, he'd been selective when giving details about his past, unwilling to leave any trail that would lead back to her. For years, he'd hidden his heart in his music, the fame, and the fans. And for every one of those years, he'd missed her more than anything else he'd left forty miles behind in Fiddler Creek.

Singing the song was a poor error in judgement. He should have refused, insisted he didn't have anything new. He cleared his throat and stood, edging in front of his manager. "We haven't decided what's going on the album. We're still in the creative process—writing and deciding what we like best." He nodded at the people crowded around the room with what he hoped was a reassuring smile before turning to glare his disgust at Becker.

Without another word, he stepped around the man and joined his best friend in the corner to his left.

Seth took the guitar and set it in the stand. "Why'd you play it now?" They'd been friends long enough that he knew the significance of the song and why Jake didn't want it out there.

"She's here."

One eyebrow arched to the center of his forehead. "Scarlett? Here, here? Like at your house?"

"Yeah. She and Cassidy are in the kitchen."

At that news, Seth's other eyebrow joined the first before his smile stretched wide enough to show the twin dimples that the ladies couldn't get enough of. "Cassidy Cagle? Scarlett's cousin?"

Jake chuckled. Some things never changed. "The one and only. Although, she may not still be Cagle. We didn't get that far."

A scowl crossed Seth's face for a split second before he shrugged it off. "I'm gonna go say hi."

"They're working, so don't keep them long." He rolled his eyes at how much he sounded like their manager. "And Scarlett's daughter is with them. She's a fan." *Unlike her mother.*

That news stopped Seth in his tracks. "A daughter? How old is she?"

"Seven maybe?" Jake hitched a shoulder. "Why?"

"Curious, I guess." He thumped a hand against Jake's back. "Didn't take her long to move on, huh?"

He winced at the forceful contact and resisted the temptation to mess up the guy's gelled-to-perfection spiked hair. "I did tell her I needed to focus on my career." *And that I didn't want a girlfriend to distract me.*

"True, and she moved away during winter break, right?"

"Yeah." Another reason he'd let her go. Jake glanced behind him when Daphne's nasally voice rose above everyone else's. A gentleman with salt and pepper hair and glasses intercepted her before she reached them. Becker stood in front of the couch, deep in conversation with a producer and two executives from the label. He turned back to Seth. "Come on. I'll re-introduce you."

As though he'd heard every word, Becker glanced up and waved him over.

Seth pounded him on the back again. "Becker beckons. I can handle myself with the ladies." He waggled his eyebrows, and those annoying dimples made a reappearance before he strode from the room.

That's exactly what I'm afraid of.

Three

"Well, if it's not the two prettiest girls this side of the Mississippi."

Scarlett rolled her eyes. Rush hour along the three interstates that met in the heart of Nashville had nothing on this kitchen. More surprises were the last thing she needed today—especially after hearing Jake sing *that* song while they'd cleared the dining room table and set out the individual strawberry shortcakes and mini loaves of chocolate zucchini bread.

Her insides were twisted so tight, they wouldn't unwind for days. Thank goodness Harmony was dawdling while cleaning up the strawberry syrup she'd spilled on her shirt when she ate her own dessert.

Scarlett swallowed a sigh as she packed an empty tray into the box on the counter beside the double oven before twisting around to greet their visitor. A grin lifted her lips at the sight of the man with spiked dirty blond hair and a chest almost as wide as Jake's standing on the other side of the island. A silver and gold belt buckle gleamed against his black T-shirt and dark-washed jeans.

"We're working." Cassidy continued scrubbing a pan at the sink without looking up.

Scarlett frowned at the back of her cousin's head before returning her attention to their new visitor. "Seth."

"Glad someone remembers me." His gaze circled the room before landing on the papers spread out on the counter in front of Cassidy. "I hear you've got a kid now."

If fate smiled on Scarlett, the girl would dillydally in the restroom a few more minutes. Long enough for them to get rid of Seth.

Her eyes narrowed. Jake used to tell his best friend everything, and no way had he been kept in the dark about Harmony. In fact, she suspected Seth had influenced Jake's decision to discard their daughter.

Right on cue, Harmony returned and lit up like a Christmas tree when she caught sight of the man who'd moved toward the back windows. "You're Seth Mason."

"The one and only." He cocked his head to the side and studied her with squinted eyes. "What's your name, little darlin'?"

"Harmony Sykes."

He arched a brow Scarlett's way before returning his attention to her daughter. "And how old are you, Harmony?"

Before she could answer, Cassidy, bless her heart, circled to the front of the island. The movement diverted him. "Seth Mason. What brings you to my kitchen?"

His gaze now locked on her. "Technically, it's Jake's kitchen."

"Jake Turnquist?" Harmony's squeal pierced the tension in the room.

Scarlett scooted beside her daughter. "You need to finish your math now that you're done coloring your plant picture. Why don't you sit at the table so you can concentrate?" She waved a hand to the adjacent breakfast nook with a view overlooking the deck and the backyard beyond it.

Procrastination was one of the less attractive traits Harmony had inherited from her dad. She picked up the girl's backpack as they passed the stool she'd occupied at the counter.

"Mom," she stage whispered. "We're in Jake Turnquist's

house. Olivia's never going to believe me. We have to take a picture to show her." And off she went, talking about Jake, her best friend, music, and anything else that came to her busy little mind as Scarlett set her up in a chair facing the French doors and away from the action behind her.

A few feet away, Seth and Cassidy spoke in murmured tones. While she couldn't make out what they said, Scarlett didn't miss her cousin's rigid stance. She owed Cass big time for sacrificing herself.

"Mom?" Harmony paused her running monologue. "Where do you think he keeps his horses? He has two. Athena and Hercules."

"I don't know, sweetie, but it doesn't matter." She glanced at her watch. "You have homework to finish." She flattened the three wrinkled pages on the table. "And I need to go."

Harmony frowned. "Are you working late again?"

It was Friday, so she'd most likely not finish her shift at the restaurant until after midnight. "Yes. You'll be in bed when I get home." She kissed the top of her daughter's head. "Be a good girl for Aunt Cass, okay?" Scarlett straightened and pointed at the book. "I know you only have a week of school left, but you need to finish your math worksheet before you read your book."

Once Harmony was settled at the table with a pencil in hand, Scarlett pulled her purse out of the girl's backpack and dug for her keys.

Seth stepped away from the powwow with Cassidy. "Don't let me run you off, Scar."

"It's Scarlett, and I have to get to work."

His eyes narrowed. "What kind of job doesn't start until four in the afternoon?"

She held his gaze, unblinking. Was he seriously asking her that? The guy who spent his evenings on stage in front of thousands of adoring fans? "The kind that's none of your business." She gave Cass a quick hug. "Take care of my baby and call if anything comes up."

"I will. Get going. You don't want Rachel giving your best customers to the other girls."

Scarlett glanced at Seth and almost laughed at the expression on his face. If his mouth fell open any further, it would hit the floor. She knew Cass phrased the statement to shut him up. Waiting tables wasn't glamorous, but the job paid the bills and provided for her and Harmony.

"Bye, Mom." Harmony shifted around in her chair and reached for a hug, wrapping her arms around Scarlett's neck when she bent over to return the gesture.

She inhaled the scent of girl, soap, and strawberries, wishing for the thousandth time she didn't have to work these late shifts. "I love you, Harmony."

"Love you, too."

"You're not leaving, are you?"

She spun around at the question. Jake's eyes held concern and something else she couldn't define. "Y-yeah." She hiked her purse strap onto her shoulder and stepped around him. "I do have to go."

"What about the tour?"

"Cass was the one who asked." As much as she'd like to check out the house, she did not want a reminder of how well Jake had done for himself. Especially now when she had to leave her daughter—again—to go to her measly job.

Jake watched Scarlett until she let herself out the back door via the mudroom and sighed. The opportunity to spend more time with her and get answers disappeared in a flash. He had managed to escape Becker again, and since he wasn't in a hurry to return to the party, he continued into the kitchen.

"Where's Scarlett off to in such a hurry?"

Seth and Cassidy stood glaring at each other beside the island. He shook his head. Some things never changed.

Scarlett's daughter, now seated at the table in the breakfast nook, slid some papers aside and pulled a book out of her backpack. "She had to go to work. Can I see your horses?"

At a shake of the head from Cassidy and a scowl from Seth, he stalled. "Maybe another time. Your mom said you had homework earlier. Did you finish it?"

"No." Harmony set the book aside and picked up her pencil before returning to the pages she'd just moved out of the way, grumbling about it not being fair.

"Can I talk to you a minute?" Seth took a couple steps toward him.

"Of course." Jake smiled at Cassidy. "Did you still want to see upstairs?"

"No, thanks. I should finish cleaning up and get Harmony home for the night. Raincheck?"

"Absolutely." He fished his phone from his pocket. "Give me your number, and we'll set it up."

She narrowed her eyes. "Not a chance, Jake. Why don't you give me yours instead?"

If he complied, the next move would be hers. He'd have no control over what happened next. "Can't." He waved his phone in her face. "Sorry, I don't give out my number. Too many crazed fans trying to get ahold of it."

"Yeah, 'cause I'd be calling you all hours of the night or every thirty seconds." She rolled her eyes and flicked a strand of hair from her forehead. "How about a compromise?"

It had always amazed him how different the two cousins were. "Night and day," Scarlett used to say. While Cassidy had short brown, almost black hair and sable eyes, Scarlett, with her red hair and deep blue eyes, was light and freshness.

They had opposite personalities as well. Cass was to-the-point and brutally honest. Scarlett hid her opinions behind a kind smile or buried her emotions. She was the thoughtful, quiet, sweet one while Cass was in-your-face, never-back-down tough. It was probably what made the two of them best friends. Jake wondered if any of the sweet teenage girl remained in Scarlett all these years later.

The clearing of a throat brought his attention back to the present, and he locked gazes with Scarlett's protective cousin.

"What kind of compromise?"

"How 'bout *you* hire me for your next party instead of your pompous manager, and I give you my business line?"

He grinned. "Perfect. I'm hosting a Memorial Day cookout. Are you available?"

"Sure. My calendar just opened up." Sarcasm laced her words. "You do realize other people hire my services, right? I'm booked for months."

"No, you're not, Aunt Cass." Harmony chimed in, and Jake could have hugged the girl. "You told Mom you don't have any parties next weekend."

Cassidy sighed. "Thwarted by a kid. A smart one, but a child, nonetheless. Guess I am available. What did you have in mind?"

"Barbecue. It's for the band." His mind raced as he put together an impromptu party. "Here at the house. We'll take the horses out afterward."

"Can I come?" Harmony wiggled in her chair. "I want to ride horses. Mom probably has to work again, Aunt Cass."

"Jake." Seth snapped his fingers with impatience.

"In a minute." He returned his attention to Cassidy. "Scar's working at the hospital?" She'd dreamed of becoming a nurse since she was twelve.

A slight twitch in Cassidy's cheek told Jake he'd guessed wrong. "No. She didn't go to college." Her eyes slid toward Harmony.

So she'd met someone soon after he dumped her, fallen in love, and had a daughter instead of chasing her dreams. He didn't want to admit to anyone, least of all himself, how painful that revelation was.

Seth stepped between him and Cassidy. "We need to talk," he said between clenched teeth. "Now."

"Okay." What was up with him? The guy was the most laid back of the group, but right now he was wound tighter than Becker during record contract negotiations. "Don't go anywhere, Cass. I'll come back to get your number."

He followed Seth to the study and closed the door before dropping into the black leather chair behind the desk. Trigger plodded over and rested his head on Jake's leg, awaiting attention. "What's wrong with you?"

"You need to forget about Scarlett." His friend paced the space between the two black wingback chairs with gold pinstripes. "She's not the same girl we knew as kids."

"Of course not. We're not the same people either." No matter how many times he wished he could turn back the clock and undo some of his choices, he'd changed. Become someone he wasn't sure he even liked.

Seth swiped a hand through the air in a slicing motion. "Look, I know you. Right now, you think her showing up here is some kind of sign. But you don't know anything about this version of Scarlett." He waved his hand at the door. "She has a kid, Jake. Probably a husband or boyfriend. At least the girl's father has to be in her life in some capacity."

Jake shifted in his seat and dug his fingers deeper into Trigger's fur. "We were friends. What's wrong with renewing that?"

"You were much more than friends." Seth's shoulders fell. "Look, it took you years to get over her. I don't want to watch you get entangled only to lose your heart again."

"That won't happen." Because he'd never taken his heart back from Scarlett Sykes. He endeavored to keep his expression neutral so Seth wouldn't read the truth.

When Seth opened his mouth to say more, Jake held up a palm. "Let me throw this cookout. I'll make it an all-day event. Just us, Cassidy, and Scarlett. If she comes, I'll talk to her about how I ended things. Apologize and make my case for renewing our friendship. Ask to meet Harmony's dad. If not, I'll give up. Deal?"

The concern in Seth's eyes said no, so his "okay" came as a surprise. "But don't say I didn't warn you."

"You sound like a woman." Jake chuckled. "Do me a favor and wrap up the celebration while I talk to Cassidy."

His lip curled in distaste. "Is Becker still here?"

"Last I checked."

"Jake, you need to fire the guy. He's making everyone miserable."

"He's also made us a lot of money and stuck with us since before we signed our first contract."

"*We've* made *him* the money, and he's smarter than to give up his gravy train."

"Can we discuss this later? I'm tired and just want my house back." One he'd only enjoyed a few weeks in the four years he'd owned the place.

"You're the boss." Seth saluted, opened the door, and pivoted to face him with warmth in his eyes. "You realize we'll support your decisions, right?"

Even if he left the band? Where would they be without their lead singer? Unwilling to voice the thought, Jake nodded but couldn't resist one last jab. "As long as I don't want to hang out with Scarlett."

"Even then. It'll be hard to watch, but I'll stand by you."

"I appreciate that, Seth. I'm blessed to have such faithful friends."

"And don't you forget it."

Four

Scarlett twisted until her backside came into view in the mirror. The jeans were tighter than the last time she'd worn them, but they would have to do.

With a sigh, she slumped onto the bed piled with the other clothes she'd tried on. Her search for something that said "look what you missed out on" and "I'm not affected by you" was futile. Ha. She flopped onto her back and stared at the popcorn ceiling. No outfit in the world would meet those criteria.

By some miracle, she'd gotten the day off and could take Harmony to Jake's cookout. She'd initially declined the invitation, but her daughter had worn her down. Cassidy had also promised they'd leave if things got uncomfortable, but her cousin needed the job, and the word of mouth would help boost her catering business in bigger circles, maybe even get her foot in the door for some big Nashville events.

Besides, after Cass had moved to Atlanta when she graduated college a year after Scarlett's parents died in order to help Scarlett out, reciprocating the favor was the least she could do. Without her cousin's steady presence and take-charge attitude, Scarlett wasn't sure how she would have handled juggling two jobs while caring for her daughter.

That didn't begin to cover the debt she owed her cousin for inviting Scarlett and Harmony to move back to this small Tennessee community halfway between Nashville and Fiddler Creek. Now, she had the freedom to carve out a new life.

"Mom!" Harmony's voice boomed through the wall, and Scarlett bolted to her feet before hurrying to the bedroom next door.

"What's wrong, sweetie?"

Harmony sat on the pink and lime green flower-shaped rug at the foot of her bed looking at something in her hand. Her shoulders rose to her ears, and she didn't look in Scarlett's direction. "Can I take this?" She held up a heart-shaped picture frame.

"Where did you get that?" Scarlett resisted the urge to snatch the frame from the girl's hands. Last she'd seen, it was tucked away in the depths of her closet. Well, except for that one moment of weakness a week and a half ago when she'd needed to compare the Jake she remembered with the way he lived now. Once again, she eyed the photo of their homecoming dance.

Jake wore a suit and tie while she glowed in an off-the-shoulder coral dress. They were so young—him a senior and her a junior. He'd told her he loved her that warm mid-September night, and she'd given him every part of herself.

Two months later, her entire world crumbled. She had nothing to be grateful for when the week before Thanksgiving Jake announced his plans to graduate early and move to Nashville at the end of the semester. After getting a recording contract, he'd wanted to focus on his music, so he'd broken up with her. That same week, her parents announced their decision to sell the farm and move in with Dad's brother and his wife. In Georgia.

Scarlett spent hours at Cassidy's house that weekend, sobbing until she made herself sick. Three weeks later, Santa left a different explanation for the previous month of nausea.

"Mom?" Harmony's impatience broke the pull of the unpleasant memories.

"What, sweetie?"

"Can I bring it to Jake's?"

She blinked back to the present and blew out a slow breath before focusing on her daughter. "First, it's Mr. Turnquist or Sir. Not Jake. Got it?"

The girl bit her lip and nodded.

"Where'd you find this picture?" Oh, she knew the answer, but Harmony needed to acknowledge she'd broken a rule.

The girl's gaze fell to the floor, and she mumbled something.

"What was that?" Scarlett crossed her arms, pursed her lips, and raised her right eyebrow while fighting off images of a contrite Jake standing before his mother. "I didn't hear you."

"In your closet."

"And why were you in there?" With her birthday around the corner, Harmony's curiosity had gotten her into trouble more than once the past couple of weeks.

Her interest in the old carpet grew more intent, confirming Scarlett's suspicions.

"Harmony? Were you snooping?" She hadn't bought the girl's birthday gifts yet. And when she did, she'd let Cassidy hide them. She bit her tongue, waiting for the truth.

When Harmony didn't answer after two full minutes, Scarlett knelt in front of her and lifted her chin until the girl's eyes met hers. "If you find out what I got you now, you won't be surprised on your special day."

"I don't care about surprises." Her face reddened, and she rubbed the back of her hand across her eyes to staunch the moisture filling them.

"Maybe not today, but you will when your birthday gets here. What's the fun in knowing everything you're getting?"

"Do you think Jake, I mean Mr. Turnquist, will come to my party? Olivia will believe me then."

"Mr. Turnquist is a busy man, sweetie. I don't think he'll be able to come." And after the way he'd rejected them, she couldn't handle watching him play nice with Harmony. Getting through today's barbecue with old friends presented enough of a challenge. She eased the picture from Harmony's fingers and set it on the dresser. "Why don't we leave this here? Maybe if Olivia sees it, she'll believe you've met him."

"Okay." She perked up and looked across the room. "Can I wear my boots?"

"You bet." Her shoulders relaxed with the relief of Harmony's acceptance and the end of a conversation that could have gone much differently.

Her daughter's excitement over meeting the rest of Jake's band and the promise of horseback riding took priority over her usual curiosity. Which might have led to more questions about her father. Questions Scarlett usually managed to gloss over with vague generalities, but with the truth of the situation hovering like an angry storm cloud waiting to unleash its torrent, she considered Harmony's quick acquiescence a victory.

She bopped her daughter on the nose. "You can't ride a horse without boots." The allure of horseback riding had won Scarlett over to going to this cookout. She'd not been on a horse since her parents had sold the farm and everything with it.

Even with Cassidy's help, motherhood was hard and bound to get harder when Harmony reached the teenage years. And doing it on her own? Formidable. Yet she did not regret one second because Harmony was the greatest gift God had given her. And no one would take her away.

J ake paused before the picture window in the living room and peered down the driveway for the twentieth time. Would she come? Cassidy had been noncommittal about whether Scarlett would make it.

Over the past week, he had written three songs. One driving, angry tune in which he expressed the injustice of time moving forward. The second, upbeat but with much less angst. A ballad about second chances rounded out the trio. He didn't need a less hectic schedule to write. All it took was the return of his muse.

A green minivan made its way down the drive, and Jake restrained himself from rushing outside to see the occupants of the car. Instead of rushing to the kitchen to greet them immediately, he remained in place.

When someone knocked on the back door, he tried to calm his racing heart and stop the tremor in his hands. He felt like the nervous teenager who'd picked up Scarlett for the homecoming dance instead of a successful musician. A second rap sounded before he finally swung open the door in the mudroom. Disappointment at finding only Cassidy and Scarlett's daughter hit him square in the chest.

"Hey, Jake." Cassidy lugged two bright purple reusable totes on her shoulders and another two weighed down her arms. "Are we setting up in the dining room again?"

"Nope. We're relaxing outside today. I set out a couple long tables alongside the house." He leaned out the door and pointed up the short flight of stairs to the deck that stretched the length of the house. "There's an outlet right there if you need it, and you can use the French doors in the breakfast nook to come inside if that makes it easier to get to the kitchen. Make yourself at home." He took a quick breath. "Can I help you carry something?"

"I've got it. Come on, Harmony." She turned toward the deck and walked up the three steps.

"Mr. Turnquist, when can we ride the horses?" Harmony's arms wrapped around a bag almost as big as her.

"I'm sorry. She's excited." Scarlett came into view balancing two large boxes. All Jake could make out were jean-clad legs from her thighs to the tips of her brown cowboy boots and the top of her honeyed strawberry hair.

Once he regained his senses and his manners, he took the burden from her. "Let me get these."

"Thanks." She spun and headed back toward the van parked to the side of the house, giving him an excellent view of just how well her jeans fit. His fingers itched to undo her braid as they had when he was a teenager and his feelings for Scarlett had started to shift from friendship to something more.

"Harmony," Scarlett called. "Come help us unload."

"Okay, Mom." The girl grinned up at Jake as she passed him. "Can I ride Athena today?"

"Um..." He paused on the top step. He didn't know a thing about the girl, and his horses were spirited. Scarlett would never forgive him if her kid got hurt while riding one of them.

She answered for him. "Harmony, we talked about this. If there are enough horses, you'll ride with me or Aunt Cass. You're not riding by yourself your first time out."

Jake frowned. Hadn't the girl ridden a horse before? It was Scarlett's favorite thing to do when they were kids. In fact, he'd realized he wanted more than a friendship with her during a ride one day when Scarlett raced him across the pasture on her white mare.

He set the boxes on the deck and followed her to the rear of the van backed into the spot nearest the garage. "How long's it been since you've ridden, Scar?"

"It's Scarlett." She handed Harmony a bag of ice and another of clear plastic cups before giving him a sad smile. "And I haven't been on a horse since we moved."

"Ten years?" Incredulity coated his question. "What happened to Snow?"

"Sold with the farm." She shrugged as though it didn't matter.

A smart man would read the signs and change the subject. Turned out, Jake Turnquist could not claim the title. "And no one ever took you? No boyfriends? Not your husband?"

She disappeared behind the van again without responding.

Cassidy approached with her reusable bags tucked under one arm. The glare she shot his way burned with intensity. "Since you're here, you can make yourself useful and carry the cooler for us."

He lifted the ice chest Cassidy pointed at and led the way to the deck but couldn't resist one more glance at Scarlett.

"She'll follow in a few minutes." Cass nudged him forward with her elbow.

When they climbed the stairs onto the wood deck Seth had helped him build last year, she dropped another bag at the end of the table. "Harmony, why don't you go help your mom?" She took the ice and cups from the girl, then looked at Jake. "Do you want the drinks with the food or somewhere else?"

"Doesn't matter to me."

"Just put it by the table, then." Cassidy set the ice on the ground, and he deposited the bulky chest under the table.

Cassidy's index finger jammed into his chest multiple times as she spoke. "You listen to me, Jake Turnquist. You have no right to pry into Scarlett's life. As I recall, you gave up that privilege to pursue this." She threw her arms wide to encompass the house and the vast expanse of verdant Tennessee hills stretched before them. "Do not bring up the past, and don't ask about the men in her life. Got it? You almost broke her spirit when you chose your career over her and your d—" Her gaze flitted behind Jake.

He spun around to see Scarlett approach with Harmony skipping alongside her and forgot about Cassidy's tirade.

Had she been crying? He frowned at Scarlett's red eyes and blotchy face. Was he to blame? He wished more than anything he could apologize and make her smile, but he had no desire for another lecture.

"Can I play with Trigger, Mr. Turnquist?" Harmony bounded over to him while Scarlett walked to the other side of her cousin.

"You can call me Jake."

The girl glanced at her mom, who nodded once.

"Okay, Jake."

He stuck two fingers in his mouth and whistled. Trigger jumped up from the dirt area around the firepit, barreled up the few stairs, and dropped to his haunches halfway between him and

Scarlett. The dog's gaze bounced between them as if deciding who to greet first.

"Come here, boy." Harmony slapped her hands against her thighs, making the decision easy for the confused dog.

Trigger plopped in front of her and rolled to his back, lapping up the attention. While he appreciated his neighbor's willingness to care for the animal when Jake was on the road, he wanted to spend more time with his dog. How many more years did they have to roam the countryside together?

"I can't believe you kept him." Scarlett's quiet statement reached his ears.

"Of course, I did. He's the best gift anyone's ever given me." One she'd had a hand in choosing. And a reminder of the idyllic days he'd spent with her.

"I'm going to get the rest of the food out of the car." Cassidy stopped in front of Jake. "Why don't you get the grill started while we finish up?" With that demand, she stomped off.

"I should help her."

Jake stared after Scarlett as she practically ran away. What did he say wrong this time?

Five

"I can't do this, Cass." Scarlett slumped in the front seat of the van and swiped tears off her cheeks for the second time since they'd arrived. How could he say what he did about the dog with Harmony right there in front of him? He had no clue what a gift he had rejected.

Cassidy stood beside the open door, dug in her pocket, and held the keys out to her. "I'm so sorry. You go. Just take the van. I'll call when I'm done, and you can pick me up."

With a shuddering breath, she shook her head. "Harmony would never forgive me for taking her home."

"Leave her here with me, then."

"No. You're working and don't need her underfoot. I'll suck it up and endure this afternoon. Maybe when everyone else gets here, it won't be so awkward." She leaned her head back against the headrest and closed her eyes. *Lord, give me the strength to get through this day.*

"I have to admit, I'm looking forward to hanging out with the gang again." Cass gave her a tremulous smile. "After you left, and they made it big, Fiddler Creek wasn't the same. And now look at us." She waved her hand toward Jake's large brick house. "We're at a fancy celebrity home in Franklin. We've come a long way."

A black truck flew up the drive and skidded to a stop beside them, halting their conversation. A petite woman with jet black hair leading to ombre teal tips hopped down from the driver's seat and squealed when she got close enough to see inside the van's windshield. "Scarlett Sykes and Cassidy Cagle. I'm so glad you came. I about throttled Seth last week when he neglected to mention you were here. It's been forever. How are you? What's going on?"

Scarlett swiped at her eyes again and took a quick peek at herself in the mirror before she got out of the van. She gave Cassidy a tremulous smile before they joined Seth's little sister at the front. Mia Mason may have grown up, but she hadn't changed all that much. If her sleeveless yellow sundress with white polka dots was any indication, her fashion sense was still on point, and her mile-a-minute chatter remained consistent. She'd even give Harmony a run for her money.

"Take a breath, Angel Face." A short guy with glasses approached and held out his hand to her.

Cassidy grumbled under her breath, and Scarlett pressed her lips together to keep from laughing. "I'm Scarlett." She stepped forward and shook his hand, then once he let go, pointed her thumb over her shoulder. "And that's Cassidy."

"I'm Peter."

Mia ignored him and clapped while hopping on her toes a few times. "This is so much fun. Like we're all back in Fiddler Creek." She turned back to Peter. "We hung out when we were teenagers. Scarlett's mom and dad had a farm next to Jake's and enough horses for all of us to ride. We spent a lot of time out exploring before we'd come back to the house where Scarlett's mom gave us fresh-baked cookies." She turned to Scarlett. "How are your parents doing anyway?"

The question tore open a wound that bled all over again. Questions like this brought fresh waves of pain and grief. "They passed away five years ago."

"Oh no." She covered her mouth with one hand. "I'm sorry. I didn't know."

"It's okay." Tears pricked her eyes. Ugh, this was so not the place for this. "Some days, it still feels like we're taking it one day at a time."

"How long have you been back in Tennessee?" She glanced between them.

"About a year." Scarlett glanced at her cousin with a grateful smile. "Cass inherited a house from her aunt last summer and invited Harmony and me to live with her."

Mia's perfectly shaped, black eyebrows scrunched together. "Who's Harmony?"

"Scarlett's daughter. She's a sweetheart and a superfan of the band. Follow me, and I'll introduce you." Before she led Mia and Peter away, Cass mouthed an apology to Scarlett.

When she was alone again, Scarlett sagged against the bumper and braced her hands on her knees. Making it through the day without a breakdown would take more than the couple prayers she'd tossed heavenward.

Several minutes and a quieted spirit later, she went to the tail of the van and gathered the last two bags. At the sound of another engine approaching, she walked to the driver's side door. Who would be next? A luxury SUV parked on the other side of Mia's truck, and Scarlett couldn't tame her grin when Levi Sinclair hopped out. The vehicle was so like the man—dependable under the flashy exterior.

"Scarlett Sykes." Levi strode to her and lifted her—groceries and all—in a bear hug. Once he set her back on her feet, he held her at arms-length. "You're prettier than I remember."

"And you're just as big a flirt as I remember." She laughed, and the weight of her unease lightened some more. Despite his impressive six-foot-three height, Levi radiated warmth and comfort. Plus, he could always cheer her up. "It's good to see you."

He commandeered her bags with one hand and wrapped his

free arm around her shoulders as they walked toward the house. "Notice I didn't bring a date. I heard two pretty fillies were coming today, so I'm hedging my bets."

"You would know better than me if Mia and Andi are available." She peeked up into his face and blinked an innocent expression.

A loud guffaw escaped his lips. "Ah, as quick witted as ever, I see. You'll keep me on my toes." He squeezed her closer. "Now, take pity on me, and tell me there's not a special man in your life."

She bit her lip. She'd dated some, but nothing serious. Levi was a friend, and she preferred to keep it that way. Discouraging a full press from him was in her best interest. But if Jake believed she had a boyfriend or husband, a buffer separated them and protected her heart from wishful thinking.

"You took too long to answer." Levi stopped walking and turned to face her. "Which either means it's complicated or you're working out how to let me down easy." He bent his head and whispered in her ear, "Maybe it's a little of both."

"The truth?" She gazed up into his hazel eyes, and he nodded. "I have a daughter who gets all my attention. Most days, I don't have time for a shower let alone another relationship."

"A daughter, huh? What's her name?"

"Harmony."

"And I bet she's as pretty as her mama." The corners of his mouth turned down. "But surely her dad lets you have some freedom now and then."

"He wants nothing to do with us. He signed away his parental rights when she was less than a month old."

"Too bad. I'm sure he's missed out on a lot." He removed his arm as they stepped onto the deck and lowered his voice. "Be sure and get my number before you leave today. You call me anytime you need anything."

"Thank you, Levi." She pecked his cheek. "You may be the biggest flirt in Tennessee, but you've got a heart of gold."

He winked. "Don't give away my secrets, Scar."

This time, she let the nickname she hated slide.

∿

When Scarlett stretched up on her toes and kissed Levi's cheek, white-hot jealousy poured through every vein in Jake's body. How had *he* gotten past the icy wall she'd erected?

To avoid viewing any more intimacies between them, he turned to Cassidy. "Is it time to get the burgers on the grill?"

She pulled her phone from her pocket and looked at it before glancing around. "Is everyone here?"

"We're here. Time to start the party." Seth's pronouncement preceded him and a brunette wearing white shorts, a hot pink tank top, and flip flops. "Everyone, this is Nikki. Nikki, everyone." They headed to the edge of the deck where Mia and Peter sat on one of the wooden benches at the patio table.

Jake turned to Cass. "We're just waiting on Andi, and she's usually fashionably late."

"Then yes, you can get them going." Cassidy shifted a bowl and moved the tray of burger toppings to the end of the table. "I can take care of it, though, if you want to mingle."

"You've done plenty, and I already spend all of my time with these guys. Let me handle this." He moved to the built-in grill island a few feet to the left and took the preformed hamburger patties from the minifridge where Cass had stowed them when she'd arrived. Within seconds, Trigger sat next to him, his tail swishing from side to side and his full attention fixed on the food. Jake shook his head at the dog who'd abandoned Harmony in hopes of a treat and transferred the meat to the rack before shutting the lid.

When Andi arrived with her boyfriend, Jake failed to hold in a snicker at Ridge's choice of clothing. Who wore a suit—even a linen one—to a beginning-of-the-summer cookout in the south?

"Mom, it's Andi Buchanan." Harmony's enthusiasm elicited a few chuckles from the others.

"I hear you're a fan." Andi pulled a bottled water from the ice chest under the table. "Maybe we can have a little sing-along later, and you can join us."

"After the horses, right?"

Scarlett's laugh rang out. "You can tell what takes priority. She's begged to go riding since she could talk."

Andi gaped at her. "Your parents never took her out?"

"We lived in the city and didn't have access to horses. My dad wanted to wait until she was older but..." Her voice broke, and she hugged her arms to herself.

Jake stepped closer.

"Sorry." Scarlett sniffled. "My parents were killed in a car crash when Harmony was four years old." She scanned the deck. "I should go help Cass."

Jake watched her pull in a breath and square her shoulders as she walked toward her cousin as if determined to move on to the next task.

"I didn't know." Andi bit her bottom lip, then narrowed her eyes at him. "Did you?"

"Yeah. My mom emailed me an article about the accident. It included information about the memorial." He'd almost left the tour at the time to go, but Becker had talked him out of it.

She scowled at him. "Why didn't you say anything?"

Because he was trying to get over her and talking about her, remembering her family, would have hurt. "What would you have done? We were in the middle of the tour."

Her eyes flashed with challenge. "Not stick my foot in my mouth for starters."

Yeah, he was done with this conversation. "I think Ridge needs saving." He pointed toward her date, who shifted from one foot to the other and darted his gaze around the space as if seeking an escape.

"I don't know why I brought him." She rolled her eyes. "He's not into any of this, but since we're only home a month, I thought it might be nice to spend some time together." She left to rescue her boyfriend.

Harmony tugged on the hem of Jake's black T-shirt as he lifted the grill lid to flip the burgers. "Are there enough horses for everyone, Mr. Turnquist?"

"You bet." Once finished, he set the spatula down and rested a hand on the crown of the girl's head. "Not everyone here will ride today." Ridge probably wouldn't last long, and Nikki wasn't dressed for it. "But my neighbor raises horses, and we can borrow as many as we need." Borrow may have been the wrong word since Jake would pay the man, but he'd keep that to himself. "Andi, Levi, and I board our animals with him."

He glanced at Scarlett as she set plates and plasticware on the table. He wanted to say something about her parents, to express his sympathy, but the moment had passed.

"I have something for you, Mr. Turnquist." Harmony raced to the table, pulled her bright green backpack from beneath it, and opened the zipper.

"It's Jake, not Mr. Turnquist, okay?" He motioned Seth over and passed him the black-handled spatula before following the girl toward the table.

"That's my fault." Scarlett's features relaxed as she walked back over and watched the girl with a small smile. "I told her not to call you Jake."

"Why not?"

"To show respect."

"Here." The girl shoved a heart-shaped frame in his hand.

Scarlett gasped, and all the peacefulness he'd just witnessed in her expression dissipated. "Harmony, I told you to leave that at home."

"But I wanted Mr. Turnquist, I mean Jake, to see it."

He flipped the frame around and stared at the same photograph that sat in the bottom drawer of his desk. The one of a naive boy who'd fallen for the girl next door before life had really begun. But she'd kept the picture, too. What did that mean?

"Do you remember this?" Harmony leaned nearer over the photo, obstructing his view. But he didn't need to see it because it was burned into his memory.

"You bet I do." He lifted his gaze to Scarlett. "One of the best nights of my life."

"Better than hearing your songs on the radio?" Good grief, the girl had questions.

He returned his attention to Harmony. "Yep."

"Better than getting a music award?"

"Mm-hmm." He bit back a grin.

"Better than your first number one hit?"

He peeked at Scarlett, whose cheeks pinkened. "Better than every one of my number one hits combined."

Scarlett's eyes glistened, but he couldn't decide whether it was a good or bad sign. She broke eye contact and focused on her daughter. "Okay, you got your answers. Why don't you put that away with your backpack, and we go help Aunt Cass with the food so everyone can eat?"

"No need." Cassidy carried a large bowl of whipped potato salad past them and set it on the table. "Levi and Mia gave me a hand, so lunch is ready whenever you are."

Jake glanced around and noted most of his friends were now seated at the patio table chatting or inside the kitchen where Cassidy had been. Seth shook off his overdressed date and scowled as he slapped the burgers onto the serving tray Jake had left beside the grill. Had he brought her in hopes of making Cass jealous? Surely, he wouldn't attempt the same stupid stunt that had blown up in his face in high school.

"Those burgers smell amazing." Mia moved closer to the long table and stole a handful of chips. "I'm starving."

"Ladies first." Jake held his hand out in invitation. "We'll follow."

He realized his mistake as soon as the ladies settled onto the two benches at the rectangular patio table.

"Excellent suggestion." Holding a plate loaded with food in

one hand, Levi paused at the railing beside Jake. "As if I don't have to look at your ugly mugs enough."

"Shut up." Seth walked past them and stomped toward the firepit as Nikki scooted over to make room for Ridge at the table.

A chuckle escaped Levi. "Rejection from two women at once has gotta hurt his pride." He swung his gaze back to Jake. "So, Scarlett's got a kid."

"Yep." He squinted to where Scarlett and Harmony sat side by side facing them. "There's no denying Harmony's her daughter, is there?"

Levi looked at the ladies, then turned to fully face him. "Take a closer look." He slapped Jake on the back and walked off.

Jake grabbed a paper plate before glancing at the mother-daughter duo. The girl's hair was a shade or two darker than her mother's. Her eyes were wider but the same color as Scarlett's. What exactly was Levi hinting at?

Six

The moment Scarlett walked into the barn, she inhaled the potent scents of hay and horses. This right here was what she missed most from her youth. Well, this and... She peeked at Jake from her periphery as he spoke to the older man with crinkle lines around his eyes who owned the stable. They'd left the others to figure out the logistics of who would join them at the stables and who needed to get going. When Jake had offered her and Harmony a ride, Scarlett couldn't refuse her daughter's pleading eyes.

Since they had time, she took Harmony's hand and wandered down the well-kept aisle. The skylights above provided plenty of light. Two large doors at the other end of the walkway opened to a green pasture where three horses rested beneath a tulip poplar dotted with yellow blooms and another lazily drank water from a large trough. A fawn-colored Palomino with a blond mane stuck her head out of a stall, and Scarlett stroked her velvet nose. "You're a beauty and you know it."

"You always could spot the best." Jake joined them and held his palm flat with fingers together while the horse took the carrot stub he offered. "This is Athena."

"She's yours." Of course this beautiful animal belonged to

him. From his home to his fancy truck to his animals, he'd graduated from small town to big time in every way imaginable. Was it any wonder he hadn't wanted her to hold him back?

"Yep." Pride laced his words. "Her and that one." He inclined his head toward the next stall where a magnificent rust-colored bay with a jet-black mane stood watch. "That's Hercules."

"Strong names." She struggled to get the words out with him standing so nearby.

"Mom." Harmony came to her rescue. "I want to ride this one." She pointed at a black and white splotched pinto.

Scarlett turned and crossed the aisle. "This one?" She eyed the large horse that stood at least sixteen hands high as it shied away from the girl's enthusiasm. The flicking ears broadcast its unease, but would she be able to talk her daughter into a different horse? "You sure?"

"Yeah. What's his name?"

Jake smirked. "*Her* name is Daisy."

Scarlett wrinkled her nose. Who named such a large horse after a dainty flower? Cass would have something scathing to say about the name. She vehemently opposed cutesy animal names almost as much as she hated the endearments couples used for each other.

"Maybe Cassidy should ride this one." He didn't even try to hide his laughter as though he'd read her mind. He leaned down until he was nose-to-nose with Harmony. "I had an extra special one in mind for you and your mom."

He strode to the far end of the barn and crooked his finger. Scarlett bit her lip and followed as if a string was tied between her and that finger. A gasp escaped her lips when she laid eyes on the gorgeous blue roan.

"This is Quicksilver." Jake stroked the animal's forelock.

"Surely, he's not to ride. He's purebred."

"Yes, he is, but he's done racing." Jake rested an elbow on the gate at the front of the stall. "I got the okay from Tom. He's all yours today. If you want him."

With an outstretched hand, she stepped to the other side of the horse. "You're beautiful." He snorted and nuzzled her fingers.

"I couldn't agree more." Jake's rough voice hinted he wasn't talking about the horse, but her tender heart wouldn't allow herself a glimpse. This was an interlude, an intersection in their lives that crossed for a time before they continued their separate ways after today.

Harmony ran toward them with all the energy of an almost-nine-year-old, and Quicksilver shied away.

"Shh." She rested a hand on his neck and held out the other to her daughter. "You have to be careful and quiet around the horses, sweetie. If they get spooked, it's hard to calm them back down."

The girl stared up at the big animal in awe and whispered, "He's so pretty, Mom."

"He is." She smiled at Harmony's sudden stillness and slack mouth. "I get to ride him today."

"Can I ride with you?" Her daughter stared up at the horse.

"You sure can."

"With this much energy, it might be better if you ride with your aunt." He tweaked Harmony's nose. "This big guy might prefer to warm up to a new rider before he's ready to take on two."

Scarlett swallowed around the lump in her throat. Why hadn't he asked anything about her? And if he didn't want anything to do with Harmony, why was he being so kind to her?

As she saddled Quicksilver, the others arrived, and a stable hand helped Cassidy tack a cinnamon quarter horse with a black mane. Not even Harmony's begging convinced her to ride Daisy, and Scarlett suspected Cass had chosen Goliath because his name was the complete opposite of the Pinto's.

Across the way, Andi, Jake, Levi, and Seth chatted as they prepared their horses. Scarlett alternated between watching them, keeping an eye on her daughter, and finishing up with her animal.

"Mia's not coming?" Jake said.

Seth shrugged. "You know how she is. She can take or leave riding, so she volunteered to drive Nikki and Peter home. She'll meet us back at your place in a few hours."

"What about Ridge?" Jake looked over his horse's saddle.

"We drove separately because he had to get some work done this afternoon." Andi sighed. "I'm breaking up with him."

Seth and Jake groaned.

"Give him a chance." Levi led his horse to where Andi stood. "It's been three months."

A pang of envy bubbled up at their easy camaraderie. If she'd stayed in Fiddler Creek—if Jake hadn't broken up with her—would she still fit in with the gang? Her gaze darted to Cassidy, who helped Harmony onto the saddle before swinging up behind the girl. At least she had her best friend in her corner.

Once the horses were ready, the group made their way out of the corral closest to the barn.

"See you in a couple of hours." Tom waved and closed the gate behind them.

As they rode through the first pasture, Scarlett relaxed in her saddle. Riding on horseback and guiding a powerful animal with her legs and the reins held something freeing. If she were alone, she'd give Quicksilver his head and let him fly.

"You want to run him, don't you?" Jake rode on her left.

"Am I that transparent?"

His lips pinched together and made a slight curve downward before he answered. "No, but you do have an expression when you ride." He waved an arm in front of him. "Your daughter should witness the beauty of you on a horse. Go ahead and fly."

"*My* daughter will only ask me to do it again with her along for the ride." She stared out at the vibrant green hills in front of them. "Responsibility takes priority." She turned her back on Jake and swiveled to her right and behind to check on Cass and Harmony—who grinned from ear to ear. "I have to consider how my actions affect Harmony. But I guess you wouldn't understand that, would you?" She bit her tongue to staunch the flow of bitter words.

"I guess not." Jake tapped his heels against Hercules and trotted ahead toward Levi, Seth, and Andi before she could apologize.

Why had she said that? She'd put the past behind her, hadn't she? Decided not to let the choice he'd made matter. But it did. His rejection of Harmony was a rejection of her.

"You alright?" Cass eased her horse alongside Quicksilver and eyed her for several long seconds before turning her attention ahead.

"I'll survive. We'll talk later." She focused on her daughter. "What do you think, Harmony?"

Her smile hadn't faded since they'd arrived at the stables. "I don't want a dog for my birthday anymore. Just a horse."

Not in my budget. "We'll see, sweetie." She wished she could give Harmony one, but between boarding, lessons, and tack, it wasn't feasible.

"Scarlett?" Levi dropped back from the lead group and hollered over his shoulder. "Wanna race?"

While tempted, the words she'd uttered to Jake only minutes ago reverberated in her head. "No, thanks."

"What? Afraid I'll beat you?"

"Hardly." She tossed the words his direction, a challenge laced with memories. Not once had he beaten her. The notion was laughable.

"Do it, Mom." Harmony leaned forward as if she would race him herself. "Show him that girls are better than boys."

How could she deny that request? She shot Levi a grin and thumped her heels against Quicksilver's flanks. The wind whipped and loosened her hair from its braid as the horse's powerful legs moved beneath her.

"Hey!" Levi's protest barely reached her on the breeze, and genuine joy filled her for a few short minutes.

When Scarlett reined the horse to a stop beside the rocky creek and danced him around, Jake couldn't take his eyes off her. Her cheeks flushed, and her eyes sparkled. Her hair flowed wild around her, and happiness, true happiness, lit her face.

"You cheated." Levi caught up with her.

"I would've beaten you anyway." Their conversation carried on the breeze.

The guy leaned over and whispered something in her ear. She laughed and slapped his hand off her arm. Jake growled at their easy interaction.

"She's comfortable around him."

"What?" Jake's saddle creaked as he turned the other way to where Andi and Seth kept pace with him.

"You're jealous." Andi didn't miss a beat. "But Scarlett has always let her guard down around Levi because she's comfortable with him. They don't have a relationship history—one that didn't end well—to navigate around." Empathy filled her eyes, probably due to her recalling her own relational heartbreak years ago. "Give her time, Jake. She'll see you're still the same guy from Fiddler Creek we all know and love."

But was he? He'd chased after fame and fortune, leaving everything and everyone behind. And with his success came a whole new set of challenges he hadn't anticipated.

"Mom, can I ride with you now?" Harmony's voice floated their way.

Andi winked and nudged his leg with her knee. "Go help her change horses so the ladies don't have to get down."

He pulled his reins to the left and steered Hercules toward the cousins. But before he reached them, Levi had already dismounted to assist. With a heavy sigh, he continued their direction. "Are you enjoying yourself, Harmony?"

She beamed at him with shining blue eyes and rosy cheeks.

His breath caught in his lungs for a moment as if the years had rolled away and eight-year-old Scarlett stood in front of him. He studied the girl for any hints of her father. What had Levi seen that Jake hadn't?

"Did you see Mom beat Mr. Levi? I told her girls were better than boys."

"Always." Cass tugged the end of a lock of Harmony's hair before Levi lifted the girl off Goliath and deposited her onto Quicksilver's back in front of Scarlett.

"Your mom always could beat the boys." Levi glanced at him. "Jake was the only one of us who ever came close to challenging her."

"Really?" Harmony twisted her neck to look at her mom, who leaned to the right until they made eye contact. "Did he ever win?"

"Sometimes." She shrugged, but the grumbled word proved those handful of losses remained sore spots for her.

"Only because she let me." Jake winked at the girl before locking gazes with Scarlett. "And she didn't do that often."

"Because she's not a pushover." Cassidy edged her horse into his line of vision and glared at him. "She's strong and capable and doesn't need to prove herself to anyone."

Whoa, where had that come from? Scarlett had never had to prove herself to him. He'd always admired her strength and determination. If he hadn't broken things off with her when he did, she would have given up her dreams to follow him. He never wanted her to sacrifice for him but couldn't help to wonder what his life would have been like if they had stayed together. Would the pressure have gotten to them or drawn them closer?

"Mom, I want to ride horses at my birthday party."

A shadow fell over Scarlett's face. "We can't afford that, baby. We'll do something small at the house."

While tempted to offer to pay, Jake sensed it would only make Scarlett more upset. "When's your birthday?"

"June fourteenth, but my party is before my birthday. Want to come?"

"When is it?"

Scarlett answered. "It's on Saturday, the eleventh."

The tour would kick off again at the end of June after their concert during the weeklong music festival in Nashville. If he switched a few things around, he could swing it. "I'd love to come to your party."

She rewarded him with another brilliant smile and looked around at the others who had gathered around. "You can all come."

"I'm not sure what everyone has going on, but if they're free, I'm sure they'd love to celebrate with you."

Levi and Seth nodded their confirmation. Andi shrugged. A kid's birthday party wasn't her scene, so she'd probably have a pressing engagement that day.

But Jake would make it a priority. "How old are you going to be?"

"I'll get you the information later." Scarlett nudged Quicksilver into a walk and left before Harmony answered his question.

Jake stared as Cassidy and Andi followed her toward the barn with Seth trailing behind the ladies. Should he have disappointed Harmony and declined the invitation? Why couldn't he do anything right when it came to Scarlett?

Levi mounted his horse. "I'm definitely going to that party."

"Hey." Jake moved closer. "How'd you get Scarlett to talk to you without taking everything personally?"

"Easy. I'm not you." He watched the ladies, who talked to each other while ignoring Seth's presence, before turning to Jake and opening his mouth. Then, he snapped it shut again without uttering a word.

"What?"

Levi stared at Jake as if trying to communicate something.

"Just say it, Levi."

He sighed. "She told me that Harmony's dad wants nothing to do with her. Why do you think that is?"

The knowledge saddened him. Harmony was a bright, energetic girl. Any man would be blessed to have such a daughter. "No idea, but he's missing out."

"Yeah. He sure is." The normally easygoing Levi kicked his horse into motion and trotted toward the others, leaving Jake to wonder what burr had gotten under his saddle.

Seven

Scarlett walked into Jake's family room and headed toward the huge sectional. The two-hour ride and caring for the horses before and after had worn her out, but she didn't regret a minute of it. She groaned as she settled into the corner of the sofa.

A smile tickled her lips as Harmony sat beside her with a similar sound.

"Does anyone want something to drink?" Jake carried a stack of plastic cups and a large bowl of ice into the room and set it on the wet bar built along the wall to her left. "There are sodas in the fridge here and lemonade and tea in the kitchen."

A glass of iced tea sounded refreshing, but her seat was too comfortable. Still, Harmony probably needed some hydration, too. She scooted to the edge of the couch, but Jake put a hand on her shoulder.

"Don't get up. What would you and Harmony like?"

"Iced tea for me and lemonade for Harmony." She turned her head and mouthed a thank you.

"Can I get you anything, Cass?" Jake moved to the front of the room.

"I'm good, thanks." Cass sat on the other side of Harmony and didn't lift the back of her head from the couch.

He put his hands on his hips and peered around the room. "I just ordered pizza if anyone's hungry."

Cass leaned forward. "You didn't have to do that. While I packed most of the leftovers in the van before heading to the stables with Andi, I could have whipped something up."

When she moved to get up, he motioned her to stay in her seat. "You've done plenty of cooking today. Dinner's on me."

As he left the room, Seth looked at Levi sitting in the armchair across from his. "He didn't ask me what I wanted to drink."

The lines at the corner of Levi's eyes crinkled. "Me either. I hope he's not expecting a good tip."

Mia, who had been waiting at the house when they returned from the stables, sat cross legged on the round ottoman in the center of everything and heaved a throw pillow at her brother. The toss went wide and hit the huge television mounted on the wall.

"Nice aim." Seth steadied the wobbling screen.

"Like you could do better." Mia stuck out her tongue. "And you can get your own drinks or be a gentleman and offer to get the rest of us something. You know where everything is."

"So do you." He crossed his arms over his chest and leaned farther into the chair.

Andi plopped down on the other end of the sectional and looked at Scarlett with a smirk. "Things haven't changed so much, have they?"

Scarlett chuckled as she ran her fingers through Harmony's hair. Today had been reminiscent of many of the summer days they'd spent together as kids on the farm. Scarlett's mom would feed them lunch before sending them outside where they'd ride or play with the other animals or explore. Once they'd expended their energy, they would return to the house for snacks or dinner before everyone went home.

"Here you go." Jake held a cup out to her. "But Harmony

doesn't look like she'll need this any time soon." He lifted his other hand.

Scarlett peeked at Harmony. Her chin rested on her chest, and if she stayed in that position, she would wake up with a crick in her neck.

"I'll take it." Mia stood from the ottoman and took the lemonade from Jake. "Why don't you and Scarlett take her upstairs so she can rest more comfortably on one of the beds?"

"That's okay." Scarlett had stopped carrying Harmony several years ago when she grew too heavy for her, and lugging her up a flight of stairs when she was already sore was not an option. "We should get going." She glanced at Cassidy, who was close to drifting off, too.

Without asking permission, Jake scooped the girl into his arms. "You'll all be more comfortable this way." He shifted his stance. "Levi, if I leave some cash on the table by the door, will you pay for the pizza when it gets here?"

"I can do that."

As Jake carried Harmony from the room and down the hall, the girl nestled against his shoulder. Scarlett bit the inside of her cheek to keep from railing—whether at Jake or the injustice of the situation remained to be seen. She followed them to the entry and up the stairs. When they reached the second floor, Jake turned left and opened the first door on the right. He laid the girl on the brown comforter. Scarlett unfolded a blue blanket at the foot of the bed and placed it over her daughter before stretching out beside her and resting her back against the headboard.

At Jake's raised eyebrows, she shrugged. "I don't want her to wake up in an unfamiliar place without me." And she really needed some space from him and the rest of the gang. The memories continued to wash over her, but she had to be realistic. Today was not normal, and she couldn't allow the walls of defense surrounding her heart to erode any further.

He nodded. "You're a good mom." He pulled his wallet from

his back pocket. "Let me run down and leave the money for the pizza. I'll be right back. We need to talk."

About what? Was he finally going to confront her about bringing Harmony here? Did he think she'd told the girl that he was her dad? She couldn't figure the man out. Why would he refuse to meet his daughter all these years and then invite them to his home? Whatever he had to say, it wouldn't be good. If she could, she'd bundle Harmony up, sneak out of Jake's house and life, and move far away.

But, even if that were a possibility, she refused to take the coward's way out. She'd always prayed he would change his mind and want to spend time with his daughter. Now that they were here—in his home—she questioned the authenticity of those prayers as doubts crept in.

Scarlett blew out a long breath and closed her eyes. *Lord, help me through this. You know what's best for Harmony. Give me wisdom to speak my mind and strength to accept Your answer.*

A peace fell over her as she smoothed Harmony's hair back from her face. "I love you more than anything." She scooted down on the bed and rested her hand on her elbow to watch Harmony sleep while inhaling traces of her grape-scented shampoo.

When Jake returned, Scarlett started to sit up, but he waved her back to her seat. "Stay. You both look comfortable." He muscled a chair around to Harmony's side of the bed and closed the door. Once he was settled, he stretched his legs out and ran his fingers through his hair, disturbing the line from the hat he'd worn earlier.

She'd once loved doing that for him after they'd gone riding. To stem the tide of memories, she closed her eyes and concentrated on the present. "Jake, I—"

"No need to apologize. I told you to move on. To live your life."

Her eyes flew open. She wasn't going to apologize. For anything. He owed her that, not the other way around.

"You know you could have called me if you needed help." He leaned forward, and his gray-eyed gaze bored into her.

"No, you made certain I couldn't." The nondisclosure agreement she'd signed made that abundantly clear. To this day, she hadn't forgiven herself for taking his hush money. Money that ran out after the first three years of his daughter's life.

He stretched his hand over their daughter and brushed Scarlett's hair from her cheek much the same as she'd just done to Harmony. "I would have helped. I loved you once, but we were friends long before that."

Loved. Past tense. The ache that had resided in her chest all day grew. He had indeed given up on her.

"Why are you doing this? Why now?"

His forehead creased. "What are you talking about?"

"You know what I'm talking about." They locked gazes, neither saying more.

A soft knock sounded on the door, and Jake rose to answer it.

"Sorry to interrupt." Levi looked at her. "The pizza just arrived. I tried to pay for it, but the kid is insistent there isn't enough cash."

Jake heaved out a long breath. "He wants an autograph, doesn't he?"

"Yep." Levi slapped him on the back as he walked out the door.

"Levi?" Scarlett sat up.

He stuck his head into the room "Yeah?"

"Will you tell Cassidy I'm ready to go?"

"You sure?" His forehead creased.

"Positive."

He entered the room and handed her a scrap of paper. "My number. Call me if you need anything."

She stared at the scribbled digits, wondering when he'd written his number down. And why? Was this an act of friendship or something more? "Okay."

"Scarlett?" He waited until she met his eyes. "I'm serious.

Anything at all, you call me."

She nodded and shoved the paper in her pocket. As soon as he left, she woke Harmony, telling her it was time to go and hoping she'd wake enough to move when Cass showed up. If Jake returned, she wanted an excuse to leave immediately.

"Scarlett?" Cass tapped on the door, and she pulled it open.

"Where's Jake?"

"He's in the family room. Levi said he'd keep him there for a few minutes."

She could hug Levi for watching out for her, but that would have to wait.

Cassidy led the way down the stairs, then pointed at the front door. "Why don't you go out this way, and I'll get our purses from the kitchen. I need to get my salad bowl out of the fridge, too."

"Come on, Harmony." She took her daughter's hand and stepped outside.

The girl dragged her feet as they walked to the van. "I'm hungry."

"We'll ask Cass to go through a drive-thru on the way home, okay?" Scarlett eyed the vehicles in Jake's driveway. Thankfully, everyone had parked behind the person in front of them, leaving plenty of room for her cousin to get out.

Her heart pounded. Would Cassidy get caught up with everyone? Would Jake discover her absence and come looking for her? She released the breath she'd been holding when her cousin approached carrying a mixing bowl with a plate balanced on the lid.

Scarlett stepped toward her. "Let me take those so you can unlock the van." The aroma of tomato sauce and cheese made her mouth water as she placed a hand on each side of the salad bowl.

"Mia insisted we take some pizza to go." Cass chuckled. "That woman is hard to say no to." Her cousin mumbled something else.

"What was that?" If Scarlett had to guess, it had something to do with Seth.

"Nothing." Cassidy unzipped her purse, dug her keys out, and pushed the fob to unlock the van.

"Can I have some pizza, Aunt Cass?" The note of pleading in Harmony's voice grated on Scarlett's already frazzled nerves.

"You bet." Cassidy answered first. "Hop in the car and get situated. Then you can have some." She turned to Scarlett and dipped her head toward the bowl. "Do you mind putting that in the cooler in back?"

"Nope." She marched to the back of the van and put the bowl away. The sooner they got out of here, the better.

Once they were all buckled in the van and Harmony munched on her pizza, Scarlett took a full breath. She'd escaped for now.

She leaned her head against the window and swiped a tear from her cheek. This wasn't over yet. They still had Harmony's party to get through.

~

J ake shut the door with a satisfying click and glanced up the stairs. Why had Cassidy gone up there?

He rolled his eyes at himself and walked to the kitchen. It was none of his business. After setting the boxes on the island counter, he walked down the hallway to the family room. "Pizza's here."

"Great." Seth stood. "I'm starving."

Mia hopped up and elbowed her brother in the side. "You're always starving."

The siblings continued jostling with each other as they passed him and entered the hallway.

Andi rose from her seat and swiped her palms down her thighs before rounding the couch and walking toward the exit at a more sedate pace. She paused beside him and turned to look at Levi. "Are you guys coming?"

"Actually, I need to ask Jake something." Levi stood from the chair and crossed the room. Tonight, he wore the disapproving expression of a father as he scowled at Jake. "What'd you say to Scarlett?"

"None of your business, Levi." He turned, intent on going upstairs and finishing his conversation with her.

"Okay, fine." Levi stepped in front of him. "I'm worried about Andi breaking up with Ridge."

Jake cocked his head. "Why? It's not the first time she's broken up with someone."

"That's the problem." Levi shoved his hands in the pockets of his jeans. "She doesn't let anyone get close enough to truly know them."

Two years older than Jake, Seth, and Andi, and four years Mia's senior, he'd earned the nickname *"BB,"* shorthand for *"Big Brother,"* from the band because he'd taken on the role of responsibility from the time they'd signed their first contract.

"Can you blame her? After Bo broke off their engagement, I was sure she wouldn't ever trust a man enough to even accept a date." He thought she'd made progress these past three years.

"She's going through the motions but not connecting with anyone."

Jake studied the other man. "Do *you* have a thing for her?"

"What?" Levi's head jerked back as if Jake had thrown a physical punch instead of a verbal one. "No. I just want her to open up and let people in. It's almost like she's created a formula for when to break up with a guy for minimal impact on her emotions."

"Why are you asking me about this?" Jake stepped back, ready to be finished with this conversation. If Andi came in and heard them discussing her, she'd blow a gasket. "Talk to her about it."

"Yeah, right."

"Are you guys going to get something to eat before Seth eats it all?" Mia grinned at them as she carried a plate with two slices of pizza in one hand and a can of soda in the other.

"Hey." Seth's holler reached them just fine. "I only took four pieces."

"We're going." Jake walked down hall and turned toward the entryway, intent on returning to his conversation with Scarlett.

"She's gone."

He spun back around and glared at Levi. "What?"

"After you *talked* to her." The guy rested an arm on the stair rail and jerked his head toward the second floor. "She couldn't get out of here fast enough."

Jake rushed to the front door and yanked it open in time to see the red glow of taillights at the end of the driveway before the vehicle turned left onto the main road. He raked both hands through his hair, his frustration mounting.

"Sorry, man." Levi gripped his shoulder.

"I was trying to make amends, to apologize for the way I left things." He stared at the now-dark driveway. "Left her."

"And?"

He sighed and shut the door before turning to his friend. "I don't know, Levi. I feel like there's more to her anger, but don't have a clue what it might be."

"Guess you can try again at Harmony's birthday party." He emphasized the word birthday.

Jake frowned. What was the guy's deal? Why didn't he just come out and say whatever it was that bothered him? "Two weeks from now?"

"More like a week and a half to give Scarlett some space." He shoved his hands in his pockets. "In the meantime, we both know Becker's breathing down your neck for new material, so concentrate on that."

Jake lifted his chin. "Actually, I wrote a few songs this week that I'd like to play for you guys. Since Cassidy and Scarlett left, this is as good a time as any."

"Sure." Levi quirked a smile. "Wonder what got your creative juices flowing again. Or should I say *who* got them flowing?"

Jake socked his shoulder. "Let's go get some food and join the gang."

Levi chuckled as he followed.

When they returned to the family room with their loaded plates, Jake strode to the chairs opposite the couch. "I worked on three songs this week and would like your opinions."

Levi eased onto the couch cushion beside Mia and inched his plate up. "There was plenty left."

Jake plugged his phone into the surround sound system and pulled up the song downloads. Once the music began, he sank onto one of the armchairs and chewed his pizza while watching his friends' faces.

After the first listen, Mia twirled her hand in the air. "Two more times, so we get a good feel."

He obliged. Mia swayed, and her fingers twitched as if her keyboard was beneath them. Andi tilted her head and hummed some harmonies with the chorus. Levi's head bobbed to the beat. The fingers on Seth's left hand moved over an invisible fingerboard as his right hand sawed back and forth holding an imaginary bow.

"The first one is too dark and angry for us." Mia set her cell phone on the ottoman, hopped up from the couch, and moved behind it to pace. "The second could work if we take out some of the references to Scarlett." He opened his mouth to object, and she held up a hand. "You can't deny every one of those songs— every one of *your* songs—is about her. Don't get me wrong, she's the reason you write so well, but these are too personal."

"I agree." Seth leaned forward and rested his elbows on his knees. "Let's sing about someone other than the blue-eyed, red-haired beauty. But the second song's a money maker if we change it up. And maybe the third as well."

"Maybe it's time to put 'Rain' on an album." Andi scooted to the edge of her seat and crossed one knee over the other. "Now that it's out there."

"No." Jake stood and unplugged his cell, not willing to budge on that song. "I never should have played that in public. It's not going on the album."

"Okay, since that doesn't seem to be up for discussion..." Andi leaned over, picked up her purse from the floor, and dug inside until she retrieved her phone. "I've been working on a little something myself." She tapped the screen several times, then held it out to Jake.

He plugged it in and played the music featuring a soaring melody and poignant lyrics about broken dreams. Andi had more talent than the rest of them put together. Not only was she part of the select club of bassists who could sing, she excelled as a song writer. And using her songs would take some pressure off him.

They listened to the song two more times before anyone spoke.

"Why are you trolling with us again?" Levi broke the spell.

She swept her platinum hair behind her shoulder and folded her hands in her lap. "We made a pact, remember? We're a team until we all agree it's time to go our own ways." She arched an eyebrow at Jake. "And until that time comes, I'm following Jake's lead."

"What if I wasn't around anymore? What would you do then?" He wouldn't be where he was today without the others in this room, and it was high time others figured that out. "Why sit on the bench, Andi? The world needs to know this band is more than just me, and I'm not above providing *you* with background vocals."

"You're the face of the band." She twisted the bracelets on her arm. "Fans won't appreciate getting me instead. Besides, Becker would never agree to it."

"Let me handle him. People should hear this. You're talented. You shouldn't be content standing at the edge of the spotlight." He spread his arms out to encompass everyone. "None of you should."

"Uh, Levi definitely should." Seth's statement ushered in a round of relieved laughter. The guy couldn't carry a tune in a bucket, but he could count a beat, which made him one of the best and most humble drummers in the business.

"Okay, I'll concede that one." Jake unplugged Andi's phone and stood to give it back to her. On his way over to her, he passed Levi and slapped him on the shoulder. "Levi will not sing on this new album, but I want the rest of you to take the helm on at least one song. Let's shake things up this time around."

Levi exaggerated a hand-swipe across his forehead to everyone's amusement.

"I'm in as long as I don't have to write my own songs." Mia's gaze bounced between Jake and Andi. Unlike Seth, who played by ear, she needed sheet music in front of her until she memorized every nuance.

"I'm okay with sharing what I write." Jake winked at Mia. "I'll even give you first pick."

She grinned. "Perfect. This will be fun." Her phone chimed, and she headed to the ottoman. She read the message and looked at him. "I have to run, but keep me posted." She hustled out of the room and down the hallway.

Andi stretched her long jean-clad legs and stood. "I should get going, too."

"Are you onboard with this?" Jake moved aside so she could pass.

"I am. If Becker approves it." She shrugged, then wiggled her manicured fingernails at Seth and Levi. "See you guys soon."

Seth leaned over, lifted the lid of the ottoman, and pulled out the remote. He glanced at Levi then Jake. "If you write something that stands without a fiddle, you can count me in, too." He pointed the remote at the television, then dropped it and eyed Jake. "Maybe I could play guitar on some of the new stuff?" He'd been teaching himself to play for the past couple of years.

"I don't see why not."

"Excellent." He lifted the remote again and turned on the television. "Since the ladies left, let's find a baseball game."

Now, all Jake had to do was sell his manager and the record label on Andi, Mia, and Seth stepping up. This next album could change the band's course, and he predicted success.

Eight

Scarlett sat on the dark brown couch with the midmorning sun warming her as she folded Harmony's clothes. The mail resting on the corner of the scratched pressed wood top of the coffee table caught her eye.

For the past week, she'd waited for the fallout from Jake. She wasn't sure how it would happen—a phone call from his lawyer stating she'd broken the nondisclosure agreement or a letter in the mail—but she sensed it coming.

A flash of light outside caught her attention as Olivia's mom parked at the curb. She'd taken the day off work to spend the first Monday of summer vacation with the girls. Scarlett was grateful the woman often included Harmony in her plans.

"Harmony, Olivia's here." She set aside the stack of shirts in her lap and stood to wave out the picture window.

The girl ran into the living room. "I can't find my horse shirt."

"The green one?" Harmony nodded, and Scarlett pulled it from the stack of clean laundry. "It's right here. Hurry up, they're waiting."

When the doorbell rang, Scarlett cut her daughter off from

answering it, and nudged her toward her room. "I'll get it. You go put your shirt in your bag."

As Harmony raced back across the beige carpet to her bedroom, Scarlett answered the door and smiled down at her daughter's best friend. "Hi, Olivia. Harmony's almost ready."

"Hi, Miss Scarlett."

She'd liked this little girl with big coffee-colored eyes, silky brown hair, and a timid personality from the first time she met her. "Are you excited to go to the water park today?" Between that and Harmony spending the night at her friend's house, Scarlett had time to pick up her daughter's birthday present.

"Yeah." She nodded and watched the hallway.

"Mom." Harmony raced into the room with her backpack bouncing against her. "Don't forget to call Jake about my birthday, okay?"

Scarlett acknowledged she'd put it off as long as possible. With the party just five days away, she had to pass along the information. "I won't." She held out her arms, and her daughter stepped into her hug. "Love you. Have fun with Olivia."

"I will." The girl leaned her head back and grinned up at Scarlett before grabbing her friend's hand. "Let's go."

Scarlett watched Olivia get dragged along and waved at Olivia's mom before returning to the couch. After picking up her phone from the cushion, she scrolled to the contacts. Should she? Could she? No, not yet. She'd finish the laundry first. She set the phone aside. Maybe by then, she'd muster up the courage.

An empty laundry basket, a made bed, and thirty minutes later, she returned to the living room. She folded the blanket and shifted a throw pillow out of her way before sitting down. She couldn't stall any longer. He was busy, right? Maybe he wouldn't pick up, and she could leave a message. Her heart pounded as the phone rang once. Twice.

"Hello?"

"Hi, Levi. It's Scarlett." She pulled the pillow she'd just moved onto her lap.

"Hi. What's up?" The warmth in his voice eased some of her nerves.

"I'm calling with the details for Harmony's birthday party next week. Would you mind passing them along to everyone else since yours is the only number I have?" She drew in a breath, both thankful and disappointed Jake hadn't offered his personal number.

"I can do that. Hang on a minute." His voice muffled as he spoke to someone. "Sorry about that."

"It's okay. I didn't mean to interrupt you."

"You're fine. We're just wrapping up here." She heard shuffling on his end of the line. "What are you doing today?"

"I'm hoping to pick up Harmony's birthday gift while she's out with her friend."

"Would you like some company? I could use a suggestion or two of what to get her." His eager tone encouraged her.

That would solve one of her problems. "Sure."

"I'm leaving Nashville right now. When and where should we meet?"

"I need to see someone in Franklin." She twisted the corner of the throw pillow around her finger. "Will that work?"

"Perfectly." A door closed on Levi's side of the phone. "Have you had lunch?"

She shook her head, then remembered he couldn't see her. "Not yet."

"Want to meet at Mandi's off the square in Franklin around noon?"

She glanced at the clock. That gave her thirty minutes to freshen up and change into something presentable before driving over there. "I'll see you there." She'd text him the specifics about the party so he could forward them on to the others.

Fifty minutes later, she parked in the red brick garage on Fourth Avenue and crossed the street to the popular deli. Levi stood under the bright blue sign with white lettering, his arms crossed over his chest. One side of his mouth tipped up in a lopsided grin when he saw her coming. When she reached his side, he bent down and kissed her cheek.

Was this a date? Did he think it was one? She looked into his eyes and tried to discern the answer. Levi was a friend, but no heat consumed her at his touch. No butterflies took flight in her stomach because of his proximity. The only thing she felt in his presence was comfort.

"I'm glad this worked out because I wanted to talk to you without everyone else around." He opened the door and waved her inside.

Scarlett's steps paused, and her pulse spiked. Was he going to ask her out? Ask about Jake? "Talk about what?"

"Let's order and find a table first." He steered her to the counter.

After a small disagreement about him paying for her meal, she gave in and left to find a free table. He found her a couple minutes later while balancing their drinks, napkins, and a metal stand with their order number clipped to the top.

Once he set everything down, he placed an elbow on the table and rested his chin on his fisted hand as he studied her. "What are you getting Harmony for her birthday?"

"A puppy." She leaned back in her seat and grinned. For months, she'd gone without small splurges and tucked away extra tips to give Harmony something that was top on every Christmas and birthday list. Watching Harmony with Trigger had confirmed the girl could handle the responsibility. "I've been researching breeds and cross-referencing them with potential sellers in the area. There's a breeder near here who has some Cavalier King Charles Spaniels."

She pushed her iced tea to the middle of the table. Was this too good to be true? Someone ready to take her hard-earned money and leave her with only regret? Her stomach quivered.

Levi frowned. "What's wrong?"

"When I called, he said he already had buyers for them. Then, before I hung up, he said he wasn't sure about one of them and said if I would put down a deposit, he'd hold one for me."

"Did you?" His eyebrows drew together.

"No. It sounded sketchy to me, but I think he may be downplaying the number of puppies he has in order to jack up the price."

"If you believe he's dishonest, why buy from him?" His eyes pierced into hers.

A server delivered her salad and his Reuben along with a slice of apple pie. Scarlett rubbed her hands along her arms in an ineffective effort to ward off the goose bumps. Her knee bounced beneath the table. "I want this birthday to be special for Harmony, and with you guys coming to her party, I don't want to disappoint her with a small gift."

"Hey." Levi laid his hand over hers. "You're not going to disappoint her, Scarlett. You've got an amazing daughter. That's all you. And if it makes any difference, I'm only planning to spend twenty-five dollars. That's why I'd like some ideas from you."

"Do you know what Jake is getting her?" She wanted to shove the question back in her mouth. Why had she asked?

"No, but I can find out. Somehow, I think whatever he gets will aim more toward impressing you than pleasing his daughter."

Her shoulders fell, releasing the tension that had lingered since he'd mentioned he wanted to talk to her. "When did you figure it out?"

"The moment I met Harmony. I'm not sure why Jake doesn't see it. The shape of her eyes and nose are all him."

"He already knows." Scarlett's appetite had fled, but she took a bite of her salad to stop herself from saying more.

Levi's brows lifted to the center of his forehead. "Why do you say that?"

"I wrote him a letter right after we moved to Georgia. And again when I was seven months pregnant. After she was born, I sent one more letter and included a picture of Harmony." Even if Jake was done with her, she'd been sure he would want to know his daughter. "A couple weeks later, he signed away his parental rights, asked me to sign a nondisclosure agreement stating I wouldn't tell anyone who the child's father is, and paid me off." She clamped a hand to her mouth. "But I didn't tell you any of this. I could get in big trou—"

"That doesn't sound like Jake." His forehead scrunched as he frowned. "Something's off here. You need to talk to him."

"No." She rubbed her thumb across the back of her hand. "The way he's acting like he doesn't know anything about her tells me he hasn't changed his mind." And neither she nor Harmony needed more disappointment from the man. Levi opened his mouth as if to argue, and she held up a palm. "Enough about Jake. Will you come with me to check out these puppies?"

He leaned back in the booth and crossed his arms over his chest. "If this guy might not be on the up and up, you're not going there without me."

"Thanks, Levi. You're a good friend."

He stared at her for several seconds. "You know, I almost asked you out in high school. During my senior year, this cute little freshman caught my eye."

She picked up her fork and poked at her salad. "Why didn't you?"

"It was obvious you and Jake had a connection. I couldn't compete with that." He shrugged.

"I'm sorry." Her cheeks heated.

"Don't be. You and I wouldn't have worked." He waggled his eyebrows and grinned. "But you and Jake..."

She pinched her lips together and shook her head. "Not going to happen again."

"I don't believe that for a second. And if you're honest with yourself, neither do you."

∾

J ake hummed the melody of the new song he'd written as he drove through Fairview Saturday afternoon. For the past week or so, he'd taken Levi's advice to heart and concentrated on his music.

The GPS instructed him to turn left from the four-lane road onto a residential street.

As he steered the truck down the tree-lined lane, he chuckled as he recalled his short meeting in Nashville last week. When he'd mentioned the idea of the other band members singing lead on some of the tracks, the record execs were thrilled with the idea. Becker spent the entire time arguing why it wouldn't work.

When he reached his destination, he eased his black truck to the curb in front of a small white house and double-checked the address. This was where Scarlett lived? How did she stand living so close to neighbors after living on a farm? He glanced at the other vehicles but didn't find any he recognized. He must have beat the others here.

He could only hope he'd given Scarlett enough time and space to get used to the idea of him being in her life again. After lifting the large box wrapped in a full roll of pink floral paper from the rear seat of the extended cab, he strode to the front door. Perhaps his present for her daughter would smooth things over further.

After he knocked, he waited less than a minute before the door swung open. Harmony's sparkling eyes and infectious smile telegraphed the girl's excitement. "You're finally here. I've been waiting *all* day." She gripped the hem of her red T-shirt and pulled it down. "I wore this special."

He never had gotten used to people wearing his face below their own. "I wouldn't miss this party for the world." He hefted the large, rectangular package. "Where are we putting these?"

"Out back. You have to meet my best friend in the world." Her ponytail swung as she twirled around. Her chatter kept pace with her steps.

Chuckling, he followed the girl through the tidy living room and small combination dining room and kitchen. He nodded at Cassidy, who scowled at him before returning to frosting the round cake on the counter.

Harmony opened a sliding glass door behind the table. "Olivia, he's here! I told you he'd come."

Jake ignored Cassidy and trailed the girl outside. A wood fence enclosed the large yard. Harmony ran to a group of a half dozen girls in the corner near a swing set he guessed hadn't been used for a while. Several adults lingered near two long tables on the left side of the cement patio. A pile of gifts sat on one, and Jake tucked his present under it. The other table held an array of sandwiches, chips, and punch. A few more people sat on a grouping of chairs arranged in a semi-circle on the lawn not far away and four empty blankets lay past them.

"Oh, Jake, I didn't realize you were here." Scarlett wheeled an ice chest from the side of the house to the end of the food table. "Did you get something to eat?"

"Not yet. I just got here. Harmony let me in."

She nodded. "She's been watching for you." She turned to watch the group of girls. "Thanks for coming. It means a lot to her."

"It's my pleasure. Seth and Levi should be here shortly. Mia's going to try and come, but Andi can't make it."

She swung around to face him, and a citrus scent wafted from her hair as it settled back around her shoulders. "It's fine. Harmony will be over the moon with just you here."

"See, Olivia. I told you." Harmony dragged a brown-haired girl whose gaze remained on the ground to the patio. "It really is Jake Turnquist."

He lifted his black cowboy hat up an inch with a knuckle. "The one and only. It's a pleasure to meet you, Olivia."

The girl squealed, and the others rushed over to talk to him.

Scarlett patted him on the shoulder. "I'll leave you to your adoring fans."

"By myself?" He raised an eyebrow.

She rolled her eyes. "Something tells me you can handle this crowd." She stepped away and lowered her voice. "It's their moms you should worry about." She tilted her head toward the food table where several women casually dressed for the warm summer darted surreptitious glances their way.

He exaggerated a shudder, and she laughed as she returned inside. Heat radiated through his chest at her show of happiness.

Before any other guests approached him, Seth and Mia arrived. He showed them where to put their gifts. After talking to them a few more minutes, he made an excuse and ducked inside in search of Scarlett. "Hey, Cass, need any help in here?" With no sign of Scarlett, he might as well lend a hand.

"Nope." She waved him back outside. "Go on and relax."

He scanned the small space. "Where's Scarlett?"

She narrowed her eyes and frowned at him. "In the garage with Levi. They'll be out in a few minutes."

Jake couldn't hold back a scowl at the news. Had Levi's encouragement to give Scarlett space been a ruse to keep him busy so he could home in on Jake's woman? *Whoa, man. She's not been your woman for a long time. You made certain of that.*

He returned outside, and Seth called his name. Soon, Scarlett and Levi approached. Together. His hand rested on her back. When she peered into Levi's face with a soft smile, Jake felt as if he'd been kicked in the gut. As if sensing his disapproval, the couple moved apart.

Scarlett squeezed Seth's forearm. "Thank you for coming." She turned to Mia. "Both of you. Harmony will be talking about this party for weeks."

"We wouldn't miss it." Mia hugged her. "Andi sends her apologies and a present."

"She didn't have to do that." She blushed. "Having the four of you here is plenty." She motioned toward the tables. "Did you get some food? Cass went a little overboard, so please help yourselves. We'll do presents shortly."

"Sounds great." Levi winked at her, and Jake's fingers curled into a fist. Never had he wanted to hit someone as badly as he did that minute.

Jake had just finished loading a plate when Scarlett set the girls up in the chairs. The other adults gathered around to watch the birthday girl.

"Okay, Harmony." Scarlett sat in a chair between the girl and the gift table. "Which present do you want to start with?"

"Jake's." She pointed to the biggest package under the table.

"I'll get it." He waved Scarlett back to her seat, handed his plate to Seth, and stepped forward with a little thrill of victory zapping through him as he crouched to get the large box from under the table. After he set it on the ground in front of Harmony, he retreated to where his friends stood and turned to watch the girl.

Harmony ripped off the wrapping paper and lifted the flaps on the box, then peeked inside. Her squeal pierced the air. "Mom, it's a guitar. And Jake signed it."

He glanced at Scarlett.

Her smile fell, but she recovered quickly. "What do you say, sweetie?"

"Thank you, Jake." Harmony gave him a radiant smile. "I really wanted a new guitar."

He'd remembered. "You're welcome. Maybe you'll play something for me later?"

"Okay." Her gaze shifted back to the table overflowing with packages.

When she'd opened all the presents—he'd tried to hide his smugness when Harmony opened the stuffed horse from Levi—and Scarlett had stuffed all the paper into a trash bag, the girl turned to her mom. "There wasn't one from you."

Scarlett nodded at Levi, who strode back to the garage door. "I saved mine for last. It's coming in a few minutes."

The moment Levi returned, Harmony screamed and bounced out of her chair. "A puppy!"

A brown and white Cavalier King Charles Spaniel with a

green bow tied around his neck squirmed in the crook of Levi's arm. He passed the tiny dog and a brown leash to Scarlett. When she had a firm hold on the dog, he walked to the spot next to Jake.

She held it to her chest and knelt in front of her daughter. "You'll need to take care of this little guy. Make sure he has food and water, take him for walks, and clean up after him."

"I will, Mom." She reached for the dog. "What's his name?"

"That's another one of your responsibilities. You get to pick the perfect name for him."

When his parents gave him Trigger, he'd taken days to settle on a name. Scarlett loved teasing him with names like Taco, Wonton, or Meatball. He'd roll his eyes and fight his laughter so he didn't encourage her.

Harmony screwed her lips together, and Jake chuckled at the expression that she'd so obviously inherited from Scarlett.

"Max. His name is Max."

"An excellent name." She hooked the leash to the dog's collar and held it out to her daughter. "Why don't you show Max around his new home while Aunt Cassidy and I get the cake?"

"Okay." Harmony started toward her friends but twisted around and ran to Scarlett to give her a one-armed hug. "Thanks, Mom. This is the best birthday ever."

"You're welcome, sweetie."

While Scarlett and Cassidy went to get the cake, the other moms chatted among themselves while they watched ten little girls follow the puppy around the yard.

"You ever consider getting one of those, Jake?" Levi tipped his head toward the group.

"I have Trigger."

"Not the dog. The kids."

The only person he could imagine having children with wanted nothing to do with him. "Nah, I've got too much on my plate to add a kid to the mix."

Levi sucked in a breath as Cassidy shuffled outside carrying the cake.

"Oh, that's beautiful," Mia said. "Let me take a picture." She took out her phone and snapped a couple photos.

Jake moved closer to the table and read the words piped on top.

HAPPY 9th BIRTHDAY, HARMONY

Something niggled at his conscience, but before he could zero in on it, the puppy darted past his boots, and he stepped back to avoid the herd of giggling girls who gave chase.

Nine

The lessons she'd scrimped to pay for showed as Harmony strummed her new guitar and lost herself in the music. Scarlett settled into her chair next to her daughter and lifted another bite of cake to her lips, smiling as the song came to an end.

"Play another." Levi's request got no resistance from the birthday girl.

Harmony's soprano rang out clear and high before the song registered. Scarlett darted a glance at Jake, who aimed an accusing glare her way. He wouldn't cause a scene over her teaching Harmony that particular song, would he?

The first time Harmony had asked about her daddy, Scarlett wanted to give her something to hold on to. A piece of the man she loved. No matter how much pain pinched her heart every time her daughter asked her to sing the song again or sang it to herself in a voice filled with longing, she could not regret sharing it with her.

Unaware of the storm brewing around her, Harmony closed her eyes as she led into the chorus. "When the morning comes and the storm blows through, I'll be waiting. Watching over you.

When life disappoints, and you can't help but cry, let the rain of my love get you by."

Scarlett blinked back tears at the broken promises and years of loneliness those lyrics represented.

A fierce scowl marred Jake's face. "Where'd you hear that song?" He took a step forward, crushing a cup in his hand as his gaze bounced between her and Harmony.

The music stopped mid-note. Scarlett stood and moved in front of her daughter as his face grew redder. Why was he so angry? She hadn't broken her word—he was the expert at that. All she'd done was taught a little girl—one desperate to understand why she didn't have a dad who loved and wanted her—a song.

"My daddy wrote it." Harmony's small voice ignited every protective instinct within her.

All color drained from his face before he spun on his boots and stomped away, disappearing around the corner of the house.

She stood frozen with his wounded and confused expression playing on a loop in her mind.

"Go." Cassidy grabbed the plate from Scarlett's trembling hands and nudged her shoulder. "Talk to him before it festers."

Before what festers? Scarlett stumbled after him. Was this really about the song? If anything, she had more cause to be angry. He'd abandoned her and their child. Made promises and broken every one of them.

One night of dancing, followed by kisses in the barn, had led to confessions of love and much, much more. Yes, she regretted the choices they'd made back in high school. Her life would be less complicated if they'd refrained from intimacy, but God had given her a beautiful daughter despite their impetuous mistake. Without Harmony, would she have healed from the heartbreak of Jake's silence?

She caught up to him as he yanked open the door of his black truck, snatched off his hat, and tossed it inside. "Jake?"

His back stiffened, and both hands furrowed through his dark hair—that needed a trim because the wave was showing—before he faced her. The hard edge of his jaw halted her forward progress.

"Is it true? Her daddy...?" He choked up.

Her jaw fell as she stared at him. What kind of game was he playing with her? "I taught her the song but never said *who* wrote it."

He slashed a hand in the air. "I don't care about the song. Why, Scarlett? Why keep this from me?" His shoulders fell, and he slumped against the side of his truck. His voice ground so low she had to lean in to hear him. "What did I do to make you hate me this much?"

Fury boiled inside until the edges of her vision blurred. *He* rejected a relationship with his daughter. Why was he blaming her for his choices?

His voice grounded lower. "Nine years? I've had a daughter for nine years and not one peep from you."

"That's not true, and you know it." She jabbed a finger in the air toward him. "You're the one who wanted nothing to do with our daughter. *Your* daughter."

"You think I didn't deserve to know *my* daughter?" He glared at her. "What gives you the right to make that decision?" His volume rose again as he stood to his full five-foot-ten height. "You're going to pay for this."

She already had. Every single day. "Jake, this is what you wanted." He couldn't change his mind and take her daughter now.

"I'm so livid, I can't think straight." He put one foot inside the truck before pivoting her way again. "You can expect a call from my lawyer."

Her legs turned rubbery at the pronouncement before the truck engine revved, and Jake sped away.

She couldn't afford a legal battle, especially not against someone who could hire the best lawyer in the state. Why was Jake so angry about this, and what had changed to make him want his daughter now?

And Harmony would be caught in the middle. Her breath

caught on a sob. Oh, Harmony. She was going to feel so betrayed when the truth came out. Would she blame Scarlett for keeping this from her? Want to live with Jake? The singer she already loved before she knew he was her dad?

An arm wrapped around her shoulders, and she glanced up. Levi's solid presence broke her resolve, and she buried her face in his chest, letting her tears loose. Seeing the anger and disgust in Jake's face had been far more painful than receiving his letter with the nondisclosure agreement and check a decade ago.

When she calmed enough to speak, she pulled away and swiped at her cheeks while avoiding eye contact, embarrassed by her show of weakness. "I don't understand why he's acting this way. He didn't want her before, but now he's blaming me, as though I kept her from him on purpose."

"Did you ever talk to him?" He tightened his arm and held her in place. "In person, not through a letter or email?"

"I tried." She inhaled a shuddering breath. "Every time I called, someone else answered his phone and said he didn't want to speak with me."

"The same person?" His somber tone drew her gaze to his as she searched her memory.

"No. Three or four different people, I think. Definitely a man and a woman."

"I don't know what happened, but like I said before, none of this sounds like Jake. You two need to sit down and hash out exactly what went down. Who else knows he's Harmony's father?"

"Cassidy figured it out. Mom and Dad did, too, but they never told a soul, and we moved out of state before I started showing."

"Anyone else?"

"Jake."

Levi's lips turned down. "So, his parents have no idea they have a granddaughter?"

Tears started anew, and she shook her head. "I wasn't allowed to say anything, and when they find out, they're going to hate me more than Jake does." She longed for Harmony to meet her other grandparents, especially now that her parents were gone, but never believed it was a possibility.

"He's upset, but he doesn't hate you. Will you do me a favor?"

She wiped her eyes again and sighed. His eyes held compassion when she looked into them this time. "What?"

"Make an effort to talk to him. Tell him every detail." He smiled wryly. "But first, give him a day or two to cool off."

"I'll try, Levi, but I'm not giving Harmony up without a fight." Even if it took every spare minute on her knees and every penny she had, she would fight for her daughter.

~

Jake barreled down his driveway, not remembering one bit of the thirty-minute drive from Scarlett's house. Too worked up to do anything inside, he turned the truck around and steered it toward his neighbor's barn. He'd take Hercules for a run.

Once the horse was saddled and outside, Jake pressed down on the crown of his hat to secure it, swung into the saddle, and kicked Hercules into a trot. The questions in his mind kept cadence with the horse's hooves as they pounded the ground. Harmony was a vibrant girl full of happiness who sang like an angel, and he'd had no part in developing her big personality or her musical talent. What would it have been like to hold her in the crook of his arm or hear her first word? He would have happily read her a story and tucked her into bed each night. Given her advice about boys, most of which would be to avoid them. He let out an incredulous laugh. Look at him, already worried about his daughter. Wow, he had a daughter. His parents would be over the moon when they found out.

He frowned. How could Scarlett do that to them? To him. She'd stolen so many precious memories.

She was to blame for this situation. Did she already know she was pregnant when he'd broken up with her? Was moving to Georgia a way to keep their baby a secret?

He sighed. That wasn't fair. She'd had no choice in the move. And he was the immature child who pretended to be a man when he asked her to prove how much she loved him. A real man would never ask that of someone he cared for. He swallowed and brushed the thought away.

Hercules stumbled, and Jake jerked his head up in time to glimpse the large hole the horse had stepped into before he sailed from the saddle and over the horse's head. He landed face-first with his right shoulder taking the brunt of the impact. After giving himself several minutes to catch his breath, he tried to sit up. Pain shot through his upper body, and he bellowed as he rolled to his back. He stared at the cloudless blue sky.

"I know it's been a while since I talked to You, God, but I'm in a pickle." He sucked a lungful of air between his teeth. "No one knows where I am, and I have no way of contacting anyone. Give me the strength to get back to the barn or send someone this way." He closed his eyes as moisture pooled in them. "And if You see fit, please help me forgive Scarlett and be a good dad to Harmony."

He opened his eyes when a nicker sounded nearby, and he tilted his head to the left. Hercules stood a few feet away, watching him with wary eyes. He breathed a sigh of relief. His horse hadn't broken any bones, but he wasn't sure the same was true for himself. He needed to check them both for injuries but couldn't do that lying on the grass.

He shifted into a sitting position with his legs stretched in front of him and waited for the wave of nausea to pass. A minute later, he shifted to his knees and grit his teeth, holding his right elbow to his side as he lumbered to his feet. His hat sat a yard away, so Jake retrieved it and stuck it on his head.

After confirming Hercules was unharmed, he gripped the saddle horn with his left hand and stuck his right boot in the stirrup. While it wasn't how he normally mounted, Jake counted it a blessing he'd trained his horse to accept saddling from both sides. He ground his teeth as he pushed off the grass with the sole of his boot and came back down before he could swing his leg over the back of the horse. He took several deep breaths and tried again. And again. On the fourth attempt, he pushed through the pain and settled onto the saddle.

As Hercules plodded toward the barn, every contact of hoof to ground sent a wave of pain into Jake's right shoulder. He fought to keep his balance and watch the terrain as sweat beaded on his upper lip. The last thing either of them needed was another fall.

Finally, the barn's brown siding came into sight, and Hercules's ears perked up. "We made it." He patted the horse's neck with his left hand.

Levi walked out of the barn and opened the gate. Jake growled under his breath as he begrudgingly acknowledged the assistance with a tilt of his head. The guy had become way too friendly with Scarlett. Jake had seen him in his rearview mirror after he'd driven away from his argument with Scarlett. Seen him stride to Scarlett and wrap her in his arms.

"You here to do Scarlett's begging?" He grimaced as he tugged on the reins, and Hercules came to a stop once in the corral.

Levi walked to his side and squinted up at him. "You okay? You're almost white."

He tugged the brim of his hat down to hide from Levi's pitying gaze. "I'm fine."

He swung his leg over the saddle and landed on the ground. The impact sent searing agony through his shoulder, and his knees buckled, sending him crashing to the dirt as Levi hollered Tom's name.

"Jake?" Someone called him from a distance. "Can you hear me?"

He squinted an eye open enough to make out two heads

above him with two sets of eyes peering down at him. "What happened?" The words came out as a croak.

"You fell off Hercules." Levi's forehead creased with concern.

Jake blinked several times and tried to breathe through the pain and nausea that swirled worse than it had in the field. "Again?"

"What?" Disapproval dripped from Tom's single word. "You fell before this?"

"Earlier." He tried to sit up, panting with the effort. "When we were... riding. He stepped in a hole."

"Those blasted moles." Tom took his hat off and slapped it against his leg. "They've torn up the east pastures." After replacing his hat, he walked to Hercules and ran a hand down each leg, murmuring reassurances to the animal.

"Where'd you land?" Levi bent lower and studied Jake.

"Probably one of the east pastures." Jake bit his tongue. That had slipped out without thought. How had he forgotten, even for a few seconds, those looks between Levi and Scarlett?

Levi cupped a fist over his mouth, but the lines around his eyes exposed his humor. "What part of your body broke your fall, Jake?"

"Shoulder." Which throbbed like a hammer struck it with each pulse of his heart. He needed to stall a few more minutes before he attempted to get to his feet. "You got any aspirin, Tom?"

"Aspirin?" The old wrangler scowled. "Did you land on your head? You need to see a doctor. I'm liable for any injury that occurs on this property, and the last thing I need is bad press because some spoiled country singer couldn't keep his rear in the saddle."

Jake heard the man's teasing but wanted to assure him in case any truth resided in his statement. "What are you talking about? I won't even mention your name."

"Come on." Levi held out his left hand, and Jake reluctantly gripped it. "I'll drive you to town."

On his feet again—a feat much easier with Levi's help—Jake nodded at his friend. "Thanks."

"I'll take care of this guy and keep an eye on him." Tom unbuckled the rear cinch.

"Appreciate it." His energy faded, and he stumbled forward.

"Whoa." Levi came to his left side. "Why don't you use my shoulder for support?"

Defeated, he grasped Levi's shoulder as they shuffled to the parking lot. He gave a regretful look at his truck before settling into the SUV. He groaned as he leaned against the leather seat and closed his eyes.

"I'll let you take me to the hospital, but we're not going to discuss Scarlett."

Levi buckled Jake's seat belt, jerked a nod, and slammed the door before rounding the front of the vehicle. After he slid behind the steering wheel, he looked at Jake. "You might want to lose the hat." He reached in the backseat and handed over a tattered red and white baseball cap. "Try this."

While most people in Nashville and the surrounding suburbs left him alone when they recognized him out and about, some fans were on the lookout for musicians and the handful of other stars who lived in the area. And then there were the photographers out to get a picture they could make a profit on. If Becker got wind of his injury from someone other than him, Jake would never hear the end of it. Especially if this delayed the tour, and he had a sinking suspicion his manager would have an earful of opinions about how he'd spent his Saturday.

Despite his insistence they not speak of Scarlett and Harmony —his daughter, how long would it take for that to sink in?—he couldn't shut off his brain. As he stared out the window watching the rocky hills and green trees fly past, today's events marched through his brain in much the same way. What was she afraid of? Did she think he'd be a bad father? They'd dreamed of having a family, kids of their own when they were kids themselves, and he'd shared everything he hoped to do with them one day. So why—

even if the timing wasn't right for his career and she had another year of high school to go—did she keep this to herself?

Unable to keep the questions inside any longer, he turned his head toward Levi. "Why didn't she tell me about Harmony?"

"Are we discussing it now?" He shifted to the right lane and glanced at Jake. "You signed away your parental rights and paid her to keep quiet."

"What?" He flinched at the outright lie. He would never do that to Harmony. Or Scarlett. "Who told you that?"

"Scarlett did."

Jake took shallow breaths as twin pain stabbed him. His shoulder would heal with time, but would his heart ever recover? Why would she say that? He swiped the ball cap from his head and dropped it in his lap. He ran his left hand through his hair and released a sigh of frustration. "I'd never do that to Harmony or Scarlett."

"I know, but she believes it. Has for nine years now. It'll be a challenge to dissuade her."

"I'm mad at her." But with Levi's insights, his anger eased a tad. "There are so many things I've missed. I have a daughter, Levi, a little girl, and I didn't get to share any of her life before now." He could have been the one to sing to her on nights when she couldn't sleep because of a nightmare or written silly songs with her.

"Can I give you some advice?" Levi's tone softened like he, too, had missed out on those years.

He hesitated, unsure whether he wanted more advice from his bandmate. "I'm going to get it whether or not I agree, so go ahead."

"That little girl is Scarlett's life. I heard you threaten her with a lawyer, but if you try to take her away, I'm not sure it's something either of you could recover from."

Perhaps, but could he overcome Scarlett's omission? Even forgive her?

He studied Levi from the corner of his eye. Why wasn't he

freaking out about Jake being a dad? The hints he'd dropped at the Memorial Day barbecue came back to him. "How long have you known?"

"From the moment I laid eyes on Harmony. She's the right age, and she favors you."

He thought of the girl who'd answered the door that morning with her red ponytail, sparkling blue eyes, and a wide grin. "She looks exactly like Scarlett."

"No." Levi exited the interstate and yielded right into cross traffic. "She's a combination of both of you. I bet Scarlett can point out the similarities to you."

As they turned left at a light three blocks from the emergency room, Jake leaned his head back and stared up, picturing the heavens above. "What am I supposed to do now?"

Ten

S carlett put away the last of the lunch dishes and walked to the back door to check on Harmony. She smiled at the girl's laughter as she played tug with Max using one of his toys.

Her daughter's confusion and frustration after Jake's abrupt departure from the party yesterday had added another level of frustration to Scarlett's distress. Levi had once again stepped in and smoothed the waters when he stayed at the party a while after Jake's abrupt departure and gave Harmony some dog training tips.

Scarlett's phone rang, and she grabbed it from the kitchen counter, grateful for the interruption to her thoughts. She didn't recognize the local number, but one of Harmony's friends had left a jacket yesterday, and this could be one of the girls' parents calling about it. "Hello?"

"Scarlett?" Jake's voice sent fear and agitation through her system.

"How did you get my number?" She glanced toward Cass's room, but her cousin wouldn't dream of betraying her like that. Which meant Levi had passed it along. She should have known he'd eventually side with Jake. "Never mind. Did you call to rant some more?"

Hadn't he said enough hurtful things to her yesterday? Was he calling to throw more verbal darts her way? She glanced out the window to make sure Harmony hadn't tired of playing with the dog before she stomped to her room and shut the door. "Or is this a courtesy call to remind me that I'll be hearing from your lawyer?"

"Calm down."

"Don't tell me what to do, Jacob Michael Turnquist." Her volume rose with each syllable as she paced beside her bed. "You have no place."

"You're right. I'm sorry." His quiet, placating tone smoothed her irritation from tornado to thunderstorm proportions. "I'm calling to ask a favor."

How dare he? They weren't friends. They weren't anything to each other anymore.

"You still there?"

"Yeah, I'm here."

He blew out a breath. "I, um, got thrown from Hercules yesterday."

"What?" Her anger melted away like ice on a summer sidewalk. No matter what Jake decided to do about Harmony, she didn't wish ill on him. Much. "Are you okay?"

"Not exactly." He barked a humorless laugh. "I broke my collarbone and have to wear a sling for the next four weeks."

He had to be in a lot of pain. One of Cassidy's twin brothers had broken an arm when they were kids. He couldn't even perform simple tasks. She sucked in a breath. "Oh, Jake, your tour."

"Becker's working on postponing the shows. I got an earful from him when I called to explain what happened, but the man knows how to do his job. He's already found replacements for our appearances at the music festival at the end of the month, and instead, we're filling in at an acoustic showcase the second week of July."

"I'm glad he's taking care of the logistics for you. Do you need anything? Can I bring you a meal or drive you to the doctor?" What was she doing? She wished she could shove the words back inside. Her memories of Gavin's injury had given her sympathy for Jake.

Agreeing to such an offer would not remove him from her life. She'd been counting down the days until he was on the road and states away from her confused daughter and Scarlett's own bruised heart. Now, he would have time on his hands to follow through with his lawyer.

"There is one thing." He hesitated too long.

What could he possibly want? An apology? A date? Full custody of Harmony? "What is it? You're scaring me. Just spit it out."

"It's difficult to do most everything with my left arm. Would you consider staying here and helping me out for a month? Since school's out, you can bring Harmony. I'd like to spend some time with my daughter."

Hearing him say *my daughter* broke something loose inside of her. She sank onto her bed and breathed through the ache. Could she do what he asked? It meant being near him all day, every day.

"Jake, I have a job." One she couldn't afford to lose. Not to mention, if they were at Jake's house, her drive would be thirty minutes longer each way. And who would watch Harmony when she worked? Jake with his one good arm?

"Take some time off. I'll pay you."

"I don't know." She twisted a loose thread from her green and white quilt around her finger. Rachel could find another server for the next few weeks. Plenty of her coworkers asked for extra shifts, but would she hire Scarlett back when Jake drove out of her life again?

"Look, Scarlett, I'm not going to push or beg. Think about it, okay? I'll pay you the same as I would any in-home care provider, and you're welcome to anything in the house." When he spoke again, the smile in his voice carried over the airwaves. "And Tom's stables are only five minutes away."

Her shoulders fell. She was more than tempted to take him up on the proposal. "I'll consider it." She could spend more time with Harmony. The girl would be on cloud nine at Jake's house, but she'd have to keep the possibility from her daughter until she made her decision.

"Thank you. I do need to find someone else if you can't, so I need to know in the next day or two."

Was he alone in his big house? Was someone making sure he ate and took his pain medicine? "What are you doing for help now?"

"Andi's here today, and Seth's coming tonight."

Something she hadn't experienced in a long time pricked at her, and she jerked her finger to break the thread. Andi was his friend. His coworker. She and Jake weren't a couple.

"I'll call with my answer before noon tomorrow."

"Perfect. Even if you don't want to do it, we do still need to talk."

"I know." Her response came out so quiet he probably had to strain to hear it. "Bye, Jake."

She disconnected the call and dropped her phone on the bed, grabbed a pillow, and curled herself around it. "I wish you were here, Mom. I could really use your advice."

But she could always speak with someone. The One who wanted the best for her, even if it meant walking through trials to get there. *Lord, I don't know what to do. I'm confused and scared for my baby girl right now. Give me clear direction in answering Jake's request, and please, please protect Harmony's heart.*

"Mom?" Harmony's distress had her on her feet and out the door in seconds.

"I'm here." She froze at the end of the hallway.

Max sat under the coffee table with white feathers surrounding him like a dusting of snow. He pawed at the torn throw pillow, widening the blanket of white on the carpet.

Scarlett put her hands on her hips and looked at her daughter. "Harmony, what is Max doing in the house?"

"I had to go to the bathroom, and he wanted to come with me." Her bottom lip jutted out.

"We talked about this yesterday. Max needs to stay in the garage until he's house trained." What would she do with the dog if they went to Jake's house? She shook the concern from her head and concentrated on the more important issue. "Go put the dog in his crate and come back in to clean this up."

"But Mom..."

"No buts, Harmony." No time like the present to teach the girl a lesson in the responsibilities of dog ownership. "You agreed to take care of Max, and that means cleaning up after him. You go get some grocery bags from under the kitchen sink, and I'll pull the vacuum cleaner out for anything you can't get with your hands."

Harmony had stuffed a second handful of feathers into a grocery bag when Cassidy walked in the front door. She glanced at the mess, strode down the hall, and shut her bedroom door without uttering a word.

"Is she mad?" Harmony's eyes were round as she stared after her aunt.

Scarlett had seen the amusement in Cass's eyes and fought her own grin. "When you finish up here, you should go apologize."

"I can buy a new pillow with my birthday money."

Her heart softened at the girl's generous heart. "Why don't you tell Cass that." No way would her cousin accept, but she didn't want to discourage Harmony.

When Harmony finished vacuuming the last of the feathers from the carpet, Scarlett perched on the arm of the couch. "Go talk to Cass, and then I want you to spend an hour in your room."

The girl nodded and blinked back tears. "I'm sorry, Mom."

"I know you are, sweetie. But you broke a rule, and there are consequences for that."

"Okay." With slumped shoulders, Harmony trudged to the end of the hall and knocked on Cassidy's door.

When Harmony came out and went to her bedroom a few minutes later, Cass walked into the living room, shaking her head the entire way. "I don't know how you do it, Scarlett. I couldn't keep a straight face."

She laughed. "I can't always." With the diversion over, her thoughts returned to Jake's call. "Today I had something else on my mind. Jake called me earlier."

"Oh, no." Her hand flew to her mouth, and she sank onto the couch cushion nearest Scarlett. "What'd he say?"

"Not what I expected." She plucked a stray feather from her cotton capri pants and recounted their conversation. "What should I do?"

"Maybe if you go, he won't fight for custody. Once he realizes how much work caring for her is, he'll back off."

"Jake's not like that." Her defense came unbidden. "A little hard work won't deter him. His career is evidence of that."

"That's another reason he shouldn't get Harmony. How much did he say he'd pay you?"

"The same as an in-home caregiver." She shrugged as if it didn't matter, but she knew it would be more than she made at the restaurant. She glanced at the clock on the wall across from them and stood. "Guess I should look that up when I get home from work."

"I'll do it. You go get ready."

"Thanks." She squeezed Cassidy's hand. If she didn't get going, she wouldn't have a chance to talk to Rachel before her shift about taking time off. If her boss said no, she could deny Jake's request with a clear conscience.

Jake checked his phone for the dozenth time since he'd woken up.

"Knock it off." Seth filled two mugs with coffee, returned

the pot to the machine on the counter, and sat in the chair across from him, sliding one of the cups his way. "She'll call."

He put the phone face down on the table and wrapped his right hand around the handle, but his sling prevented him from lifting the brew to his lips. He grunted and grabbed the mug with his other hand. Everything felt backward lefthanded. He stared over Seth's shoulder into the backyard.

Would Scarlett come or turn him down? He'd rushed to assure her he'd pay her. When he looked up the average salary of a care provider, he'd groaned. Five hundred a week wasn't enough. Surely, she'd realize his celebrity status would demand a private provider, which would mean better pay. Right?

"Jake?"

He took another sip of coffee. Should he call and give her an exact dollar figure? How much could he offer without offending her?

"Jake?"

And what if she said no? How would he spend time with Harmony then? Levi was right. He couldn't take her away from Scarlett. It would destroy any chance of an amicable future between them.

"Jake? Oh, forget it. Hello?"

His head snapped up.

Seth smirked across the table with Jake's phone pressed to his ear. "Yeah, he's here. Just a second." He lowered the phone with the speed of a turtle.

Jake abandoned his coffee and snatched it from his hand as soon as it was within striking distance and lifted it without looking at the screen. "Hello?"

"Hi."

He'd never been so relieved to hear a voice on the other end of the line. "Scarlett, I'm glad you called."

Seth stood and lifted his coffee cup in a salute before exiting the room.

"I had a couple of questions about helping you out," Scarlett said.

"I'll pay you a thousand dollars a week." Too late to second guess himself now.

"I wasn't going to ask about money, but that's too much."

It wasn't, but he'd cross that bridge later. "What would you like to know?"

"Harmony has Max now, and I want to teach her responsibility—"

"Bring him. Trigger needs a pal."

"A-are you sure? He's not housebroken, and he tore up one of Cassidy's throw pillows yesterday."

"Positive." If agreeing got them here, he'd replace the carpet and every pillow in his entire house later. "Anything else?"

"Well..." She hesitated, and he pictured her biting the inside of her bottom lip. "What are the sleeping arrangements?"

He'd given this some consideration, not wanting her to feel uncomfortable or like she was intruding. "Harmony can sleep in the same room she stayed in last time, and you can use the one beside hers or the one across the hall. My room is at the far end, but if you're uncomfortable with that for propriety's sake, Seth can help move me into the family room."

Yeah, he hadn't mentioned that to Seth, but if it convinced her to come, he'd gladly take the chiding sure to come from his friend.

He held his tongue, unwilling to push too hard and tip the scales in the opposite direction. Several minutes ticked by. Or perhaps it was only a few endless seconds.

"Okay."

Did he hear correctly? "Okay? You'll come?"

"Yeah. One month, right?"

A grin stretched across his face. "Yes."

"But we need to get something straight. I probably should have started with this. Please don't say anything to Harmony about you being her father."

His smile faltered. "Scar—"

"No, Jake. If you can't agree to that, you'll have to find someone else. Harmony will not get caught in the middle when you change your mind again."

Why she thought he would abandon her and Harmony confounded him. With his injury, he hadn't been able to dig into it more, but he knew what he wanted now. Maybe more than he ever had. "I won't ch—"

"Not today, but what about when the next tour or album comes along? Or when you fall in love and get married and start your own family? Please don't set my daughter up for that kind of heartbreak."

"Our daughter." Harmony belonged to him, too. If he couldn't tell the girl the truth yet, he'd remind Scarlett every chance he got. "And I won't say a word." For now. "As long as I can spend time with her. Get to know her."

"She'll love that."

He'd love that, too. Love her. Already did.

"When should we come?"

Now. "Any time today. I can talk Seth into staying until then, but he'll want to get out of here soon."

"That works. Should I pick up groceries or anything on my way?"

Groceries? He glanced at the box of donuts Seth had brought with him. His meals usually came from a delivery driver or the freezer. He doubted either of those options would appeal to Scarlett. And he wouldn't complain about a homecooked meal or two. "Um, yeah. That would be great. I don't have a lot here. If you include some stuff for me, I'll pay you for everything when you get here."

"Of course, I'll pick up some food for you. Isn't that what you're paying me for?"

"It's the least I can do." As long as they were in his home, he'd take care of them. Like he would have done if she'd told him about the pregnancy. Like he hoped to do in the future. "I'm sorry you'll have to do most of the cooking while I'm incapacitated, but I do have a cleaning company that comes in twice a week to take care of the house."

"Jake, I can do the housework. You don't have—"

"It's my normal routine, Scarlett. I'm already taking advantage of your kindness."

"You're not."

"Yes, I am, but that's not the point. I don't want your staying here to cost you a thing. Think of it as a working vacation."

"Fine." Her frustration carried over the phone.

"Thank you. I'll see you in a few hours." Before she could argue further or change her mind, he hung up.

He took a sip of his now-cold coffee as the buzz of elation hummed through his body. He had four weeks to convince Scarlett he wanted her back in his life. From this day forward. Permanently.

And he would start tonight.

Eleven

After ensuring Harmony had a tight grip on Max's leash, Scarlett gave her one of the lighter fabric grocery totes. She grabbed several others to carry herself and led the way to Jake's back door. Had she made the right decision, or was she setting both her and her daughter up for disappointment? Her heart thumped harder with every step closer.

Harmony knocked, and Seth swung the door inward. "Hi, ladies. Come on in." He stepped aside to let them pass, and the puppy pulled at his leash in his excitement to check out the new surroundings.

"Don't let go of Max, Harmony." Scarlett set her load on the island counter and took the girl's bag from her hand. "Why don't you take him outside until I get this stuff put away, and then we can let him explore." The activity would do her daughter good and maybe run off the sugar from the piece of birthday cake she'd eaten after lunch.

"Okay." She turned around.

"And don't let him off his leash." Scarlett got the last instruction out as the girl raced out the door.

Seth walked over to the opposite side of the counter, crossed his arm over the back of one of the barstools, and eyed the totes. "Wow. That's a lot of food."

She laughed. This was nothing compared to some of the hauls Cass brought home for her catering jobs. "And there's even more in the car."

He straightened. "Can I bring those inside for you? I can also grab your luggage or whatever else you need." He lifted his arms and flexed his biceps. "May as well take advantage of these while you have them at your disposal."

She pressed her lips together to keep from smiling. Despite his antics, he was being a gentleman. She'd have to remember to tell Cass he wasn't a complete neanderthal—her cousin's words not hers. "That would be a tremendous help. Thank you."

He headed back toward the door, and Scarlett stepped in front of him. "Wait. Where's Jake? Where should I put the food?"

"Jake's taking a nap." He chuckled. "The pain medication knocks him out, but he's switching to regular aspirin in a couple of days. He'll probably be down for a little while yet." He glanced around the kitchen and shrugged. "And do whatever you like with the food. Make yourself at home."

She dug her keys from her pocket and held them out, extremely aware of her rundown sedan with the peeling tan paint on the hood and roof. "The rest of the groceries are in the backseat with Max's kennel. Everything else is in the trunk."

When he took them from her, he tossed them in the air, then swung the keyring around his index finger. "Got it. I'll be back in a flash."

When he left, she opened several cupboards and drawers to familiarize herself with the location of Jake's dishes, pots, pans, and cooking utensils. She opened the fridge and found ketchup, mustard, and barbecue sauce in the door. A half-gallon of milk and three Chinese food takeout containers occupied the shelves. The pantry contained three cans of soup and a questionable loaf of bread.

Wrinkling her nose, she tossed the bread on top of four

Chinese food takeout cartons in the three-quarters full trash can at the end of the island.

She looked out the window to check on Harmony and chuckled. The puppy held his head high as he bounded ahead with a long stick in his mouth, and her daughter raced along with him. A light clicking came from the front entry, and Scarlett turned around. Trigger meandered into the kitchen and headed straight to her.

"Hey, big guy." She scratched him behind the ears. "Are you okay sharing your house with us?"

The black lab leaned against her leg.

"Maybe you can teach Max a few things, hmm?" The back door opened, and she spun to the left.

Seth muscled in four grocery bags in one hand, Scarlett's black suitcase in the other, and Harmony's smaller purple one tucked under his arm.

She hurried over to the counter and made some more space for him to set the rest of the food down.

Once he'd unburdened himself with the totes and set the suitcases along the far wall, he walked over and leaned over Trigger to scratch his chest. "You need to go outside, big guy?"

"Uh." Scarlett bit her lip. Trigger was well-trained, but she had no clue how Max would react to him. What if one of them got hurt? Or worse, what if Harmony got in the middle of them.

Seth looked up at her. "Is there a problem?"

"It's just..." She pulled a couple of boxes of pasta from one of the bags. "I don't know how Max will handle a much bigger dog."

"I'm sure he'll be fine." Seth stood up again and strode into the mudroom.

Scarlett frowned at the empty opening. Was that conversation over?

Half a minute later, he returned with a blue leash in his hand. "Why don't I take Trigger out and introduce them? I'll stick close by, and when we come back in, I'll give you gals a tour before Jake wakes up."

"Don't let us keep you." She separated the groceries into piles —fridge, freezer, and pantry—as she continued emptying the shopping bags. "Jake mentioned you needed to leave this afternoon."

"I don't have any plans." He hooked the leash to Trigger's collar, then gave her a crooked grin, complete with his dimples. "Besides, I'm hoping to snag an invitation to dinner." He waggled his eyebrows.

"That can be arranged." Scarlett laughed. "I'll even let you choose what we have tonight. Chicken and broccoli casserole or beef stew?"

"With rolls?" His green eyes brightened as he waved a hand at the bag of Cassidy's homemade rolls resting on the counter.

"And salad."

"Yum. Beef stew gets my vote." He peered down at the dog. "You ready for this big guy?"

Scarlett opened one of the windows so she could listen for any problems that might arise. As she set to work putting away groceries—leaving those she'd need for dinner out—to the accompaniment of Seth and Harmony's voices. Once everything had found a home, she opened the lower cupboard beside the stovetop and reached in back of the bottom shelf for a large pot.

"You made it."

She bumped the back of her head on the underside of the top shelf and pulled the pot out. She rubbed the sore spot as she twisted around. "Jake, you scared me."

"Sorry." His forehead creased as he rested a hip against the island. A black sling kept his right forearm snug against his lower chest. And the gray button-up shirt he wore not only matched his eyes but fit him well. "Are you okay?"

"I'm fine." She twirled around and set the pot on the burner harder than necessary before she flipped the heat to medium high.

"Did Seth show you around?"

She picked up a bottle of olive oil and poured enough to coat the bottom into the heating pan. "He's outside with Harmony and Max right now but said he'd give me the tour afterward."

When he moved to the window she'd opened and looked outside, she studied him from the corner of her eye. Her fingers itched to fix the brown hair crushed at the back of his head. When he twisted her way, she gasped at his wistful expression. Did he wish he could be out there instead of Seth?

"They seem to be getting along fine."

"Good." She grabbed the package of stew meat from the island and set it beside the stovetop. "I was a little concerned about Trigger giving up his independence."

"He plays well with others. Mia's little dogs love him."

"Oh." She chided herself as she ripped the plastic off the beef. It wasn't any of her business. Besides, wouldn't something have happened between him and Andi or Mia already? They'd been performing together for a long time. She had no reason to be jealous.

"What are you doing?" He edged closer to her.

"Starting dinner." A sharp sizzle filled the air when she added the meat to the pot. "Seth requested beef stew." She glanced at him. "Oh, I hope you don't mind. I invited him to stay."

One corner of Jake's mouth lifted. "Not at all. You're the one doing all the work."

"It's not that much more than I'd do at home." When his smile fell, regret gripped her stomach, and she returned her focus to searing the beef. Why had she said that?

Twelve

Winning her over was going to be more difficult than he realized. Scarlett's presence filled his kitchen with light and warmth, however, even though it wasn't as thick as when he'd rashly vowed to sic a lawyer on her, a wall still surrounded her. *Pull it together, Jake. It's not going to happen in an hour.*

"I'm looking forward to a home-cooked meal." He inhaled the aroma of seared beef, and his stomach rumbled. "It's been a while. Probably Mom's last visit."

Scarlett tensed even more as she used some tongs—did he own tongs?—to turn the cubes of meat.

How did he keep saying the wrong thing? "Can I help with anything?"

She sent a pointed look at his sling.

"I can carry and stir even if I can't chop vegetables or unpeel potatoes."

Scarlett laughed, and relief flooded through him. "It's peel potatoes, Jake, and you know it."

He grinned. "Yeah, I do. Just wanted to see if I could make you smile." Which he would do every day of his life if she'd let him.

The back door banged open, and Jake spun around as Harmony rushed inside with wild hair and pink cheeks.

"Mom, can Max come inside now?"

Scarlett leaned around him. "Where is he?"

"With Seth." The girl glanced over her shoulder. "He really wants to come inside."

She stunned him when she winked his way. "Seth can come in anytime he wants."

"Mom." Harmony drew the word out into three syllables, and Jake chuckled.

"If it's okay with Jake, Max can come in, too."

Harmony folded one fist into the other and held them under his chin as she looked up at him. He never could resist that look from Scarlett, so why should it be different with his daughter? "It's fine with me."

Seth leaned in the door and unhooked Trigger's leash, and Jake watched his worn-out dog trudge down the hall toward his bed in the study.

"Keep Max's leash on for now, Harmony." Scarlett's voice brought his attention back to his daughter kneeling beside the squirming puppy.

Seth strode in from the mudroom and inhaled. "Man, it smells amazing in here." He approached Scarlett and investigated the inside of the pot. "How long 'til dinner?"

"A few hours." Scarlett tapped the spoon against the side of the pan before setting it aside on a small plate as Seth groaned. "Haven't you heard?" She patted her palm against his chest. "Good things come to those who wait."

"It better be amazing if I have to smell that for the next three or four hours." He went over and opened the upper cabinet closest to the fridge. "Harmony, would you like some water?"

"Yes, please." The girl looked up at him. "Can Max sleep with Trigger?"

"Trigger usually sleeps in my room." Jake couldn't stand to see the slump in Harmony's shoulders. "But maybe he'll stay in the study if he has a friend."

Scarlett moved beside him and shook her head at her daughter. "I don't think that's a good idea. He can stay in the garage like he does at home."

"But Mom—"

"No whining, Harmony. It's the garage or Max stays with Aunt Cass."

"Fine." The girl's bottom lip poked out as Seth handed her a glass of water.

"Why don't I go get his crate, and we get him set up?" He glanced at Jake. "You can help us find the perfect spot."

Torn between helping his daughter and spending more time with Scarlett, Jake's gaze bounced from Scarlett to his daughter and back. At Scarlett's slight nod, his decision was made. Seth took Harmony's now half-full glass and set it on the island next to his before leading the way through the mudroom to the garage.

Fifteen minutes later, Max was conked out in his crate in the back corner of the garage. Harmony had made sure the dog had a couple chew toys, his blanket, and food and water dishes nearby before draping a cover over the top of the metal cage. She was already taking responsibility, and Jake's heart swelled watching her care for her pet.

"What are we going to do now?" Harmony looked between Seth and him.

"I don't know about you, but I could use a snack before dinner." Seth grinned. "Let's go see if we can talk your mom into something."

"It will have to be healthy." The girl's brows scrunched together. "She doesn't let me eat too much sugar."

Seth's grin slipped. "How healthy?"

She shrugged. "Fruit or vegetables. She might let us have some crackers, too."

"Let's see what we can find." Jake laid his left hand on

Harmony's shoulder, and she slipped out from under it. He frowned. Had he done something to upset the girl?

The three of them entered the kitchen via the mudroom, and Scarlett spun from the island counter with a knife in her hand. "Did you get Max set up?"

"Yep." Harmony rushed to her. "Seth wants a snack."

Jake ground his teeth. What did Seth have that made the girl accept him without a second thought?

Scarlett's eyebrows rose, and a slight smirk lifted her lips. "Seth, huh? And is anyone going to share with him?"

"I am." The girl nodded with enthusiasm.

"There are apples and bananas." Scarlett gestured to the counter beside the fridge. "Or grapes in the fridge. You can also have a few pretzels or crackers, but not too many." She set the knife down and pointed to the two glasses in front of her. "And finish drinking your water."

As Seth and Harmony gathered their food and took it to the table, Scarlett carried the cutting board to the stovetop and added potatoes, carrots, and onions to the pot of meat and broth. She then returned to the island, put the cutting board and knife in the sink, and swiped the remnants of the chopped vegetables from the island into the garbage can.

"Are you done?" Jake itched to show her around more of his home.

"For a while, as soon as I finish the dishes."

"I'll take care of them." Seth looked up. "It's the least I can do for you feeding me."

For all his caution to Jake a few weeks ago, his friend sure was giving him an opening today.

Despite the dull pain returning to his injury, Jake wasn't ready to take more pain medication yet. He hadn't spent enough time with Scarlett to scratch the itch that grew now that she was here with him. He inched in beside Scarlett and held out his left hand. "Let me show you around." When she took it, years dropped away. He'd have to be careful not to slide into other past habits around her. Pet names and stolen kisses could wait. He cleared his throat. "You've already seen everything down here—"

"What's in that room?" Scarlett pointed to the first door past the breakfast nook.

The one room he kept closed off from company. He coughed into his shoulder and winced at the ache. "It's intended to be a bedroom, but I use it for storage. There's some old equipment in there along with boxes of merch and some old demos from the days we used to burn them."

Scarlett studied him with an intent gaze as if she could read his embarrassment.

"You can look in there if you like." He swallowed. "When I bought the house four years ago, I let the decorator have free rein, but have tried to make it feel more like my home whenever I'm here." The place was much bigger than one person needed, but he'd given up so much for his career, he wanted to enjoy a few of the rewards.

"I'll get Seth to help move some of my clothes to the family room and a few necessities to the guest bathroom before he leaves."

"With Harmony as chaperone, you might as well stay where you're most comfortable to rest and recover from your injury." Scarlett squeezed his hand. "But speaking of that, I'm really curious about the rest of the second floor I haven't seen yet. You have a gorgeous home."

He heard the unspoken *but* in there and waited. She didn't say more.

He released her hand and inclined his head toward the stairs to their right in an invitation for her to lead the way. When they both reached the landing at the top, he turned left. "You already saw this room where Harmony can stay, so we'll start over here."

When he opened the door to the bedroom across the hall, Scarlett gasped. He'd asked his decorator to do one of the bedrooms in lavender. Watching Scarlett's reaction, his subconscious request of her favorite color became clear. A queen-size canopy bed with lavender and white bedding sat in the center of the room with soft gray walls, and a white wardrobe stood guard at the wall along the hallway.

Scarlett circled the room, her fingers trailing along the small white desk, then the backs of the twin deep plum armchairs as she stared out the window showcasing the pastures and hills surrounding the house. He couldn't pull his gaze away. This house had never felt so much like home as it did now.

Her soft smile warmed him from the inside out. "I've never seen anything so beautiful."

I have. Swallowing the words, he backed out of the room and pulled air into his struggling lungs.

"Are you alright?" Scarlett's concerned blue eyes met his. "Do you need more pain medicine?"

"I'm fine." He waved his left hand for her to follow. "There's a bathroom here off the hall or the blue room has a small private bath, if you prefer that." *Smooth, Jake. Way to ruin the moment.*

She shook her head as they walked. The room they'd just left was the one for her.

"My studio is there." He pointed at the closed door to the right, then pushed open the last door on the left. "This is the third bedroom, and the washer and dryer are in the closet across the hall."

He paused outside the final door. Would it be awkward to show her—

"Is this the master?" Scarlett leaned closer, and he resisted taking her hand again. "Cass insisted I give her all the details. I can't leave this one out and disappoint her."

"No, we can't have that." He opened the door and stepped inside.

Scarlett followed him and walked to the end of the enormous sleigh-style bed.

He winced at the rumpled comforter, but she didn't seem to mind. She turned in a slow circle. "This room looks like you."

Was that relief? He glanced at the oak armoire and chest of

drawers. The browns with touches of gold and tan here and there gave the room a masculine overtone.

Could she imagine drinking coffee in the morning or winding down at the end of the day in the club chairs at the far corner of the room? His face heated.

"This and the studio were the only rooms I gave much input on." He waved a hand at a door to their right. "But since you're reporting, you have to tell Cass all about this."

She entered the master bath. "Oh my." Her voice filled with awe.

He peered over her shoulder. Did she like the large jacuzzi tub sitting under the picture window or the glass-enclosed shower stall that occupied the corner at the foot of the tub more? Maybe it was the walk-in closet at the far side of the room.

"You're welcome to use any of this." Anything to make her see this place as home.

"I don't think so, Jake." Her blue-eyed gaze met his in the mirror as a pretty pink blush crept into her cheeks. "It feels like an invasion of your personal space if you're staying here."

"Not at all. I don't mind finding something else to do while you enjoy the amenities." Stillness settled about them. A belonging together in this moment, in this space. Did she feel it, too?

"Mom?" Harmony's shout broke the spell.

Scarlett stepped away and hurried to the hallway. "I'm up here, sweetie. Come see your room."

Jake followed as the girl thundered up the stairs. She pulled to a stop when she saw him, a slow scowl marring her normally bright face. He winced. Harmony was definitely upset with him, and it seemed he had more fences to mend. He pressed his left hand to his aching shoulder. For now, he'd give them space.

"I'll leave you two alone to get settled." He brushed a hand lightly on Scarlett's back as he passed. "Let me know if you need anything."

Their voices followed him down the stairs.

"Harmony, that was rude."

"Mom, he ruined my party. And he made you cry."

And those two statements explained the girl's hesitance around him. This had nothing to do with Seth. It was on him, and he had a long road of making amends ahead.

A yipping urged him toward the kitchen as much as the tantalizing scent of beef and potatoes. Was Max in the house again?

Seth set a plastic bowl four times the size of the puppy on the floor.

Laughter bubbled out of Jake at the sight. "Are you giving him something to drink or trying to drown the little guy?"

Seth's head came up. "He's small, isn't he?"

"Yeah, but he's also a small breed. How'd Trigger do with the pup?"

"Just fine. He laid down and let Max climb all over him."

"Excellent. I'd hate to traumatize Harmony more since I already ruined her party."

"Kids are resilient. Or so I've heard." Seth leaned against the counter and eyed Jake with compassion. "You'll have to determine for yourself if that's true."

"Jake?"

He strode from the kitchen at Scarlett's call and found her peering down over the stair rail. "Do you need something?"

"Will you or Seth stir the stew, so it doesn't burn to the bottom of the pot?"

"Sure."

She started to turn away but twirled back around. "Do you mind if Harmony takes the yellow room? She likes it more."

"Of course not. This is your home for the time being."

"Thank you." Her brilliant smile stole his breath.

Thirteen

❧

Who knew yellow curtains would change her daughter's mind so fast?

Scarlett heard someone coming up the stairs and peeked out the door of Harmony's chosen room. Jake should be resting and not taxing himself worrying about them. The words of censure building up died on her tongue when Seth appeared with their bags.

"Where would you like these?"

"Oh, you didn't need to carry those up, but thank you. The black one goes in here." She pointed toward the purple room. "And the small one goes in here with Harmony."

Once he dropped them in the appropriate spots, he leaned against the door. "Do you need anything else?"

She shook her head. "We're all set." As he retreated down the stairs, she went to the door and called after him. "Will you turn the oven on to three hundred fifty degrees?"

"You got it." He waved a hand over his head.

She returned to the room, lifted Harmony's suitcase onto the bright yellow bedspread, and zipped it open. "Let's put your stuff away before dinner."

Scarlett and her daughter transferred her clothes into the

dresser. As Scarlett stowed the suitcase in the closet, Harmony stacked her books on the nightstand.

"Come talk with me for a minute, sweetie." Scarlett sat on the bed and patted the space beside her.

The girl climbed up next to Scarlett. "I'm sorry for being rude."

"I know, baby." She wrapped her daughter in a hug and smoothed the wavy curls in her hair. "I'm sorry I didn't ask you if you wanted to stay here before I agreed. I thought you'd be happy about it."

The girl wrinkled her nose. "I will, Mama."

The use of the name warmed Scarlett. It'd been a long time since Harmony had called her anything other than Mom. But had she made the right choice? Would helping Jake come at the cost of her daughter's heart? Was keeping Jake's true identity from the girl the right decision?

"If you want to stay with Aunt Cassidy, that's okay with me." She would miss Harmony terribly, and Jake wouldn't be pleased with the arrangement, but her daughter's well-being came first. "Jake asked if we could come help take care of him." Her insides churned. That wasn't quite the arrangement, but the best explanation for the time being.

"What happened to him?" The girl tugged at the hem of her light blue tank top.

She'd done a terrible job explaining the situation. "He fell off his horse and broke a bone in his shoulder." She ran a finger along Harmony's right collarbone. "This one here."

"Does it hurt him?"

"He says it doesn't, but I'll tell you a little secret." She leaned her forehead against Harmony's. "Sometimes people pretend they are strong and immune to pain, but it's okay to cry when you're hurting."

The girl nodded as though she understood the gravity of the statement.

"I love you."

"Love you, too."

Scarlett squeezed her one more time. "I'm glad. Now, let's get downstairs and set the table. I'm starving."

"Okay." Harmony hopped off the bed, and Scarlett followed down the stairs and around the back to where Seth and Jake sat across from each other at the small table in the breakfast nook, each checking their phones. Max slept curled in a ball beneath them with his head resting on Jake's socked foot. Harmony stiffened and leaned closer to Scarlett.

He looked up, glanced between her and Harmony, and raised an eyebrow. Once upon a time, she could interpret his expressions, but it had been a long while.

"Max seems to have settled in." She squeezed Harmony's shoulder and nudged her forward.

"He's a handsome little pup. You chose well."

"Levi picked that one." She owed him a debt of gratitude for going with her. Not only had he taken care of the haggling with the breeder, he'd also talked her out of leaving with another of Max's litter mates.

Jake's eyes darkened, but he made no further comment.

Harmony approached him with her head hanging low. "I'm sorry I was rude earlier."

Seth stood. "I'll be right back." He walked down the hallway, and a few seconds passed before a door closed.

Her daughter's courage to take the initiative and tender-hearted apology stirred a pride deep inside Scarlett. She followed Seth's lead and turned away.

"I forgive you."

She peeked over her shoulder as Jake took her daughter's small hand in his.

"And I'm the one who should apologize. I'm sorry I rushed out of your party the way I did. That wasn't very considerate of me."

She crossed the kitchen and gave the stew a quick stir, then checked to confirm Seth had preheated the oven.

"It's okay." Her voice was quiet. "I was maddest because you made my mom cry."

Scarlett winced as she opened the refrigerator, but when she glanced at Jake, his intent gaze was focused on her. "I'm sorry about that, too."

Scarlett mouthed the word *forgiven*, then gathered vegetables as Seth returned. "Harmony, come wash your hands and set the table while I make the salad."

"Mom." The whine in the girl's tone had Scarlett nipping the complaint in the bud with a raised eyebrow.

Harmony tromped to the sink with her head hanging low.

Fits of male coughing erupted. Both men covered their mouths with their fists and looked away, but not before she caught the twinkle in their eyes.

A few years' experience single parenting would wipe that merriment right off their faces. "Seth Mason, you've got two good arms, so you can help. We'll eat in the dining room tonight."

"Yes, ma'am." He stood and shot a glare Jake's way, reminding her of the trouble they'd gotten into as boys. Once he reached the sink, he made a face at Harmony, making her giggle, and washed his hands.

Scarlett set bowls, plates, and silverware on the counter. Seth picked up a stack of dishes, and Harmony grabbed two fistfuls of spoons and forks. The two jostled each other as they left the kitchen through the butler's pantry. She shook her head at their antics as she lined a baking sheet with the rolls Cassidy had baked yesterday and put them in the oven to warm.

"What can I do?" Jake leaned back in his chair and fidgeted with the strap of his sling.

If he believed for one second his injury excluded him from chores, especially after she'd scolded Seth, reality was about to hit him square in the face. "You can take the butter and the salad dressing to the table."

He looked at her with wide eyes. "Me?"

"Yes. You can handle this."

He slid his foot out from under Max and stood. Instead of going to the fridge, he walked to her side. His fingers wrapped around her wrist. "I *am* sorry about the other day. It's not an excuse, but I was shocked and upset."

"I know, and I promise we'll talk about everything." She glanced toward the other room and lowered her voice. "Later."

He released her and stretched to open the fridge door. "I don't see any dressing."

She smirked at the comment she'd heard so many times from Harmony when looking for something in the kitchen. "It's in the door."

"Where?"

She moved next to him and pointed at the shelf at his eye level. "Right there."

"I've missed you." His voice rasped. "More than you know." He wrapped his fingers around her hand.

She couldn't do this. Couldn't let him draw her into his orbit again only to be left brokenhearted and alone. After yanking her hand away, she returned to the safety of the island and dumped the bagged lettuce into a bowl. "I need to finish this salad."

"Scarlett."

"Don't, Jake. I-I can't go there with you again."

He grabbed the bottle of dressing from the fridge and shut it with more force than necessary. "Because of Levi?"

Her eyes narrowed. Did he think something was going on between them? "No, not because of him. I've spent Harmony's lifetime doing what's best for her, and I'll continue to do so."

"What's best for Harmony?" He thumped the bottle onto the counter. "*I'm* what's best. I'm her f—"

"Don't finish that sentence." The knife clunked against the cutting board as she sliced a cucumber. "She's one room away, and her little ears hear everything. Besides, you promised."

He scrubbed his hand over his face.

"What about drinks, Mom?" Harmony skipped into the room.

"Want to make lemonade?"

"Okay."

"Can I help?" Jake tucked the bottle of dressing into his sling and picked up the tub of butter. "After I put these on the table?"

"Sure." Scarlett pulled a stool to the counter, grateful for an excuse to diffuse the conversation. Keeping her distance from Jake Turnquist was proving more difficult than she'd imagined.

Once Harmony sat, Scarlett rummaged through several cabinets until she found a glass pitcher. When Jake returned, she handed it to him. "Fill it three-quarters full of water. Harmony can take it from there." She set the drink mix and a long-handled wooden spoon in front of her daughter.

"What else can I do?" Seth joined them.

"You can fill four glasses with ice and put them on the table."

Once she'd set out the salad, the group gathered at one end of the long table. Seth lifted a ladle filled with the stew as Jake reached for a roll.

"We didn't pray yet."

Both men froze at Harmony's declaration.

"Would you like to do the honors tonight?" Scarlett smiled at her daughter.

"Okay." The girl folded her hands in front of her and bowed her head. "Jesus, thank You for this food. Thank You for Mom and Max and my new friend Seth. Help Jake get better. Amen."

Scarlett lifted her head. Jake's Adam's apple bobbed when he swallowed. Had the simple prayer affected him? Which brought up another question. Had fame and fortune replaced faith in Jake Turnquist's life?

Fourteen

~~~

J ake woke to the scent of bacon and squinted at the blue numbers on his alarm clock. Wow, he'd slept in but felt good. Must have been the pain pill Scarlett had insisted he take after dinner. But he didn't like how they knocked him out, so he'd skip this morning's dose, even if a good night's rest was a blessing.

Help Jake get better. Harmony's childlike faith amazed him. How long since he'd had a real conversation with God? Years if he was honest with himself, and he missed it.

"Jake?" Scarlett rapped on the door.

Having her in his home was another answer to prayer. He scrubbed his left hand over his face, the hair on his chin rubbing against his palm. "I'm awake."

"Good morning." She opened the door. Her damp hair hung straight past her shoulders. She wore jeans and a black tank top. "Did you sleep okay?"

"I did. You?" He braced his left hand on the bed while keeping his other arm tight against his body as he tried to sit up.

"We slept well." Trigger barked, and she glanced over her shoulder "Do you need anything?"

"Will you let the dog out?" He glanced down at the track pants and button-down he'd worn yesterday. "I'll get ready and come down in a few minutes." He blinked and smiled at her. "Breakfast smells wonderful, by the way."

"Do you need any help?" Her cheeks turned as red as her name as she glanced toward the bathroom door.

"I got it." If he took his time, he could dress himself without much pain. After all, he'd done it yesterday because he didn't want to impose on Seth.

Once he'd donned a new pair of black track pants and a green button up shirt and put his sling back on, he opened his bedroom door and followed Scarlett's and Harmony's voices to the kitchen. Harmony sat at the counter reading a book while Scarlett worked at the stove with her back to him.

"Good morning, ladies." He ruffled the girl's hair, noticing for the first time the curl. Had she inherited that from him? The possibility warmed his heart. "What's on your agenda this fine Tuesday?"

"We haven't decided yet." Scarlett spun around and set a plate with three pancakes and five pieces of bacon at the space next to Harmony. "Go ahead and eat."

He pulled out the stool and maneuvered onto it from the right to keep from bumping into the girl. "I'll wait for you guys."

"Oh." She winced and glanced at her daughter. *Their* daughter. "I wasn't sure how long you'd need to get dressed, so we went ahead and ate while it was hot. Sorry."

He poured syrup over the pancakes, trying to hide his disappointment at missing a meal with them. "It's fine." He set the syrup down and looked at Harmony. "What are you planning to do over summer vacation?"

She looked up from her book with sparkling eyes. "I want to ride the horses again."

"You're just like your mom when she was little." He glanced at Scarlett and winked. "She always preferred to be outside on her horse."

"I'm not sure we'll get to ride for a while, sweetie." Scarlett set a cup of coffee in front of him, then picked up her own mug and took a sip. "We're here to take care of Jake, remember?"

He swallowed the bite of salty bacon in his mouth. "I don't expect you to spend every minute in the house. Why don't you go this afternoon?"

Scarlett cupped her hands around her mug. "We'll see. I need to run home and grab a few more things to keep Harmony occupied. Somehow, I doubt the books we brought along will last more than a week."

"Can I bring my guitar, Mom?" She wiggled in her chair.

When Scarlett opened her mouth to answer, Jake cut her off. "That's a great idea. We could write a song together."

The girl's blue eyes brightened with her grin. "And I can tell everyone Jake Turnquist helped me write it."

"You bet." He took a bite of the fluffy pancakes.

"What do you need me to do today, Jake?"

After he'd pleaded with her to stay here, he had to give her something to do. Especially after he'd turned down her offer to help him get ready for the day. As he chewed, he composed a quick list—meals, caring for Trigger, basic cleaning, driving him to and from the doctor. He swallowed and blurted the first thing to enter his mind. "I have some laundry that needs washed."

"Surely, that's not all." Scarlett lifted an eyebrow and watched him steady the plate with his right arm.

He tilted his head toward Harmony, a reminder he wanted to spend time with his daughter. "I'm assuming you're handling lunch and dinner as well." He relaxed a little when she sighed.

"Of course." She took another drink of her coffee. "I'll make another run to the store tomorrow, but we're covered for the next few meals. Let me know if you have any special requests for what to eat."

"You know my favorites." He toasted her with another forkful of pancake and stuffed it in his mouth.

She rolled her eyes and rinsed out her mug before putting it in the dishwasher. "What are you doing today?"

"Andi's coming over to write at eleven." He glanced at the clock on the microwave above the stove. If he and Andi could knock out another song or two today, they might have enough to present to the label before the tour started back up and the never-ending chaos of the road sapped his creativity.

"Hmm." Scarlett snatched the syrup bottle from in front of him and stomped to the pantry.

Jake's forehead creased as he watched the now-empty space as she banged cupboards and muttered. Was she upset he planned to work instead of spending the day with her? Despite his injury, he had obligations to fulfill, which meant spending time in the studio.

"You want any more to eat?" She returned to her side of the counter and crossed her arms over her chest.

"No, thanks." He pushed his plate aside while trying to figure out what he'd done to upset her this time. "This was more than I usually eat, but it was delicious."

Scarlett's chin poked forward. "Is Andi joining us for lunch?"

"Probably. I expect we'll work several hours this afternoon."

She nodded. "Since she'll be entertaining you, I can put off my errands and take Harmony riding instead."

"Yay!" Harmony jumped down from her stool, ran around the island, and hugged her mom around the waist. "This is the best birthday ever."

Jake froze. The girl had mentioned her birthday party was before her actual birthday, but he hadn't given it any further thought. Where had he left his phone? He'd give Andi a call and cancel their songwriting session.

"After lunch." Scarlett rinsed his plate under the running faucet as though his world hadn't just tilted on its axis. "For now, you can either help me load the dishwasher or finish reading your book."

No, he'd better not change his plans now. Scarlett could probably use some time away to thaw that cold shoulder she was giving him.

"Can I play with Max?"

"Not right now. I don't want you outside by yourself."

"If you give me a couple of minutes to put some shoes on, I'll go out with her." Jake stood and smiled at Harmony. "And happy birthday."

The girl beamed at him. "Thank you. I'm really nine now."

Scarlett peered into his eyes. "Are you up to going outside?"

Give up more time with Harmony on her birthday? The first one he got to celebrate with her? Not a chance. "Absolutely. Let me do this."

"It's not that. I don't want you to hurt yourself trying to keep up. She's got a lot of energy and the puppy adds to it." Her gaze slipped to the girl. "You're supposed to be resting and healing."

"I promise not to overdo it." He got the message loud and clear. His injury wasn't what she was most worried about. "I appreciate your concern, but I'm a big boy. Let me determine how much is too much."

"And let me remind you that I'm here for thirty days. No longer." Scarlett stiffened and straightened her shoulders. "If you reinjure yourself, you'll have to hire someone else."

If that happened, he'd find another way to keep them around.

～

Scarlett parked her sedan at the stables Jake's neighbor owned. At the sight of a trio of horses grazing in the paddock, the tension building since that morning finally flowed away.

Lunch had been a challenge as Andi and Jake talked and joked with each other the entire meal. They had practically ignored her and Harmony, the hired help. What did it matter, anyway? If Jake wanted to get involved with Andi when she was on the rebound, that was his business.

After unbuckling her seat belt, she looked over her shoulder at Harmony in the backseat. "Ready?"

"Yeah." The girl reached for the door handle and scurried out.

When they reached the front of the car, the lanky rancher with a beat-up straw cowboy hat glanced up from cinching the saddle on a fawn-colored horse and waved. Scarlett squinted her eyes. Was that Jake's palomino?

The rancher led the horse over to the fence and rested his boot on the bottom rail. "Jake called and let me know you were coming."

She blinked several times at Jake's thoughtfulness. She didn't think he'd paid any attention to her and Harmony after Andi's arrival at his place.

"Athena's ready and waiting for you." He held out a hand. "We didn't officially meet before. Name's Tom Corbin."

"Pleasure to meet you. I'm Scarlett, and this is Harmony." She smiled. "We could have saddled her, but thank you for taking the time."

He waved her off. "I'm out here anyway." He tweaked Harmony's nose. "This one's going to be a natural if she takes after her mother."

How did he know that? She frowned.

"I saw you on Quicksilver last time you were here." He inclined his head toward the trail they'd ridden with a knowing grin. "You ride beautifully."

"I used to have a horse." She smiled at the memory. "...rode every chance I got until..." Her spirits fell at the memory of not only losing Jake, but the four-legged friend who held all of her secrets. "When my parents sold their ranch, I lost Snow, too."

"You come ride anytime you want. My horses are yours."

"That's kind of you." Scarlett put a hand on her daughter's shoulder to keep her from inching any closer to the big horse. "Do you have any ponies? Harmony wants to learn to ride, but I'd like to start her out on something a little less spirited."

"I have two." He took a step toward the barn. "Want me to saddle one up?"

"We'll ride together this afternoon." She stroked the gorgeous horse's neck. "Maybe next time we come, we'll get her up on her own horse."

"Alrighty, then. Call whenever you think she's ready, and I'll have one of them waiting."

Scarlett climbed into Athena's saddle, and Tom lifted Harmony up in front of her. "Stay out of the east pastures. That's where Jake got thrown."

"We will." She smiled her appreciation.

Harmony's body went rigid.

"Are you nervous, sweetie?"

"I don't want to fall and get hurt like Jake." The girl's voice wobbled.

"You won't." Scarlett tucked her daughter closer and glanced at Tom. "I'll be careful, and we'll go slow."

He nodded and patted Harmony's leg. "Trust your mom. She'll take care of you." His kind gaze lifted to Scarlett. "I'll get the gate behind you."

Scarlett scanned the terrain ahead for potential issues and skirted the horse around any large rocks or branches.

"See how I'm holding the reins?" She lifted her hands with their loose grip on the leather. "I don't want to put much tension on them so Athena stays relaxed."

Harmony set her hands on top of Scarlett's. "How do you know she's relaxed?"

Scarlett smiled. "The best way to tell is her ears. See how they're pointed up and down?"

The girl leaned forward. "Yeah."

"That means she's happy. If her ears lay back, she's scared."

"Don't be scared." The girl patted the horse's neck in front of her.

Fifteen minutes into their ride, Harmony twisted in the saddle with pleading eyes. "Can we go faster, Mom?"

"A little bit." The ride on Quicksilver a few weeks ago had been amazing, and today of all days, Harmony deserved a taste of that freedom. Scarlett nudged the horse into a trot, relishing the combined fragrances of her daughter, the horse, and the loamy earth.

When the afternoon sun grew hot and the humidity rested heavy, she turned Athena back to the barn.

Tom walked outside as they approached. "I was beginning to wonder if I should go search for you." His wink added weight to his teasing tone.

"We were having so much fun, I lost track of time." She leaned down to Harmony's ear. "Tell Mr. Tom what you said after we ran."

"I want to ride horses every day." Joy flowed through every word.

He lifted his hat and chuckled, making the smile lines along his eyes more pronounced. "That's what I like to hear. Jake called looking for you."

She gasped as tension filled her body, making the horse shift beneath her. Oh no. Was something wrong? Had he needed help while she was out having fun? "Did he say why?"

"No." Tom grabbed the bottom of Athena's bridle. "But I got the impression he was fretting over you."

Her muscles loosened with the knowledge he wasn't lying injured on the floor, and she climbed out of the saddle. When her feet hit the ground, she put one hand on Harmony's leg and patted her back pockets with the other before remembering she'd left her cell phone in the car because she didn't want to lose it. "Let me call him back, then we'll cool Athena down." She lifted her arms toward her daughter. "Come on, Harmony."

Tom shifted his grip on the palomino's bridle and took two steps toward the barn. "I can do that."

"Wait." When the older man turned around, she held his gaze. "Please allow me to show Harmony that owning a horse involves more than an afternoon ride."

Tom chuckled. "When you put it that way, I can hardly object."

"We'll be right back." She grabbed Harmony's hand and

started toward the parking lot but slowed her pace when she noticed her daughter's stiff legs. Scarlett felt a little saddle sore herself. When they got to the car, she unlocked it, snatched her phone from the center console, and winced at the time. They'd been out almost three hours, and even though she had a missed call from Jake, he hadn't left a message. She dialed him anyway.

"Scarlett?" Jake's voice held a mixture of worry and relief. "Are you okay?"

"We're fine. I'm sorry, I didn't realize we were out so long."

He blew out a breath. "It's fine. I suppose I'm more cautious after my accident. How did Athena do?"

"She's wonderful." She glanced to where Tom stood with Athena in the shade of the barn. "We enjoyed the ride."

"Good..." His voice trailed off.

She glanced at her daughter slumped against the back door. "We're going to brush her down and get a drink of water before heading home. I'll start dinner when I get there."

"No rush. I'm just glad we all had a productive day."

Another peek toward Tom, who had started untacking Athena, lit a fire under her. "Bye, Jake." She tossed her phone onto the front seat and closed the door. "Come on, Harmony. Let's see if Mr. Tom has some water for you."

They were halfway to the corral before she remembered that she'd forgotten to ask if Andi was still at Jake's house.

Fifteen

J ake couldn't contain his smile as he hung up the phone and
set it on the console. Home. Scarlett had called his place
home. Quite the change.

Then again, he'd been the paranoid invalid watching the clock
after Andi had left at three. Wondering if Tom had warned them
about the moles. Or if Athena had gotten spooked. He'd finally
given in to his concern and called Scarlett. When she didn't
answer, his apprehension ramped up, and he'd called the stable
owner. At the man's promise to go look for them if they didn't
return within the hour, Jake let Max out of the crate in the garage
for a bit to run around outside with Trigger. After the puppy
expended some energy, he put him back and retreated to his
studio again in a poor attempt to distract himself.

He breathed out a long sigh. They were okay and on their way
home. And the repetition of that word again wrapped around his
heart.

Now that he knew his girls were safe, he unplugged the head-
phones and wrapped the cord around them before stowing them
in the desk. He shut down the monitors and mixing board. Then,
threw the papers Andi had scribbled out lyrics on in the empty

trash can beneath one of the fiberglass acoustic panels attached to the wall.

They'd made a lot of progress today, tightening and recording two songs for the album. Combined with the five he'd already written in the past month, he figured they only needed seven or eight more before he'd need to get Seth and Mia in over the next few weeks to record.

His first year in the industry, he learned the band needed two and a half to three times the number of songs the label would put on the album. While he might love a song, everyone else would hate it. And the songs he didn't necessarily care for, they'd add to the playlist. The only one of his songs he'd ever fought for was 'Midnight Blue' because it was his song for Scarlett. An apology of sorts, even if he'd never acknowledged his intent. As he recalled singing the song in his kitchen with a little girl whose eyes were the same shade as her mother's, he realized it was also an apology to the daughter he didn't know he had.

After all these years, it was still his favorite. Hearing the crowd sing along with him when the band stopped playing always moved him. But it was a double-edged sword, witnessing the popularity of his first hit while carrying the reminder of what he'd given up almost a year before he reached the launching point of his career. And now she was here, back in his life. In his home for now. He planned to make the most of it.

But first, he had to learn what happened. Why did she believe he wanted nothing to do with his daughter?

Hurried footsteps on the stairs had him peeking his head out the door. "How was riding?"

Several strands of Harmony's long hair had escaped her braid. Her cheeks were flushed, her eyes bright. "Mom said I can ride my own horse next time."

Jake's heart took a nosedive to his stomach. She was too small. Could he dissuade Scarlett from teaching her to ride for a while? "Where's your mom?"

Harmony shrugged. "The kitchen. She told me to change and then come help."

"In that case, you best get moving." He smirked at the use of one of his own mother's phrases.

Once she closed her bedroom door, he hurried downstairs.

Scarlett glanced up when he entered the kitchen. "Hi. I'm throwing together dinner now. It'll be ready in about an hour."

"That's fine." He settled on one of the barstools at the island. "Harmony mentioned she's going to ride solo next time you go out."

"Yep." Her beaming smile lit his insides up like a Fourth of July fireworks display. "She did great with me, and her posture is almost better than mine. I'd like her to learn while she has this opportunity."

"Are you sure she's ready?"

Twin vertical lines appeared in her forehead paired with a slight scowl as she spooned a meat mixture over noodles in a glass baking pan. "I just told you she was."

"What if she falls off?" He didn't ever want to see pain in his daughter's eyes.

"I'm starting her on a pony, and we've both fallen off horses, Jake." She raised one eyebrow as her gaze shifted to his sling. "She'll be fine. I'll keep close until I'm certain she's ready." Her expression softened. "It's hard, isn't it?"

His fingers itched to touch her cheeks. Were they still as soft as they used to be? He lifted his gaze to her eyes. "What?"

"Figuring out the balance between how much freedom and independence to allow and how to protect her at the same time." She sprinkled a layer of cheese over the meat.

He kneaded his neck with his good hand and tried to rein in his errant thoughts of romance to those of parenting. "How do you manage?" How had she done it by herself for so long?

"Lots of prayer and almost as many tears—both mine and Harmony's." She gave him a wry smile.

As if summoned by her name, Harmony skipped into the

room with a book in her hand and skidded to a stop next to Jake. "Can I sit there?" She pointed at the stool beside him.

"You bet." He scooted it out and patted the seat.

The oven beeped, and Scarlett carried the pan to the other side of the room and slid it inside. "If you two are okay for a bit, I'm going to take a quick shower and change."

"Go ahead. As long as I don't have to do anything with dinner, we're fine." His lips lifted into a half smile as he remembered her teasing him about burning their lunch of grilled cheese sandwiches while plying him with cookies.

"It has to bake for an hour, so you're off the hook." She laughed. "And you're off the hook for dessert, too."

Harmony bounced on her stool. "Can we make cookies?"

"We don't have all the ingredients. Why don't we save that for tomorrow after we go to the store?" At Harmony's acceptance, Scarlett rounded the island and kissed the girl on top of her head. "You be good for Jake."

"Okay, Mom." Their daughter opened her book with a smiling dog on the cover and shifted a glittery purple bookmark from the middle to the back.

He watched her as she read, swinging her short legs in the air. A hunger to know, to understand the miniature human beside him reared inside. She was a part of him... his daughter... his flesh and blood. His, and yet, not his. He wanted to learn everything about her. He wanted to be a good father. One she looked up to and felt comfortable coming to with questions.

He cleared his throat. "What's your favorite kind of cookie?"

She moved the bookmark back to its original place and set the book down, pushing it aside as she rotated toward him. "Peanut butter."

"Hmm." He rubbed his chin with his forefinger and thumb as if contemplating her answer. "Those are good, but I like chocolate chip."

"Sometimes Mom makes peanut butter chocolate chip. Those

are my real favorite." Her voice lowered as her eyes grew wide. "Maybe we should ask her to make those."

He chuckled at her instantaneous change of opinion. This sweet girl already held his heart, and he couldn't wait for her to learn the truth. He sighed. Would she hate him then? Would he fail her like he'd failed Scarlett?

"Maybe you should ask since it's still your birthday." He rested his sling on the countertop and adjusted the strap. "I know you like to read and play the guitar. What else do you like to do?"

"Play with Olivia and sing. We play a dancing game on her TV sometimes, too."

"On a gaming system? I have one of those." But he didn't own that kind of game. Should he give Scarlett money to pick one up when she went for groceries tomorrow?"

"What games do you have?" Harmony leaned forward.

"The sports ones and a couple of the rock bands." He didn't mention the graphic ones he owned. Scarlett wouldn't appreciate him letting the girl play those, and he didn't want to subject her to the violence. Maybe it was time to give those away.

"Can we play later?" She held her clasped hands beneath her chin.

"We'll see." Another phrase his mom used often. She and his dad had modeled parenting as a partnership, and he intended to honor that with Scarlett. "I'm not sure what your mom has planned."

"She'll tell me to read." She sighed as though reading was the worst chore ever. "That's all she ever tells me to do."

Jake laughed. "I bet she'll let us take Max and Trigger outside to play again."

Harmony hopped off the stool. "Let's take them out now."

"We better wait and ask your mom, so she knows where we are."

The girl's shoulders fell as she traipsed back to her stool and opened her book again. As she repeated the shifting of the bookmark, he wondered if she'd made it. Did she like glitter? What other girly things did she own? Nail polish? Bracelets? He was behind the times and way over his head trying to figure out the female mind. He'd have to get ideas from Scarlett before he proved to his daughter just how clueless he really was.

～

After dinner, Scarlett watched Harmony follow Jake down the hall to the family room before loading the dishwasher. She could have used the help he'd offered, but after her day's rollercoaster ride of emotions, she needed some time to herself.

They needed to talk soon. Too many unanswered questions about his place in their daughter's life hung between them. Harmony needed a dad who was present and available, but Jake's career wouldn't provide *that* kind of security. Financial security, yes, but money wasn't the most crucial thing in life.

What about love? Or sticking around for the important events? Harmony had so many life experiences ahead of her—her first crush, her first heartbreak, prom, graduation, her wedding— and Scarlett intended to walk her daughter through every one of them whether it was alone or with Jake by her side.

After she finished the dishes and put the kitchen back in order, she wandered to the family room and paused at the door. Jake swung at the virtual baseball flying toward him on the TV screen and spun in a full circle, eliciting giggles from Harmony. Her heart pinched as she entered the room and snuggled into a corner of the sectional. They had missed out on so many evenings like this one—family dinner followed by quality time together.

"Scar?" Jake's voice cut into her haze. "Wake up. You're gonna get a crick in your neck."

She lifted her head and winced. His warning had come too late.

Jake moved behind the chair. "Scoot back."

In her sleepy state, following his voice-encased command came naturally, and she found herself upright against the cushions. Strong, skillful fingers kneaded the skin between her neck and right shoulder, releasing the tense muscles and inviting more than the spasms as she melted into the warmth of his touch.

She opened her eyes and glanced around the room. "Where's Harmony?" Had the question come from her? A cloud of contentment cocooned her in comfort as his hand moved to her left side.

His breath stirred her hair as he chuckled. "She went to bed. Guess I wore her out."

"Hmm." Every last strand of tension disappeared. And suddenly, so did his hand. She tucked her legs under her and turned to face him.

"Sorry." He smiled. "That would've been better if I had the use of both hands."

"It was perfect." She reached for his hand and gave it a squeeze. "Thank you."

He sat on the end of the couch nearest her. "Can I ask your opinion about something?"

"Sure." Was this the time for their conversation?

"There's not much to entertain her around here." He adjusted his sling against his chest. "Would you drive me to the store so I can pick up a few things?"

Scarlett shook her head. "You don't have to do that. We'll get some stuff from the house tomorrow, and she'll be fine."

"Let me do this, Scarlett." His gray eyes held a plea. "I missed years of birthdays and Christmases. And I can afford it."

She cringed at the implication she couldn't give Harmony everything. The truth—but she didn't like to admit it, especially in front of Jake.

He scrubbed his hand down his face. "That came out wrong. I'm not faulting you. I only want to give her something."

"Like what?" She didn't want him throwing gifts at Harmony to atone for his absence.

"For starters, she mentioned a dancing game."

She could allow him the small concession. He wasn't asking to buy her an entire gaming system.

"And maybe a board game or two." He smiled. "We can all play in the evenings like we used to do with your parents."

Grief dug its ugly stinger into her heart, and she blinked back tears. The ache of losing her mom and dad reared its head at the most unexpected times.

"I'm sorry." Jake moved to the ottoman in front of her. "I shouldn't have brought that up. You miss them, don't you?"

She nodded and sniffed. "Some days are harder than others." But she didn't want to dwell on the two holes in her heart, so she gave him a watery smile. "Harmony prefers puzzles anyway."

"I can do puzzles." He released a long breath. "Anything else?"

"That's enough for now. You gave her the guitar for her birthday." She scowled at him. "Which was way too much, by the way."

"I'm glad I did it, knowing what I do now."

"About that..." The time had arrived.

His eyes lit up, then dimmed. "We don't have to do this now." Jake reached over and squeezed her bare knee. "We've got time."

Her stomach churned, and her mouth went dry. "I'd rather not put it off anymore."

"Okay." He returned to the couch—was it to give her space or himself?—and relaxed into the cushions. "Start from the beginning. When did you find out you were...?"

She wrapped her arms around her stomach. His shocked and wounded reaction at Harmony's party had made her question whether he'd dismissed them without a care. A niggle of doubt remained, though. Was he acting clueless about her letters and the one she'd received from him to protect his reputation? She would answer his questions, but doing so didn't mean she trusted him.

"A couple weeks before Christmas." She'd keep her answers short and to the point.

"That soon?" He scowled at the floor. "Why didn't you come

over to the house when I visited for the holidays? You could have told me then."

"At first, I didn't know what to do—keep her or give her up for adoption to parents who could give her more than I could. Once we were settled in Atlanta, it didn't take long to make my decision. Your mom gave me your address in Nashville, and I wrote you a long letter explaining everything." She'd poured her heart onto those pages. "I even included an ultrasound photo."

Jake shook his head and frowned. "I never got it. Or anything else. Mom mentioned you asked for my address, and I kept waiting for something, anything, from you." He ran his hand through his hair. "I promise I never received anything from you after you moved. Could it have gotten lost in the mail? Or maybe you had the wrong address?"

"Wouldn't the letters have come back to me if the address wasn't right?" She twisted her fingers together, feeling the pain of rejection all over again. "I tried to call, too. Every time someone answered your phone, they said you didn't want to speak with me, so I wrote another letter when I was seven months along and still got no answer."

"Who would do that? Sure, Becker encouraged me to pass my phone to others when we were working, which was pretty much twenty-four seven those first four years, but you have to believe I wanted to talk to you." His voice sounded strangled as his jaw ticked. "The others in the band saw how much I missed you and would have put you through without question. I missed you so much."

She'd missed him, too, but she had to focus on finding out what happened all those years ago. "You can't imagine what it was like. There I was, in a new place with no friends, and I find out I'm pregnant. Mom agreed to letting me do homeschool for my last three semesters." She was glad she didn't have to start over at a new school while pregnant the second half of her junior year or let someone else take care of Harmony during her senior year.

He leaned forward. "I shouldn't have pressured you that night. This is all my fault."

"Stop blaming yourself. I could have said no, and you would have let it go. It took both of us." She squeezed his hand, then released it and clasped hers in her lap. "It's in the past, and the outcome of that poor decision turned out to be the best thing in my life. Harmony is a gift from God."

"One that someone stole from me." He stood and paced the space in front of the couch. "I'm going to do everything possible to find out who was behind this, starting with remembering every name I can and finding those people to ask if they ever had charge of my phone. I'll get the others to help with that list of names."

After several seconds of muttering, he paused and focused on her. "I'm sorry you had to go through all of that alone."

"Not alone. Mom and Dad supported my decision to keep her. They loved being grandparents. I'm sad Harmony doesn't remember them much, but we talk about them often." She bit her lip. Harmony had grandparents she'd never met. Didn't even know about. "Your parents are going to be so hurt and angry."

"Let me handle them. Once the shock wears off, Mom'll be over the moon." He chuckled for a second before growing serious and returning to the couch. "Why didn't you try to contact me again? After she was born?"

"I did. That letter included a baby picture. And I tried to call you again." Scarlett sucked in a breath.

How could someone be so manipulative as to monitor all communication between her and Jake? Was she the only person this had happened with, or were there more? Had he considered someone might have blocked more than her? She could ask another time. Or wait to see if he came to the same conclusion. Right now, she had to concentrate on herself and Harmony.

"A couple weeks later I got some certified mail from an attorney. It stated if I signed a nondisclosure agreement and never revealed the identity of the baby's father, you would give me $50,000 plus pay my medical expenses."

"Fifty—?" He strangled the word. "I didn't have that kind of money back then. Even if I did, it's not enough to raise a child. Who would have called a lawyer and had the money to follow through? Who disliked me enough to steal my mail and cut off any contact I could have had with you?"

She breathed a half laugh, half cry. "I don't know. When I got no response to my letters, I thought you wanted to forget all about me." That he was too busy enjoying his fame to get saddled with a family. "When I got that certified letter, it confirmed you didn't want anything to do with us."

"Never." He scooted off the couch and sank to his knees in front of her before resting his forehead on her knees. "You and Harmony are part of me. I'll always want you."

He wanted her? Them? Then and now? The truth of his words broke through the walls around her heart and soothed her rejection as completely as his fingers had eased the pain in her neck. Tears ran down her cheeks. They'd wasted so much time.

Jake got up, moved to the arm of the couch beside her, and put his arm around her. "You know I hate it when you cry." His husky tone hinted at how close his emotions were to surfacing.

She hiccupped a laugh. Before they started dating, he would bring her flowers he'd picked in the fields around his house or share his treasures with her. When they became a couple, he would hold her tight as her tears soaked his shirt.

"I'm sorry." Two simple words weighted with regrets stretched between them, attempting to bridge the chasm of mistakes and heartbreak. "If I could rewind the clock and change everything, I would."

"Me too." She sniffled and shuddered, then looked up into his own watery eyes. "Where do we go from here, Jake?"

"First, I'm going to make a list of every person I can remember who worked with us. I'll get the others to help. While I work on that, I'm going to spend time with my daughter this month." He brushed a tear from her cheek with his finger and pressed it to his heart. "I'm not going to take her away from you, but I want to hang out with her while I can."

He had already been so attentive with Harmony. When she apologized, he listened and forgave her easily. They'd formed a quick bond playing with the dogs and laughing over the video game. "She'd love that."

"And I think we should tell her." He clasped her shoulder tighter as she shook her head.

"Jake—"

"The longer we wait, the harder it will get. How's she going to feel when she finally learns the truth? And she *will* learn about it because I plan to take care of her from now on."

What would it be like to lean on someone else for support? To not have to scrimp and save for every special celebration? Jake could ensure their daughter went to college if she wanted to. Her stomach clenched. She'd cashed that large check when Harmony was a baby. "But what about the documents I signed? If this gets out, I don't want to get sued." Someone had sent that letter and had a copy. She couldn't repay the money or legal fees.

Jake flinched and removed his arm from around her. "I wouldn't do that." He stood and returned to his seat again, as if he needed to distance himself from her. "I'll call my lawyer first thing tomorrow and find out what needs to happen to undo it. And I want to give you back child support."

She shook her head. "No. I don't want more money from you." Money had caused enough issues between them. While she now believed he had nothing to do with the NDA, what would happen if he changed his mind about her? Would she have even more to repay? "You can put it in a college fund for Harmony."

"What about one for you?" He studied her face. "You could go back to school, become a nurse like you always dreamed."

"It's too late for me." It *would* be nice to have a more stable career, but going back to school sounded exhausting. She'd rather spend her evenings helping Harmony with her homework instead of laboring over her own.

"No, it's not. You're young. Promise me you'll consider it."

Emotionally drained, she gave a tiny nod even though she knew she wouldn't follow through.

"Good." He leaned back again. "Now, let's talk about something happier. What was our daughter like as a baby? I want every detail."

Sixteen

Ϭ∾Ͽ

S carlett took the last sip of her coffee splurge as she drove to Jake's place late Wednesday morning. After staying up into the wee hours talking with Jake and her early morning jaunt home for Harmony's guitar and a few more of her favorite books plus a trip to the grocery store, she needed the jolt of caffeine.

As she pulled into the driveway, she stifled another yawn with her fist and glanced at the clock on the dashboard. Almost ten. How had Jake fared with Harmony the few hours she'd been gone? Had they played with the dogs? Found another video game? She looked forward to hearing about their time together.

Harmony ran toward the car with tears running down her face.

Scarlett's heart sank to her toes. What happened? Was Jake okay? She put the car in park, shut off the ignition, and hurried out of her seat. "What's wrong, sweetie?"

Harmony threw her arms around Scarlett's waist and buried her face in her side. "Jake's mad at me."

"Why?" She struggled to remain calm, to listen before she gave Jake Turnquist a piece of her mind. Who did he think he was?

"He said everything upstairs was ours. I heard him."

Yes, Jake had said that. To Scarlett. Had the girl gone snooping in his personal space? "Did you go in his bedroom?"

The girl shook her head and studied the ground with intensity.

"Harmony Rayne, tell me where you were." She placed her hands on her hips to add weight to her firm voice.

"The studio." Her voice squeaked like a tiny mouse. "I wanted to record my song. The one my dad wrote."

Did she break something? Scarlett couldn't afford to replace a piece of expensive equipment or an instrument.

"I didn't mean to mess up his stuff." Harmony sniffled and hugged her arms around her stomach.

"What did Jake do when he found out?"

"He yelled at me, said he would have to do everything over again, and told me I'm grounded. I said he wasn't my dad and went to my room until you got back. Can we go home?"

So many issues to address. Scarlett squeezed her eyes shut as she sorted through where to start. "Did you stop to think about all the expensive things in the studio? Or did you feel like you should stay out of there?"

When she opened her eyes again, she stared at the top of Harmony's head. With a sigh, she knelt in front of her daughter and lifted her chin with a finger. "Did you break something?"

"No." She glanced up. "I only messed up a song on his computer."

A rush of air escaped Scarlett's lungs at the confirmation Harmony's lapse in judgement would not cost her money... but it had cost Jake time. And it was an invasion of his privacy.

"Am I grounded, Mom?"

"Well, I think you knew you shouldn't go in there and did it anyway." She held the girl's gaze. "I'll talk to Jake, and we'll decide on a fair punishment."

"Why do you have to ask him?" Harmony's eyes pleaded with her.

"Oh, baby." Scarlett hugged her daughter close. Jake was right. She couldn't keep her secret any longer. "Jake's your daddy."

The girl jerked out of Scarlett's embrace and glared. "No, he's not."

"Yes, he is." She sighed and glanced toward the house as the sunshine warmed her shoulders. "I'm sorry I didn't tell you before now, but when you were a baby, I promised not to tell anyone."

"He didn't want me?" Her voice trembled.

Scarlett took her daughter's small hand and held it between both of hers. "He didn't know about you. He found out at your birthday party."

"Is that why he yelled at you and left?" Harmony's head tilted to the side as she studied Scarlett's face.

"It is." She tucked a strand of the girl's hair behind her ear. "But we talked and realized we both were mistaken."

Harmony stood motionless, not saying anything more.

The silence became unbearable. "Forgive me?"

"Yeah, Mom." She stepped away, and her eyes bugged out before she squealed. "My dad is Jake Turnquist. Olivia's not going to believe this."

"We need to keep this a secret for a little while, sweetie." Once the excitement of learning Jake was her dad wore off, they'd have to have another conversation about what she could and couldn't say.

"Can I call him Dad?"

Scarlett's eyes misted at the thought of Jake hearing the name for the first time from his daughter's lips. "I bet he would like that. If it's just you and him or the three of us, you can."

Harmony's eyes, so much like her father's except for the color, stared back at her.

Scarlett stood, hiding a wince at the sharp pain in her knee as she maintained eye contact with the girl. "Your dad and I have to figure out how we're going to tell people about you. Since he's famous, the press will eat this up, and I don't want you caught in the middle."

It was her second biggest concern about the news becoming public, trumped only by those documents she'd signed. Had Jake called his lawyer yet? What would have happened if she'd refused to sign and returned them to the sender?

She shook her head. What ifs never led to happiness. "I brought you some things from home. Can you take them inside while I get the groceries?"

"Okay."

When they carried in the third and final load from the car, Jake stuck his head out of his ground-floor office but retreated so fast she didn't have time to ask what he wanted. Scarlett glanced at Harmony as she carried her guitar toward the stairs. "Why don't you put everything away while you're up there?"

"Okay."

Once she put the last item in the fridge and freezer, Scarlett walked down the hall and rapped on the open door with her knuckle.

Jake sat in the chair behind his desk with mussed hair and a miserable expression so much like Harmony's from earlier, she held back a laugh.

He looked up. "Does she hate me?"

"No." Scarlett stepped inside, shut the door, and sat in one of the black and gold wingchairs.

"I can't believe I lost my temper and yelled at her." He ran his left hand through his wavy hair, leaving lines where his fingers had furrowed. "Andi and I can re-record the song. It's not the end of the world."

At the mention of the other woman's name, Scarlett's stomach cramped, but she tried her best to ignore it. "Harmony knew she shouldn't go in there."

"I *did* say everything upstairs was yours."

"Yes, but you said that to *me*, not her. You made the right call, Jake."

"When she started crying and said I'm not her dad..." He shook his head and stared at the desktop.

"I told her."

His head jerked up, and his eyes locked on hers. "You did? What'd she say?"

Scarlett chuckled. "She can't wait to tell Olivia." *And asked if she could call you Dad.* She'd let him discover that joy for himself. "I asked her not to tell anyone for now."

"Why not? I'm ecstatic. Everyone should know I have a daughter."

"Not if it's going to invite a media circus into our lives. I won't have us become some sensation for the news crews."

~

J ake shook his head. "I doubt anyone will care."

Scarlett shot up as if he'd pinched her and paced the floor behind the chairs.

He understood her hesitation about the media, but she was making a bigger deal out of it than necessary. He'd dealt with the press for years, and for the most part—unless he was doing something for the community or something outrageous—they left him alone.

"What'd your lawyer say?"

"He's drawing up documents for both of us to sign stating I won't hold you liable. He asked if you have the original papers you signed. I'd like to see them, too, since someone obviously forged my signature."

"They're in the fire safe at my house." She stopped pacing and slapped her hand to her forehead. "I should have brought them back with me." Her shoulders slumped as she sat again. "Who do you think did it?"

"No idea, and so many roadies have come and gone since then, I'm not sure we'll find anyone who answered your phone calls." He hated admitting that. He wanted nothing more than to solve this mystery and confront the person who created all the confusion and rejection. "We can sign the new papers whenever you like."

"Tomorrow?"

"Of course." He was as eager as she was to put this ordeal behind them.

A soft rap sounded at the door. Only one other person was in the house.

He smiled at Scarlett and sat up tall. "Come on in, Harmony."

The door creaked open, and the girl stood there. "I'm sorry I ruined your song." Her words escaped in a quiet jumble as a fresh tear trailed down her face.

He glanced at Scarlett. Heaven help him from turning to mush anytime tears glistened on his girls' cheeks.

"Come here." He crooked a finger. Once Harmony stood in front of him, he leaned down to her level. "I'm sorry, too. I overreacted and handled the situation badly. What you did cost me some time and work, but I can do it over."

"Am I grounded?" She peeked at her mom.

"We haven't discussed it yet." Scarlett's lips pinched together. "Will you give us a few more minutes and wait in your room until then?"

"Okay." She gave Jake a lightning-fast hug and backed away before he could respond. "Thanks, Dad."

The one simple word winded him. Moisture pooled in his eyes, and he blinked it back, not wanting Harmony to misunderstand. She had given him a gift far greater than she could comprehend. Her small infraction was frivolous compared to his absence in her life.

As soon as the girl left the room, Scarlett shook her head. "Don't you dare change your mind. I see those wheels turning. Harmony should be punished. She knew it was wrong to go in there and touch your equipment."

He frowned. "Grounding her seems harsh." Man, this

parenting thing was hard. He needed to buy a few books on the subject and cram.

She tapped a finger against her lips. "How about we tell her no riding for two weeks? Not only is it a consequence for her actions, she can focus on training her puppy instead."

"I guess you've done this a few times." He huffed a laugh. "I'll defer to you on this one. Are you going to tell her, or should I?"

"We should do it together, present a united front."

He stood and held out his hand, but Scarlett turned and walked out of the room ahead of him. He ground his back teeth. Just when they were making progress, she pulled away. He had three and a half more weeks to show her how much he wanted her in his life. Their talk last night only illuminated how lonely he'd been.

When they arrived at Harmony's room, Scarlett tapped on the door and pushed it open. Their daughter sat up on her bed and watched them with an expectant gaze.

Jake moved beside Scarlett. "Your mom and I made a decision."

Harmony's eyes glistened. He stopped talking and looked away from her sweet face, afraid he'd cave and throw her punishment out the window. He obviously had no backbone when it came to his little girl. He glanced at Scarlett for backup.

She rolled her eyes, then turned their daughter. "You did something you knew was wrong. We're not going to ground you, but you can't go riding again for two weeks."

"Mom—"

"That's our decision, Harmony Rayne. Don't argue, or we'll make it three weeks."

"You gave her our name. The one we chose from the song." When he'd first heard Scarlett call the girl that name, it tore him up. But now? Now, it was as if she'd given him the world.

"It's spelled different." Harmony hopped off the bed. "R-A-Y-N-E."

While her middle name was borne from the song, her first name filled him with hope. "A beautiful name for a beautiful girl."

Seventeen

ᏜᏜᎯ

A week after Scarlett told Harmony that Jake was her dad, the three of them stood in the potato chip aisle in the grocery store. Despite her protests, he'd insisted on coming along today. He had to be going stir crazy stuck at home.

"What kind of chips do you want for lunches?" She glanced at him as he tugged the brim of his baseball cap lower. Did he really think switching out one hat for another fooled people?

"Whatever you like is fine." He scooted closer. "Is this place always so busy on Wednesdays?"

"It wasn't last week, but I came earlier in the day." Scarlett looked up from her grocery list and glanced around.

At the far end of the aisle, two women whispered to each other, casting furtive glances their direction. The women maneuvered closer. Why not just ask him to shop with them and turn this whole thing into a caravan?

Scarlett ground her teeth and stepped in front of Harmony. Why didn't he wait in the car? The whispers and stares grated on her nerves. Pretending to search for a certain brand, she moved halfway down the aisle with Harmony in tow to put more distance between herself and the famous Jake Turnquist.

Spending this time with him challenged her more than she

thought possible. Sometimes, she longed to give in to the attraction, to accept the comfort and touches he offered. Just this morning after breakfast, he'd reached toward her face, then pulled his hand away as if unsure she'd welcome his touch. But she couldn't fall under his spell only to be left behind again.

While she now knew he hadn't sent those horrid legal papers, he *had* broken up with her to chase his career. If he'd missed her as much as he claimed, he could have made more of an effort to contact her.

Her cell phone rang, and she dug it out from the bottom of her purse. "Hey, Cass."

"Hi. Sorry I missed your call this morning. How's everything going?"

Scarlett wandered to the end of the aisle for privacy from the women who had moved closer. "Okay. Jake called a band meeting tonight at six." She glanced at Harmony, who studied all of the potato chip options in front of her, and inched farther away. "Can you come? I need some support." Telling Jake's bandmates about Harmony unnerved her on a whole new level.

"Won't Levi be there?"

"Yes, but he hasn't been with me from the beginning like you have." She checked her list and wedged the phone between her ear and shoulder before grabbing two bags of tortilla chips for the taco salad she'd planned for tonight. "Besides, Harmony misses you."

"Low blow." Cassidy exhaled. "Yeah, I'll come. Can I bring anything?"

"I'm making dinner, but if you bring dessert, no one will object. If you don't have the time, don't worry about it."

"Actually, I found a new cheesecake recipe I'd like to try. The band'll make great guinea pigs."

"Thanks, Cass. I owe you one."

"And I won't let you forget it." She laughed. "I'll see you tonight."

Scarlett hung up and stuffed her phone back in her purse.

When she turned around, the aisle stood empty with no sign of Jake, the women, Harmony, or their cart. How long had she been on the phone? She rushed on wobbly legs to the end of the row. Where had they gone? Had Jake gotten distracted by his fans and let Harmony wander past him? He wouldn't let anything happen to her, would he?

"What about Mom?" Harmony's voice carried, and Scarlett followed the sound two aisles over to find them adding chocolate chips to the cart.

She speed-walked to Jake and glared. "Why'd you leave?"

Jake exchanged a glance with Harmony, then raised an eyebrow at Scarlett. "We wanted to give you some privacy for your phone call."

"You should have gotten my attention and warned me you were moving on. When I turned around and you were gone, I thought..." Okay, maybe her concern wasn't so much over Harmony as it was the women ogling him. She wouldn't put it past them to strike up a conversation with a child—especially one who looked like Jake—to garner his attention.

"You do care." One side of his mouth tipped up.

"About Harmony." She rolled her eyes and tossed the tortilla chips in the cart, not caring how crunched they were after her scare. "Let's finish up here. I need to get home and start dinner."

"I told you I could order something in, so you don't have to cook."

"And I explained I need something to keep me busy. This is as good as anything." He'd used his injury as an excuse to keep her and Harmony around, but she let him believe she hadn't figured that out. "You're paying me, so let me earn my wages."

His lips formed a straight line.

"Come on, Harmony." Before he could argue more, Scarlett set the girl's hand on the cart handle and hurried to the produce department, leaving Jake to trail behind.

A few minutes later, he set a bunch of bananas on top of the other groceries they'd gathered and stepped in front of her. "I'm not sure what I did to upset you, but I'm sorry. It wasn't my intention to make you angry."

If she told him the truth—that she struggled to be around him because he churned so many emotions in her—she'd become more entangled. "I'm sorry, too. This dinner is stressing me out a little." She glanced at Harmony picking out apples and lowered her voice. "What is everyone going to say when they find out about Harmony?"

He rested his hand on her shoulder, his fingers on her neck sending electric charges down her back. "Levi knows already. Seth and Mia probably have an idea because they were at the party, and they heard her sing 'Rain.' And I'm sure someone has said something to Andi by now. Either way, they're going to be thrilled about this."

"But it's going to change your relationship with the band."

"Is it? There's no reason I can't still do everything I need to with the band." He tipped his head to where Harmony twisted the top of the bag of apples.

And that's exactly why Scarlett could not—would not—give her heart to Jake Turnquist again. Second place in his life was not good enough. She and Harmony deserved better.

"We need to re-record your song." Jake stood at the bottom of the stairs with Andi.

Her forehead puckered as she frowned. "Why?"

He glanced around to make sure his daughter hadn't come inside and could overhear them before lowering his voice. "Harmony accidentally messed up our recording."

"Just like one big happy family." She crossed her arms across her chest and smirked. "I heard what happened at the party."

So, he'd been right. Someone had blabbed to Andi. "What did you hear?"

Someone knocked on the door and pushed it open. Levi

walked into the house and nodded their way. "Hey, guys." He stopped next to Andi and cocked his head. "Did you get your hair done? It looks good."

She ran her fingers through the ends of her platinum blonde hair. "I did." She frowned at Jake. "Thank you for noticing."

How could Levi even tell? Her hair was the same as always with not one strand out of place.

The man slapped Jake on his good shoulder. "Everybody's cars are outside, so where's the party?"

"Scarlett's in the kitchen. Everyone else is out back playing with the dogs."

Levi's gazed bounced between Jake and Andi. "So why are you two out here?"

"Jake wanted to talk shop." Andi shrugged.

"Then I'll leave you to it." Levi made a beeline to the kitchen, and Jake stared after him.

"Levi!" Scarlett's joyful greeting irritated Jake. She hadn't mentioned his name in the week and a half she'd been here, but she also hadn't denied any involvement with him the one time Jake had braved to ask.

Andi cleared her throat, and Jake looked at her. "What?"

"Nothing." She glanced upstairs. "Anyway, Mia told me yesterday about what happened at the birthday party." She raised an eyebrow. "Will you put 'Rain' on the album now? Like I said before, it's a guaranteed hit."

"Shh." He grabbed her arm and pulled her into the formal living room. "That song isn't up for debate. You know I wrote it for Scarlett years ago, and I won't cheapen it by making it available to everyone."

"Um, you might want to check social media." She put a hand on her hip. "Someone filmed you and posted a video from Becker's party. Last time I checked, it had been shared several thousand times."

"Just perfect." He ran a hand through his hair. Now, he'd have to track that down. "I'll deal with it later."

"What are you going to do about the band?" Andi sat on the edge of the couch and tugged at the ends of her hair. "Now that you're a father."

Wow, that sounded better coming from someone outside the family. Like a confirmation that sunk the truth deeper. He plopped onto the chair across from her. "I don't expect much to change."

Andi's hands rested on her bare knees. "Do you really believe that? You're willing to miss out on more of your daughter's life than you already have because we've got a show or an award ceremony to attend? What happens when you're forced to choose between us and your family? Which will take priority?"

My family. His answer came without hesitation, surprising him. Did Scarlett wonder if he'd choose the band over her... like he had in high school? Was that the reason for her reluctance in rekindling anything with him?

"You've been unsatisfied with this life for a couple of years now." Andi tapped her heeled sandal against the rug. "Take some time and re-evaluate what's most important. Don't base your decision on what's best for the band but on what's best for you and your daughter."

"I will." How had his life become so complicated? He sighed. "The truth is, I'm not sure what to do. Scarlett and Harmony are part of my life now, and I don't want to let either of them down. There have already been too many misunderstandings as it is."

"Why didn't she tell you about the baby?" She touched her fingers to her throat as her eyebrows scrunched together.

"Long story. I'll give everyone the details after dinner, so I only have to explain it once."

The doorbell rang, and Andi looked at him. "Are we expecting someone else?"

"Yeah. Cassidy." He stood and moved toward the front entry. "Scarlett asked her to come tonight for emotional support."

"Seth will appreciate that." Andi rolled her eyes.

"That guy can't take a hint." Jake shook his head before he answered the door. "Hey, Cass. Scarlett's in the kitchen."

"Great." She picked up a large tote at her feet. "I brought dessert."

"Excellent."

As soon as she disappeared, Andi approached. "Are you and Scarlett back together?"

"No." His heart clenched. No matter how much he wished it, he couldn't make any headway with her and refused to force her into a relationship she didn't want. "She doesn't trust me anymore."

"You could earn it back."

"How?"

As Andi drew closer, Scarlett stepped into the entryway. "Dinner's ready. Fix your plate in the kitchen, and we'll eat at the dining room table." Her words came out clipped and angry before she spun around the way she'd come.

What had he done this time?

Andi grinned. "Hmm...winning her back may be easier than you think."

"What?" His gaze shifted from the direction of the kitchen back to his smirking bass player.

"She didn't like me standing this close to you."

He took a step away. Why were women so confusing? "No, she's probably put out we're holding up dinner. She's putting too much pressure on herself."

"Want to test that theory?" She lifted an eyebrow.

Not really. "How?"

She took his hand. "Sit by me during dinner. I'll take care of the rest."

He followed her to the kitchen, his gut churning at going along with whatever Andi had cooked up. Would this push them forward or ruin any progress he'd made with Scarlett? But he'd run out of ideas, and time was ticking away.

Eighteen

S carlett sat at the table in the formal dining room and pushed the taco salad around her plate, her appetite gone.

Across from her, Andi giggled again and leaned her shoulder into Jake. Ugh. Obviously, they had a thing going on, which left no hope for her and Jake.

She looked toward the end of the table and noticed the scowl on Levi's face as he watched the happy couple. At least she wasn't alone in her disgust at their display.

"So, Jake..." Seth was either oblivious or ignoring the tension in the room. "Why the big meeting? Did you talk to the studio about the album? How did they take the suggestion of each of us singing lead on a track?"

"They were interested in the idea when I brought it up a couple weeks ago." Jake set his fork down. "I plan to feel them out more at the meeting next week."

Seth glanced around the table. His gaze lingered on Harmony, then Scarlett a few seconds longer than made her comfortable. "Okay, I'll ask again. Why the meeting?"

"We'll discuss it after this delicious dinner Scarlett made." He treated her to that lopsided grin that sent goose bumps up and down her arms.

Did Andi notice? And what exactly was Jake doing flirting with her when his girlfriend sat beside him?

With her stomach in a twisted knot, Scarlett pushed her chair back. She stood and gathered her dishes. "Cassidy brought dessert. Who wants some?" As soon as everyone affirmed, she rushed from the room, desiring the solace of the quiet kitchen. If she remained at that table one more minute, she wasn't sure what would escape her mouth.

Cassidy stepped beside her and snaked an arm around her waist. Scarlett rested her head on her cousin's shoulder.

"Rough night?"

"And probably only going to get worse." She closed her eyes. "They'll hate me. Jake doesn't think it matters, but their dynamic will change with Harmony in the picture."

"As it should." Cassidy let go of her and opened the fridge. After she pulled out two cheesecakes and set them on the counter, she glanced Scarlett's way again. "What's really bothering you?"

Scarlett picked up the stack of dessert plates she'd set aside earlier and spread them out on the island countertop. "Is it fair to Harmony to shuffle her back and forth between us? And how often does he get her? I'm trying to do what's right for everyone here but feel like I'm the one who's giving up the most."

"First of all, Harmony's old enough to decide how much time she wants to spend with Jake." Cassidy opened a drawer and removed a pie server before pointing it at Scarlett. "But, you're still going to have to get used to sharing her. You can't keep her from him now that they know about each other. Yes, it's going to be different and take some getting used to, but God's got you. He always has and won't leave you alone now." She waggled her eyebrows. "Of course, you could always get back together with Jake and not need to share at all."

"Thanks for the reminder about God's presence in this. I needed it." She glanced toward the butler's pantry and lowered her voice. "But we aren't getting back together."

"Why not?" Cassidy sliced the dessert, keeping her attention on the pieces she placed on the plates.

Scarlett added dessert forks to each of the plates. "For starters, he and Andi are together."

The pie server in Cassidy's hand stilled, and she lifted her head. "Do you really believe that act they're putting on?"

"Did you not see the flirting in there?" She waved her arm in the direction of the dining room.

"Did you?"

"Of course I did. I was right across from them for a front row seat."

"They were putting on a show, alright." Cassidy exhaled a chuckle. "I realize you haven't dated in a while—or at all—but you're completely clueless."

"I'm telling you, Cass. They're a couple." Scarlett spun around and yanked open the silverware drawer.

"Did you not notice how Andi eyed Levi whenever she touched Jake or giggled at something he said? And Jake isn't reciprocating. At all. In your experience, is that normal behavior for him when he's with someone?"

Now that she thought about it, Jake *had* instigated every step of their relationship. Starting one day not long after her fifteenth birthday when he had searched her out in the barn after a ride. She'd taken the saddle off Snow and was brushing her down.

"You in here, Scar?" Jake's quiet voice carried to her.

"Back here." His footsteps crunched on the hay-strewn ground, marking his progress. She glanced over her shoulder. "We just returned from a ride."

"Your mom told me." He moved beside her and covered her hand holding the horse brush with his. "I wanted to talk to you about something."

At his serious tone, her strokes stalled, and she gazed into his gray eyes. She'd never noticed how thick his eyelashes were. Or how his irises darkened like a thunderstorm cloud when he grew serious.

Or how tall he was. She sucked in a breath and tamped down her sudden jitters. "Is everything okay?"

The fingertips of his free hand grazed her cheek. "I hope so. I—" He stepped back. "Scarlett, I need to tell you something. I can't keep it to myself anymore."

Now, her stomach churned. What was wrong? Jake never got that serious. He preferred to joke around and laugh at himself.

"What?"

"I like you, Scarlett."

Her muscles relaxed, and she stared at him. That wasn't news to her. They were friends and hung out all the time. "I like you, too, Jake."

He grasped her hand, his grip strong yet tender. "As more than a friend. I... Will you be my girlfriend?"

When her mouth fell open, Jake pushed her chin up with a finger, then touched his lips to hers. In her shock, their first kiss ended in the blink of an eye, a quick brush of his lips and it was over. She almost missed it.

From that moment, Jake took charge of their relationship, holding her hand, kissing her, cuddling. Even that night after homecoming, she had followed his lead.

Scarlett pulled herself from the memories she'd worked hard to shut away. Was it her fault their love died? She shouldn't have expected him to do everything. Wasn't a relationship supposed to be a partnership between two people? Yet she'd let Jake do all the work.

Cassidy stopped pouring sauce over the slices of cheesecake and rubbed Scarlett's back. "Sorry. Didn't mean to bring up the past. I know you don't like to dwell on it."

"Maybe I should. We were so young, Cass. It would never have worked out, anyway."

"Yes, you were young, but it was obvious to everyone you two loved each other. In fact, the entire school expected Jake to propose during your senior year, and the two of you to get married the summer after you graduated." She sighed. "At least they did before you moved away."

"I believed that, too." Until Jake had sat her down and explained he wanted to pursue his music and to do that, he couldn't have any distractions.

Especially not her.

∾

Jake slumped in his seat. Dinner had been a horrible idea. Or perhaps listening to Andi's advice was where he'd gone wrong. Either way, over the last half hour, Scarlett had erected and reinforced her walls, taking pains to avoid his gaze whenever possible.

As she and Cassidy gathered the empty dessert dishes and carried them to the kitchen, Jake disengaged himself from Andi.

"I'm going to help the ladies with the dishes." Levi scooted his chair from the table and stood.

"Me too." Mia grabbed the remaining items on the table and followed him.

Seth moved from the seat beside Jake to the one Levi vacated at the head of the table, turned it around, and straddled it, resting his arms across the back. "Does someone want to explain what's going on around here?"

"What?" Jake inched his chair farther from Andi even though her hands no longer lingered on his skin.

"Don't play dumb, Jake. We've known each other too long." He waved his index finger between them. "Why the act during dinner?"

"You didn't recognize it?" Andi smirked. "I took a page out of your playbook."

"Yeah, and I learned my lesson. Nothing good comes from feigning a relationship. It either unnecessarily encourages one of the parties involved or creates a rift between you and the person you're trying to make jealous."

"So, you and that girl you brought to Jake's cookout..." Andi put her elbows on the table and rested her chin on a fist. "You're still an item? What's her name again? I figured the arm candy was for Cassidy's benefit. How'd that work out for you?"

Seth eyed her and smirked. "About as well as it did for you and Ridge."

Jake slapped his hands on his thighs and stood. "Enough. You two need to knock it off now. I'm sick of your bickering."

Seth got to his feet. "Fine with me. Can we get on with the real reason we're here tonight? I have things to do."

Jake shot a glare his way. "I'll go see if they're done in the kitchen. We'll meet in the family room. You two go on in." Before they left the room, he added, "And be civil."

Only Levi and Mia remained in the kitchen when he entered.

"Where'd the girls go?" Jake glanced out the windows.

"I'm right here." Mia waved at him. "Hi."

He rolled his eyes. "You know who I mean."

"Cassidy went home." Levi paused in wiping down the counter and pointed at the back door. "And Scarlett's putting Harmony to bed." He folded the dishrag and placed it beside the sink. "She said you can share the news without her."

Jake sighed. Cass was avoiding Seth to the same extreme Scarlett was avoiding him.

"What news?" Mia glanced from Jake to Levi. "Am I missing something?"

Levi raised an eyebrow and peered at Jake as if challenging him to answer.

"You already know, but I'll give you more details. Andi and Seth are waiting." Jake squared his shoulders. "I do have something to tell all of you."

As he waited in the entry to the family room, Mia kept guessing what he had to share. Was she that clueless or trying to lighten the mood? Not that his mood would lift. Scarlett should be here, not hiding out upstairs. What a mess he'd made.

"Everybody, find a seat." He settled into one of the chairs in front of the TV and waved Seth away when he started to sit in the other, hoping Scarlett would still make an appearance.

Seth glared at him and plopped down beside his sister.

As soon as the others sat, he made eye contact with each of them. "You've all figured this out, but I want to confirm. Harmony *is* my daughter."

"Why didn't she tell you?" Mia peered at the others. "Y'all knew Scarlett better than I did, but I can't imagine her not telling Jake he was going to be a daddy."

"She did try to let me know, but none of her letters or calls got to me." He adjusted the strap on his sling. "Then someone sent Scarlett NDA documents and a check in exchange for her silence on the paternity."

"Who would do that?" Levi leaned his elbows on his knees.

"I'm checking into it. Unfortunately, when we first came to Nashville, several people came and went. My list of people I remember is short. If any of you have ideas, I'll take them, although I'm not holding out hope for an answer. But there is *no* doubt Harmony is my daughter. I've missed out on a lot, and from here on out, I plan to be present."

"How does Scarlett feel about that?" Mia remained wide-eyed. "She's taken care of Harmony for years."

"I'm okay with Harmony spending time with her dad."

Everyone's heads turned to the door as Scarlett joined them. She headed toward the chair beside Jake.

When she sat, Jake leaned closer and lowered his voice. "I didn't think you were coming."

"Neither did I." She glanced around the room. "But they'll have questions I can answer."

As if to prove her point, Seth piped up. "We all figured out Jake was Harmony's dad at that birthday party. Was the NDA what tonight's powwow was about or is there something else?"

Scarlett stiffened in her seat.

Jake laid his hand on her forearm in a show of solidarity.

"What we want is your input on the best way to make the news public."

"Why even go public?" Levi stretched his arm along the back of the couch. "You could say Scarlett's your new girlfriend, one with a daughter."

"I'm not—"

"No." Jake wouldn't lie to his fans, and he would not fake anything with Scarlett. Besides, he had a legal obligation as Harmony's biological father. "We need to be upfront about this. I don't want the press chasing down Scarlett or Harmony or people digging into their past."

"They're going to do that, regardless." Andi shook her head and looked at Scarlett. "I hope you don't have any skeletons."

Jake frowned at his friends. What was wrong with them? They had grown up with Scarlett.

"When do you want to tell everyone?" Mia put an end to any chance of a blow up before it could begin.

"I was thinking after I'm healed and Scarlett goes back home, but I'd like to get ahead of this before the tour starts back up on July twenty-third. My parents got back from their month in Hawaii yesterday." He rolled his eyes. "Mom heard I was injured, and even though I assured her I had help, she has to see for herself. So, after catching up at home, they plan to drive up next Thursday since we no longer have the festival commitment."

Scarlett gasped. "What? You never mentioned your mom and dad are coming."

He looked over to find her face reddening. Why was she so upset? He thought she'd be thrilled about the visit. His mom loved Scarlett. "This is something they should hear in person. It's not a conversation to have over the phone."

"Jake, you can't spring this stuff on me. I need to prepare myself. And Harmony."

He turned toward her and lowered his voice. "They already love you. And they'll be overjoyed to meet their granddaughter."

"Remember your initial reaction? Joy didn't make any kind of an appearance." She shot out of her chair. "What day are they coming again?"

"Next Thursday. And they plan to stay a few days like always when we can arrange a visit." He glanced at the others. Levi's and Andi's eyes ping-ponged between him and Scarlett. Seth's eyes were closed, and his head rested against the couch while Mia typed with her thumbs on her phone screen.

"Okay, Harmony and I will go home Thursday morning. Your mom can take care of you." Scarlett paced, talking to herself as though none of them were in the room. "We'll come back on Saturday. That gives them a couple days to process the news before meeting Harmony."

"No." Jake stood in front of her to halt her frantic movement. "I don't want you to leave."

"It's not a bad idea," Levi said.

Though calmly spoken, the interruption grated on Jake's nerves. "This is family business, Levi. Stay out of it."

But what if Levi and Scarlett got together. He *would* become part of the family. A second dad to Harmony. He'd have to share his daughter with another man, and Levi would keep Scarlett all to himself.

Nineteen

Sunday morning, Scarlett glanced at Jake's door. Should she knock? No. She needed a break from him and the volatile mix of emotions he stirred.

She tiptoed back downstairs to the kitchen and left a note assuring him they'd be home by lunch and to call if an emergency arose. After she set it by the coffeemaker, she quietly rushed her daughter out the door so they wouldn't be late for the service. She'd missed worshipping last week, but after feeding Jake and Harmony breakfast, she would have arrived in time for the benediction after making the drive.

A braver person would have knocked on his door, checked if he was awake, and left a plate of breakfast in the fridge for him to microwave later, but she couldn't risk him inviting himself along. Like he had Friday morning when she felt the urgent need to take Harmony to the library after he'd mentioned Andi coming over sometime during the weekend to record their song again. After she'd returned home, she learned Seth and Mia had also joined them.

She didn't have the stamina to talk him out of coming with them today. She longed for peace and calm. And none of the turmoil and chaos that showing up to the service with Jake Turn-quist would stir.

As soon as she turned the car onto the main road and headed toward her church, she breathed a sigh of relief. Why had she agreed to staying with him? They'd made it almost two weeks, and her nerves were shot. How would she manage two more?

"Mom?"

"Yeah, sweetie?" She glanced in the rearview mirror.

"Am I going to live with Jake sometimes?"

Scarlett's stomach sank at the hope in her daughter's voice. Did she want to live with him? "What do you mean?"

"Mikayla lives with her mom during the week and her dad on some weekends and vacations. Is that going to happen to me?"

"No, baby." She flipped on her left turn signal and merged into the flow of four-lane Sunday morning traffic. "Jake's job takes him away from home too much. He'll spend time with you when he can, but you won't have a regular schedule of which days you'll be at his house." She prayed he would keep his word about that.

"What will you do when I spend time with him?"

Miss Harmony like crazy. Spend the entire time wondering and worrying about what was happening. "Maybe I'll pick up an extra shift at work or do something for myself like take a long bath or read a book."

"Will it make you sad when I'm with Jake?"

Her daughter's concern smoothed some of the rough places in her heart. "A little bit, but happy, too, because your dad wants to spend time with you." Something she was just now learning to trust.

Satisfaction spilled across Harmony's face. Her pert nose went right back to her book now that all was right in her world.

On the other hand, Scarlett's world continued its tilt-a-whirl ride.

Lord, I truly am happy Jake knows about his daughter. Thank

You for opening that door and allowing both of us to share our side of what happened back then. If You'll get us through the next couple of weeks with no drama, I'd appreciate it. And please, please let Jake's parents, especially Shelly, forgive me.

She pulled into a parking spot in the middle of the church lot. Harmony unbuckled herself, hopped out of the car, and waited for Scarlett before they headed inside.

"Good morning, Harmony." The Sunday school teacher stood at the door with a welcoming smile. "We missed you last week."

"I was at my d—"

"We're helping a friend out this month." Scarlett squeezed Harmony's shoulder. "He had an accident, and we're taking care of him until he can manage on his own." She tugged Harmony to the side, bent down, and lowered her voice. "Remember our secret?"

"Sorry, Mom."

"It's okay, sweetie. If you don't talk about Jake, you won't have to remember."

"Or we can tell people." A pleading expression filled Harmony's face.

"We'll keep it quiet for a little longer. Jake's figuring out the best way to tell everyone." She gave her daughter a hug. "I love you."

"You too, Mom."

Scarlett watched her join her group of friends before turning back toward the sanctuary. After finding a seat in the back corner, she studied the bulletin while waiting for the service to begin. Oh, how she longed to rest in God's presence.

Music swirled around her, and her heart rose with it in praise. She couldn't carry a tune like Jake or Harmony, but she could rejoice and worship in her own way. As if He designed the entire service for her, the songs were filled with hope and life. "It is Well with My Soul" had been one of Scarlett's favorite songs since she was little, even more so since her parents' funeral. Today, she claimed the lyrics as she closed her eyes and raised her arms, letting the words' promise and healing flow over her.

Tears choked her until she couldn't continue. God cared. He stood by her, and no matter how difficult life got, no matter the trials set in front of her, He always carried her through. Why was it so hard to believe He would remain faithful where Jake and Harmony were concerned? Right there, in the back of the sanctuary, Scarlett gave all her fears and doubts over to God. No matter what happened, He loved her and was in control. Whatever the next two weeks or the ten years after that brought, her soul would be well.

J ake heard the back door open and relaxed against the blue couch cushions. They were back. He closed the magazine he hadn't read a word of over the past hour and set it aside.

"Why can't I play with Max right now?"

He smiled at Harmony's love of her dog.

"Go change first." Something clunked on the kitchen counter.

"Okay." Harmony's little footsteps pounded up the stairs, and the clatter of dishes and swishing of running water came from the kitchen.

He had panicked when he noticed her car missing from the driveway this morning before he found her note on the counter. In order to reassure himself she hadn't left for good, he'd rushed back upstairs and checked to make sure their belongings were still in their rooms before retreating to the family room.

One thing he'd decided over the course of the morning was that he had to come clean about Andi's ploy. Especially if it encouraged Scarlett to divulge information about her and Levi.

Resolving to get everything in the open before they sat down to lunch, Jake stood and headed down the hall.

He paused in the doorway. In a pink sundress and brown

sweater with her hair in a braid, Scarlett took his breath away. She'd always been cute, but age and motherhood enhanced her natural beauty. He could get used to her in his kitchen on a permanent basis.

She opened the oven and slid something inside before returning to the island and sorting groceries she must have picked up on her way home. When she walked to the pantry, giving him a view of the brown boots she'd paired with the dress, he chuckled. It was proof she had plenty of the country girl he once loved in her even now.

She spun around and jumped, dropping a couple of cans on the hardwood floor. "Jake, what are you doing? You scared me."

"Sorry." For startling her, but not for admiring the view. He walked around the counter and picked up a can of tomato sauce. "I couldn't help myself."

"With what?" She set everything in her arms on the counter in the butler's pantry, and he added his item before retrieving a can of corn from the floor.

When he'd set that one down, he edged close enough to Scarlett for her citrus scent to fill his senses. He wrapped his good arm around her waist and dipped his head. "This."

When his mouth found hers, every ounce of love he'd fought to reel in exploded. She tasted like comfort and promise. Like home. He never wanted to leave this behind ever again.

Several seconds later, her palms pressed against his chest. Her lips left his, and she took a step back, leaving a void between them. Shaking her head, she continued backing away, her cheeks flushed, breaths coming short.

"Wh-what are you doing, Jake? You can't do this to me." As if in afterthought, she added, "Or Andi."

"I'm not doing anything to Andi." He stood his ground, not drawing closer to her but remaining in his place. "I'm in love with you. Always have been."

She gasped. "Don't do this. Please. I can't..."

His heart thudded against his chest with the confirmation of his fears. "Why not?"

"Andi, for one."

"Scarlett." He ran a hand down his face. What a mess he'd made. Instead of drawing her closer, he'd pushed her away. She'd been avoiding him for days. "What you saw the other night was all an act. There's nothing going on between Andi and me. We're friends. We hang out and write songs together, but that's it. I've never been attracted to her." *She's not you.*

"Why would you let her hang on your arm like that during dinner?"

Should he admit he wanted to make her jealous to see if he mattered more than Levi? "Because I'm desperate." His voice cracked as he leaned a hip against the counter in the pantry. "She said you didn't like us standing close, and I dared to hope it was true, so I went along with her scheme." His eyes dipped to her lips.

"You used her?"

"No." The accusation stung. Levi had scowled throughout dinner, and Seth was more out of sorts than normal. "If anything, she used me. She's always loved to rile the guys up. Wednesday night was another way of doing that." He sighed. Sometimes it felt like they were still in high school. "I'm sorry, Scarlett. I shouldn't have played along. I never intended to hurt you. It was stupid and, as I said before, I was desperate to see if you cared even a fraction of what I do. Will you consider a second chance? For us?"

"I can't." She shook her head, her eyes glistening. "You need to spend your time and energy on Harmony. Be her dad. She deserves that."

"And what about you?" He took a step toward her. "What do you want? Deserve?"

"Nothing."

The whispered word broke his heart. She deserved the world, and now it was his turn to make the sacrifices.

~

Scarlett muttered an excuse of changing out of her dress and almost ran from the room. When she reached her room, she locked the door and flung herself across the bed.

Jake had kissed her, and almost every single part of her yearned for him to do it again. Except her brain won out with a wave of fear. Fear of loving him only to be rejected again. Fear for her daughter. The only answer was to keep their distance with their hearts locked up tight.

"Mom?" Harmony knocked on the door.

She sniffed and sat up. "Yeah, sweetie?"

The doorknob jiggled. "Can I come in?"

"Just a minute." Scarlett peeked in the mirror hanging above the dresser and swiped at her eyes before crossing to the door and opening it.

Harmony stood in the hall, now wearing black shorts and a white T-shirt with a sparkly rainbow ironed onto the front. "Can you come play with me and Max?"

"Why don't you ask Jake? I have to finish getting lunch ready." And it would get him out of the house if not her thoughts.

"Okay." Her shoulders fell.

A new pain coated her raw heart. Had she been so busy with meals and small chores that she'd neglected her daughter?

As Harmony tromped down the stairs, Scarlett moved to the railing to eavesdrop on the conversation below.

"Do you want to play outside with Max?"

"Sure." Jake's tenor carried as he talked with their daughter. "Why don't you go put Max on his leash while I wake Trigger up from his nap."

A door opened, and snippets of Harmony's words reached her accompanied by a few excited yips from the puppy.

Decisive footsteps and the click-clack of nails on the hardwood indicated Jake's return. "All set?"

"Let's go."

"Close the garage door first."

Scarlett's lips twitched. He was trying so hard with their daughter.

The door slammed, and she cringed.

"Oops, sorry." Harmony's apology echoed Scarlett's thoughts.

Jake chuckled. "It's okay."

Max's barking was cut off with the closing of another door, leaving her alone. But all she felt was lonely.

She changed into shorts and a T-shirt and returned to the kitchen. Her phone rang as she checked the chicken she'd put in the oven when they got home from church. It needed more time, so she shoved it back in to bake and answered the call without glancing at the screen.

"Hello?"

"Hi, Scar."

She smiled, the first genuine one since that moment during worship this morning. "What's up, Levi?"

"Wanted to check in. Everything alright there?"

She peered out one of the windows. Jake stood on the deck and looked on as Harmony and Max ran circles around Trigger. The scene evoked an odd mix of warmth and longing, just like fifteen minutes ago when Jake had kissed her in the butler's pantry.

"Yep. Couldn't be better." She forced cheer into her response.

"Good." He paused. "I wanted to ask you for a favor."

"Anything."

"You might change your mind when you hear what it is. I've got this benefit dinner—"

"Levi, you're a great friend but—" Her stomach cramped. Had she led him on?

"I'm not asking you to be my date," he said in a rush. "Well, I am but not in the way you're thinking. This foundation for underprivileged kids is close to my heart, and I'd like to bring a friend with me. Someone who isn't trying to monopolize my attention or get close to someone else in the band."

Did that happen often? It hurt her heart that anyone would use him that way. "And I fall into that category?"

"You said it yourself. I'm a great friend, but..." He chuckled.

She couldn't argue with that. The back door opened, and she glanced at Jake... who was entering alone. She looked out the window again. Harmony sat at the top of the stairs overlooking the yard with Trigger lying on her left and Max standing at attention, his tail wagging on her right.

"I'll have to find someone to watch Harmony." She raised an eyebrow at Jake. "What night?"

"Wednesday."

Jake waved his hand in the air to get her attention.

"Hang on a minute." She held the phone against her shoulder. "What's wrong?"

"Nothing. I'll watch Harmony if you need to go out."

"Are you sure?" Last time she'd left them alone hadn't ended so well.

"Positive. We need to get used to hanging out without you around to referee."

"Okay. Wednesday night?"

"I've got nowhere else to be, and it gives the two of us a night to enjoy before my parents arrive and you go back to your place."

She lifted the phone to her ear again. "Jake will watch Harmony. What time?"

"I'll pick you up at six."

"What should I wear?"

Jake's head jerked up at her question. He probably hadn't planned to free her up for a date. Not that this was one, but he didn't know any better. And after going along with Andi's dinner antics, she might as well let him stew for a few more minutes. Maybe he'd think twice about faking a relationship if he understood what it was like from the other side.

"A nice dress is fine," Levi said.

"I can do that. See you Wednesday."

When she hung up, Jake filled a glass of water and leaned against the counter with his gaze downcast. "Who was that?"

"Levi, but it's not what you're thinkin'." Her words thickened. "It's a benefit for a cause I could get behind."

"Can I ask you something?" He sighed and lifted his head to look at her. "Is he why you can't..." He quirked his head toward the spot where he'd kissed her.

"What?" Heat flooded her face. "No, Jake. Levi's a friend. There's nothing going on between us."

"Then why—?" He grimaced.

She held up a palm and turned to look outside. Only Max, who was now curled in a ball, had moved. "Look, Jake." She turned back around. "I want you to spend time with Harmony. That means you and I are going to spend time together, too. When we were teenagers, I gave away my physical expressions of love before I truly understood all the consequences."

When he opened his mouth, she shook her head, sure he was about to object or apologize. "It was my decision at the time. What I'm trying to say is I need to take this new relationship—the one with you as Harmony's daddy—at my own pace. I don't want to rush into something I'll regret down the road."

"You'll give me a chance? To prove myself? My love?" His gaze darted to her lips and back up, speeding her pulse.

His earnest expression, along with the doubts hammering her heart, made denying him nearly impossible. But she squelched the flame trying to ignite and held fast to her resolve. "Let's see how your parents take the news." She crossed to the island and set her phone down with a sigh. "They may not want anything to do with me after they learn they've had a granddaughter for nine years."

He covered her hand with his. "They won't. And if it is an issue, I choose you. Over everyone."

But not *everything*. He found joy and meaning in his music. Who was she to take that away or demand he choose between it and her? But could she give her heart completely to him again only to play second fiddle to his career?

Twenty

O n Wednesday night, Jake stuck another piece of the half-finished puzzle into place on the dining room table and tried to erase the image of Levi escorting Scarlett out of his home from his mind. Not that he ever wanted to forget Scarlett wearing that navy blue dress with white polka dots and a belted waist.

"What would you like on your pizza?" He remembered his promise to take care of dinner and looked at Harmony.

"Cheese." She glanced up with wide, hopeful eyes. "Can we get breadsticks, too?"

"Absolutely. Do you want something to drink?"

"The fizzy white one, please."

Her polite response warmed him with pride. "You want anything other than cheese on your pizza?" He wiggled his fingers along her side, eliciting a giggle. "How about onions?" When he'd grilled burgers last night, she'd refused to eat any of the fixings that the white rings touched on the platter Scarlett had put together.

She wrinkled her nose.

"Pineapple?"

"Gross."

"Anchovies?"

"What's that?"

"A kind of fish." He chuckled at her scrunched face of disgust. "Okay, one cheese pizza for you and a pepperoni and sausage for me."

"I get my own pizza?"

"Sure. Why not?"

"Mom and I share when she orders because it costs more to get two." She returned to her puzzle, but her movements slowed as though she'd said something she shouldn't have.

Harmony's innocent affirmation of their financial struggles weighed like a boulder on his shoulders. How much had Scarlett sacrificed while he had more money than he knew what to do with? At least he could spoil his daughter tonight without her mom getting upset.

He opened the app for his favorite pizza place and typed in their selections. "Let's get dessert, too. You can pick."

Her grin was all the affirmation he needed. He scooted his chair closer and gave her his phone with the pizza website pulled up.

"This one." She gave his phone back, and he looked at the cinnamon concoction with icing over the top. "Those are quite a bit like breadsticks. Are you sure that's what you want?" He clicked on the side items icon. "We could get chicken instead." He could go for some wings.

"Yeah." Harmony leaned against his arm and pointed at the spicy ones. "Those."

"They're hot. You sure you can handle 'em?"

"Yep." She picked up another puzzle piece and tried to fit it in a few wrong areas before it snapped into place.

Jake finished ordering more food than his entire band could devour in one sitting and set his phone aside before picking up another cardboard shape. "You like doing these?"

"Yeah. With Mom. We get to spend quality time together."

He fought a chuckle. A Scarlett saying if he'd ever heard one.

The doorbell rang, and his head jerked up. No way was the pizza that fast.

He stood. "Stay here while I see who's at the door."

"'Kay." Harmony's focus remained on the task in front of her.

He strode through the entry way and opened the door. His mouth dropped open enough to catch any bugs hanging around the porch.

"Surprise!"

"Mom, you're a day early." He hugged her with his left arm and watched over her head as his dad pulled luggage from the trunk of their sedan.

"What? We're not allowed to change our minds and surprise our favorite son?" She frowned at his sling. "I had to make sure you're being taken care of. Besides, we wanted to miss the holiday weekend traffic."

"I'm your only son, and I'm being well cared for. I just wasn't expecting you until tomorrow afternoon." *Or prepared.*

"We can get a hotel tonight." She turned toward the driveway.

"Don't be ridiculous." He had to give Scarlett a heads up, but he'd left his phone on the table next to his daughter.

"Excellent. There's an even bigger surprise coming tomorrow."

Not as big as the one I have for you. "Can't wait." He smiled as his dad reached the porch. "Hey, Dad."

"Jake. Where can I drop these off? You still have someone here helping you out?"

"Yeah, about that." He peeked over his shoulder, stepped outside, and pulled the door shut behind him. He couldn't hide Harmony from them, but he could weave an adequate explanation until Scarlett got home. "She has a daughter, and I'm watching the girl tonight while she's out with a friend."

"Oh, fun." Mom clapped her hands together and held them under her chin. "Where is she? What's her name? How old is she?"

Dad grunted, and Jake opened the door before taking one of

the small suitcases from him. How long did they intend to stay? "Let's leave these here for now." He set it down at the bottom of the stairs while wondering how to explain the room they usually used when visiting was already occupied. By his daughter. "I'll introduce you to Harmony. We ordered pizza for dinner."

As they entered the dining room, he lifted a plea for guidance. How could he break the news? Should he wait for Scarlett or was it best to get it over with, like ripping off a bandage?

"Harmony?" He kept his voice low.

She spun in her chair, her smile dimming when she saw his parents.

"This is my mom and dad." *Your grandparents.* "They surprised me and came to visit a day early."

"Aren't you a pretty little thing." Mom bustled forward. "I'm Shelly and that's Alan. Can I join you? I adore puzzles."

He had to hand it to the woman, she made herself welcome anywhere.

"My mom and I do them together." Harmony held a single piece up. "But you can help as long as you don't put the last piece in. Mom says that's my job."

"Oh, I'm old, sweetie. We won't get anywhere close to that last one before I'm ready to turn in." She squinted at Harmony in concentration. "You look so familiar."

Please no. Let me explain first. "Dad, why don't we take your things upstairs?" He snatched his phone from the table and shoved it into his pocket. "You can either stay in my room or the blue one. Harmony and Sc...her mom are in the other two." That was too close a call.

"The blue one is fine." His mom smiled at him. "We're just glad to spend some time with you."

They carried the luggage to the second floor and set it in the room. His dad clamped a hand on Jake's left shoulder. "You doing okay?"

"I am." Other than getting this confession out and warning Scarlett.

The doorbell pealed for the second time that evening.

"Probably the pizza," Jake said. "We ordered plenty. If you haven't eaten yet, you're welcome to join us."

"Sounds good."

Jake led the way downstairs and answered the door as his dad strode to the kitchen."

After he sent the delivery guy away, he set the food on a side table and dug his phone out to shoot Levi a text. MOM & DAD SHOWED UP EARLY. CAN YOU KEEP S OUT UNTIL 11?

As much as he disliked the idea of pushing Scarlett into Levi's company longer, he had no other options. His phone chimed with a reply.

WOW. AND YES. SHOULD I WARN HER?

With a sigh, he typed one more message. PROBABLY BUT DON'T RUIN HER EVENING.

Hopefully, Levi would wait until he drove her home to break the news.

PRAYING FOR YOU.

Despite Jake's envy over the easygoing relationship Levi had with Scarlett, he couldn't deny the guy was a great friend.

"Dinner's here. Let's eat before it gets cold." He carried their feast to the kitchen and spread it out on the island counter.

"Yay!" Harmony raced into the room and stopped at the sink to wash her hands.

Scarlett had instilled good habits and southern manners in their daughter.

"She sure reminds me of someone." His mom's gaze never left the girl. "Wish I could put my finger on who it is."

Jake kept his mouth shut and fetched paper plates and napkins. He had to confess soon because it would not take long for Mom to solve the mystery. But did Harmony remind her of Scarlett or himself?

Throughout dinner, Jake braced himself for Mom's conclusion.

They made it to the cinnamon and sugar dessert before she

snapped her fingers. "I got it. Harmony looks just like Scarlett did at that age. I haven't heard from her since her parents passed away."

Harmony's head perked up. Her gaze locked on his mother. Her mouth twitched, ready to blurt out something.

"Harmony, if you're finished, you can go feed Max."

The dog proved a good distraction, and she scurried outside. Jake blew out a slow breath to have dodged the conversation yet again.

Something his mom had said pinged in his brain. "You spoke to Scarlett when her parents died?"

Other than their one late night conversation about the events leading up to the NDA, they'd not yet broached any other difficult topics, but sometimes the sorrow in Scarlett's eyes said more than words could.

"Not in person, no. Someone sent me that news article link that I forwarded to you about the funeral, but I'd just had my knee surgery, and the drive was too much." Mom gathered the paper plates and napkins into a pile. "I sent Scarlett a card expressing our condolences and regrets for missing it." She wagged her head from side to side. "Anyway, she sent me a nice thank you in return. I wonder where she is now."

Right where she belongs.

"Jake!" Harmony burst through the mudroom door and raced to the table. Her chest heaved as she lurched to a stop in front of him. "Something's wrong with Trigger. He won't get up." She pulled on his arm.

The tears clinging to her lower eyelashes slammed into his heart as hard as her pronouncement. Trigger was eleven years old, and Jake had observed a slowness in his movements since he'd returned home for the band's tour break mid-May.

"Show me." He stood and took Harmony's little hand in his, aching to protect her.

When they exited the back door, Harmony pointed at the steps. Jake trudged down them and found his faithful friend curled in a ball against the deck supports, panting. He whined when Jake ran a hand along his belly. "What's going on, boy?"

"Take him to the vet." Dad stood over him. "I'll get him into your truck."

"Thanks, Dad." Why now? He could not handle another crisis.

"We can keep an eye on the girl for you."

"No." He shook his head and swiped at the moisture filming his eyes. "I'll call her mom and ask her to meet us."

"You sure?"

Scarlett would not appreciate him leaving Harmony with his parents before they knew the truth. "Positive, but would you put the puppy in the crate in the garage? And maybe let him out again before you go to bed?"

"Of course." His dad rested a hand on Jake's good shoulder. "If you need anything else, you call us."

"I will." He jogged inside the house, grabbed his phone and keys, and hurried back outside. He yanked open the back door and lifted Harmony inside beside the dog. Once they were both buckled in and the truck was on the main road, he pressed a button on the steering wheel and issued a command to call Scarlett. He was about to ruin her evening after all.

Twenty-One

❦

S carlett's clutch vibrated where it rested on top of the white tablecloth. She mouthed an apology to those around her and grabbed it before jerking her phone out.

When she saw the name on the screen, her pulse raced. Jake had promised to call if a problem came up. No sense in disrupting the other guests even more. She flashed the phone screen at Levi and held up a finger as she pushed her chair back.

The moment she stepped outside the banquet room, she answered. "Jake? Is everything okay?"

"No." His voice trembled, sending a jolt of trepidation through her. "Trigger's not doing well. Harmony and I are on the way to the emergency vet." His voice lowered and muffled a bit. "What should I do if it's time?"

"Oh, Jake." Her heart hurt for him. "Want me to come? I'm sure Levi won't mind."

"Maybe." He cleared his throat. "That might be best. Harmony will need you if this goes south."

"Of course. Where are you taking him?" She scanned the ball-room lobby until her eyes landed on a table with promotional material for the charity. She rushed over, picked up one of the pens, and jotted the information down. "We'll get there as soon as we can."

"Thank you. One more thing."

What else could there be? "Yeah?"

"Mom and Dad got here early."

She leaned her hand against the table for support as her knees buckled. "They met—"

"Yep."

"What'd they say?"

"Nothing really. I just told them I was watching my helper's daughter for the evening, but we didn't make it through dinner before Mom mentioned she looks like you."

"Oh, no. What are we going to do?"

"One step at a time, babe."

It wasn't the first time he'd used the old endearment. She touched her lips at the memory of their kiss last Sunday.

"You there, Scar?"

"Yes," she whispered, then heard a small voice in the background.

"Harmony wants to talk to you."

She pulled herself together and grabbed her clutch and the flyer. "Okay. Yeah. She's probably scared."

"It'll be alright, Scarlett. I promise. Here's Harmony. We're on speaker."

"Mama?" Her voice sounded so small, so frail.

Scarlett wished she could wrap her in her arms and promise everything would be alright. But that wasn't the way life worked. Sometimes sad and difficult things happened. Sometimes one had to say goodbye to loved ones and walk through the grief that followed.

"I'm here, baby." She pressed the phone to her ear as applause erupted in the ballroom, wishing she could hug her little girl.

"S-somethings wrong with Trigger."

"Jake told me." She kept her tone even and calm despite the

turmoil roiling inside. "You're taking him to the doctor now. He'll know what to do."

Harmony sniffled, and her voice thinned. "I'm scared, Mom."

"Me too. I'm going to meet you at the doctor's, okay? Tell Jake..." She paused. Harmony needed her dad right now. "Tell *Daddy* you need a hug. He gives good ones."

"'Kay."

She pressed her hand over her heart that ached for the two most important people in her life. "I love you, baby."

"Love you, too, Mama."

Scarlett hung up, shoved her phone back in the clutch, and squared her shoulders. Time to ask Levi a favor of her own.

Before she reached the doors, music inside swelled, and he strode out, concern etched on his features. "You've been out here a while. Everything okay?"

"I need to go. Jake's on his way to the vet with Trigger." She held up the flyer she'd written the information on.

He took the paper and read it. "I know exactly where this is. It's not far from Jake's house, but it will take us about twenty minutes if we don't hit traffic." He rested his hand on her lower back. "Did Jake leave Harmony with his folks?"

Her head snapped up, and she twisted toward him. "You knew?"

"For about an hour. Jake texted, asked me to keep you away from the house for a while."

She gritted her teeth. If not for the dog, would he have told her anything?

"He asked me to tell you," Levi said, obviously reading her mind, "but I didn't want to ruin your evening. I figured it could wait."

"Should I call Cass to pick us up from the vet? We can go home until Jake explains everything to Alan and Shelly."

"Why don't you hold off until you talk to him? If you want to go home, I'll drive you. No sense in Cassidy driving across town when Jake and I are both here." He quirked his head toward the doors he'd exited a few minutes ago. "Need anything from in there?"

"No." She lifted her clutch. "This is all I brought."

He pulled his keys from his pocket and took her elbow. "Let's get going then."

Once they got on the road, Scarlett leaned back in her seat and closed her eyes, trusting Levi to get her to the vet. "Sorry to ruin your night."

"You didn't ruin anything." The warmth in his voice persuaded her to open her eyes and turn toward him. He winked at her. "I had a nice dinner, heard some amazing stories of the wonderful accomplishments of the foundation, and enjoyed your company."

"Yeah, but it's eight-thirty. When's the last time you ended a date this early?"

"Truth?" At her nod, he continued. "Unless we're doing a show, I'm usually in bed by ten. Guess I'm more early bird than night owl."

"Seriously?" She shifted her shoulders to face him. "Bet that's hard with music." What did the life of a musician entail, anyway? The only work-related duties Jake had attended to during the past few weeks consisted of a few phone calls and writing songs with Andi.

"It's not as glamorous as people think." He stared out the front windshield at the road and shook his head with a faint smile. "It's actually exhausting. Our work hours include travel, and our days are long. It's hard when you can't remember what city or sometimes what state you're in."

"You're not happy with the travel?"

"I don't mind it, but Jake's... been discontent for a couple years now. I see the spark, the excitement, when we're collaborating on a new song or working in the studio, but the travel and the constant clamor of fans are not aspects he enjoys."

Jake had always loved writing and creating, but also was more of an observer than a leader in a crowd. Which meant concerts and touring must feel like acting, always playing the part, being *on* for an audience.

"D-do you think he might give it up? Someday?" She held her breath as she waited for Levi's answer.

"In a heartbeat for the right reason."

A bubble of hope swelled in her. Did proving himself and his love mean Jake would leave the band?

Levi pulled into a tiny parking lot beside Jake's truck. "Go on in." He pulled his phone from his inside jacket pocket. "I've got some emails to return, so I'll wait out here. Call if you need anything."

"Thank you, Levi." She leaned over and kissed him on the cheek. "You're a terrific friend."

"Story of my life." He winked at her.

Scarlett got out of the car and went inside. Her step hitched at the sight of the scuffed white tile floor and an empty reception desk. The beige walls closed in on her as memories of another waiting room where she'd hungered for any detail about her parents while trying to keep Harmony occupied rose to the surface of her mind. She blinked them away and focused on the present situation. Jake sat across the way with Harmony on his lap. The two off them fit together like pieces from one of her puzzles.

"Mama!" Harmony hopped down and threw herself at Scarlett.

She staggered in her heels at the impact. "Hi, baby." After putting her clutch on a small end table, she sat in the chair to the left of Jake and pulled her daughter onto her thighs. "How are you doing?"

"No news yet. We're waiting."

She reached for his hand, the first physical touch she'd initiated. He wove his fingers with hers and held on like a drowning man to a lifeline.

"Can we pray for Trigger?" Harmony twisted to look at her.

"Of course we can." Scarlett hugged the girl's middle tighter. "Do you want to or should I?

"Can we all do it?" She glanced at Jake.

Scarlett waited for him to answer.

"That's a great idea." He closed his eyes. "Lord, if it's Your will, heal Trigger. Give the vet knowledge and sure hands tonight." He choked up.

Scarlett squeezed his hand as she picked up the prayer. "We know You have a plan for each of us and even for Trigger. If it's not going to cause him more pain, help him get better. And if it's time, give us the strength to let him go."

"No!" Harmony jumped from Scarlett's lap and glared. "I don't want him to go. Why did you pray for that?"

"Sweetie, sometimes we have to do things that hurt. Sometimes we lose those we love before we're ready to say goodbye." Scarlett's words got stuck behind a sob. This wasn't about the dog anymore.

Jake released her hand and wrapped his arm around her shoulders. His lips brushed her temple. Once. Twice. Three times. "I'm sorry about your parents." His whispered words brushed her ear. "I wanted so badly to come to the funeral. To see you. But we were in the middle of back-to-back concerts." His voice caught. "And Becker refused to cancel. The guy even added a couple extra shows."

If he had come to the funeral and met Harmony, would they have lost fewer years together as a family? Would he have given up everything to care for her and their daughter back then? She buried her face in his T-shirt and soaked the cotton fabric with the grief she'd held inside for too long. Here she didn't have to be strong and put together. Here Jake shared in her responsibility, and would care for the girl, so Scarlett could finally grieve.

Jake took his arm from around Scarlett. "Come here, Harmony."

The girl bumped her as she climbed into Jake's lap. A light kiss touched the back of her head.

"I'm sorry I was mean, Mama." Her little fingers brushed through Scarlett's hair.

She sniffed and turned her head to look at her daughter even though words wouldn't form.

"She's not crying because of what you said, Harmony." Jake's words wrapped around her heart like his arm swathed her shoulders. He understood. "She just really misses her mom and dad right now."

"I'm still sorry."

Scarlett peeked at her sweet girl snuggled against Jake's sling.

"If I have to let Trigger go, I will." Her brave voice wobbled. "But Max will be so sad to lose his friend."

"Max has you and so do I." He choked on the final word.

Several minutes later, Scarlett lifted her head to see tear tracks on Harmony's cheeks. A twinge of guilt pricked her for ignoring the girl until she'd cried herself to sleep. She sat up fully and swiped under her eyes with her fingertips.

Jake shifted the girl to his chest and looked at Scarlett with concern. "Do you want to talk about it?"

She obviously needed to work through more of the memories. Her gaze landed on a poster of a dog hanging on the wall behind Jake, reminding her of why they were here. "Not tonight, but someday."

He nodded once and took her hand again. "Thanks for coming."

"Of course." She'd come for Harmony but instead received support from Jake.

The bell over the door chimed, and Levi entered the waiting room. "Any news?"

"I'm so sorry." Scarlett winced. "I completely forgot you were waiting."

He waved her apology off with his hand. "I finished my emails and thought I'd come see what you found out." He glanced at the empty reception desk. "Nothing yet?"

"No." Jake's wearied tone matched the exhaustion in his face.

"I can wait here if you'll take Scarlett and Harmony back to the house."

She nodded and glanced at Levi. "I have my keys with me. If you don't mind driving us, I'd like to get my car and go back to my place tonight."

"Why?" Jake's brow furrowed.

"Your parents. They don't need any more drama tonight. We'll come back once you've had a chance to talk to them."

"Okay. I'll let you know when it's done." He didn't try to convince her to stay.

She swallowed the disappointment before remembering he'd probably be here a while longer tonight. "I don't want to go inside and disturb your family. Would you mind keeping Max for us?"

"Not at all." Exhaustion lined his face.

"Call and let me know about Trigger, too." She squeezed his hand and glanced at Harmony, wondering if she should wake her up.

"I can carry her." Levi scooped the girl into his arms.

"I'll walk you out." Jake released her hand. "I'm not ready to let go quite yet."

"Please." She gave him a grateful smile.

They stood, and the doctor entered from the back. "Oh, Mr. Turnquist, we just got Trigger stabilized."

Scarlett sent up a prayer of thanks that neither Jake nor Harmony would have to say goodbye tonight.

Twenty-Two

J ake parked in the garage and stared at the door to the house. Midnight. Most likely his parents had gone to bed a few hours ago. *Thank You, Lord, for giving me more time with Trigger.* He'd not prayed so fervently or often in years, but Harmony's request earlier had unlocked a door he'd shut tight when he left Fiddler Creek.

For ten years, he'd chased his dreams and plans, running ahead of God's will and direction. He leaned his head against the seat and closed his eyes.

"I know it's been a while, God. I'm sorry I shut You out. Thank You for bringing Scarlett and Harmony back into my life. Show me Your will for where to go from here. Help me follow instead of blindly blazing my own path. And thank You for saving Trigger tonight."

The dog needed surgery. Something about his stomach twisting and needing to be put back in place, but the vet assured him it was routine. He'd have to ask Levi about it tomorrow since he had zoned out once he heard the prognosis.

Despite his parents sleeping inside, his home felt empty without Scarlett and Harmony, and he hadn't even made it inside yet. He needed to talk to his parents, smooth things over first thing in morning so he could get his girls back where they belonged.

While sitting in that waiting room with Scarlett and their daughter, they had shared the moment as a true family. He wanted more. Preferably without the sorrow and tears, but spending the quiet time with his girls had soldered his heart to theirs. No other family would do for him.

In fact, one day he'd work up the nerve to ask Scarlett if she wanted more kids because he did. He wanted to experience everything with her. From watching her belly grow large with their child to birth and early morning feedings. He yearned for all of it.

He climbed from his truck and glanced over at the sleeping puppy in the corner. He let himself into the house through the mudroom and headed straight to the freezer where he pulled out an ice pack. His shoulder ached from letting Harmony rest against his arm, but he didn't regret one second of the pain. He grabbed a towel from the counter and trudged toward the stairs, exhausted yet buoyed in spirit.

"That you, Jake?" Mom's soft question redirected his steps toward the living room. The lamp beside the couch gave the room a soft glow.

"What are you doing up?" He leaned down and kissed her cheek.

"I've been reading and praying." She set her Bible on the end table. "What happened?"

"They're going to do surgery tomorrow." He collapsed in the armchair, wrapped the ice pack in the dishtowel and held it to his shoulder as he explained what he recalled of the doctor's words.

She frowned at his movements and adjusted a white throw blanket over her lap. "You've had an eventful night."

An understatement if he'd ever heard one. "Yeah." He couldn't wait any longer. "Mom, I have to tell you something."

"Harmony's your daughter, isn't she? Yours and Scarlett's."

"How?" He shook his head. He should never doubt her gift of discernment.

"I needed something to keep my hands busy, if not my mind." She rubbed her thumb over the back of her opposite hand. "I started cleaning."

Since he was a boy, Mom had cleaned when worried or fretting over something. He wondered what the house had looked like when Jordyn started dating. Jake had left home before then, his sister five years younger than him, so he missed all that. Most likely a blessing—for both of them.

"What'd you find?"

"A picture of Harmony and her mom. In the yellow room by the bed."

Why had the girl brought a picture of Scarlett when she was next door? "You're not upset I didn't tell you Scarlett's the person helping me?"

"Not at all." She removed her bifocals and wiped them with the hem of her T-shirt. "It took me a while to put two and two together."

He chuckled. Not that long. She'd already figured out Harmony looked like Scarlett before he'd rushed to the vet.

"I mean, Scarlett moved away when she was, what? Sixteen?"

"Yes." They'd broken up several weeks before, but that hadn't stopped him from driving home and watching from the barn loft as the Sykes family left their property for the last time.

She put her glasses back on. "At first, when I saw the picture, I thought she'd gotten married and started a family right out of high school."

He removed the ice pack from his shoulder and set it on the coffee table. "What changed your mind?"

"The guitar." One of her eyebrows lifted above the rim of her wire frames. "Signed by you."

He dragged a hand over his face. "I gave her that before I found out she's mine."

"You must have sensed it, then." She leaned forward and gave him the look. The head tilted forward, lips turned down, eyes filled with a combination of warning and disapproval, one he'd received many times over the years.

"Not really." He exhaled a half-hearted laugh. "When I first saw them six weeks ago, *I* thought she was married. She and Harmony both go by Sykes, but that doesn't mean anything these days."

His mom tucked her feet to her side and resituated the throw. "Want to tell me what happened?"

It was a relief to have someone else to talk to about the adjustment of learning he was a father. "You're too calm about this. You have a granddaughter you knew nothing about for nine years." And a son who obviously didn't live out the faith she'd raised him with.

"My first reactions weren't something I'm proud of. I'm sad I missed out on those years." She laid her hand on her Bible. "But while waiting for you, I remembered that bitterness and harboring grudges don't heal relationships. They drive a wedge. And if I want to spend time with my granddaughter in the future, I can't alienate Scarlett in the present, can I?"

He shook his head, awed by his mom's wisdom and capacity of forgiveness. "This is not how I imagined this conversation going."

"Good. That means I'm following Jesus's example and not my human tendencies. Now, why did none of us know about that little girl until now? How about you fill me in?"

Over the next hour, he shared everything he'd learned from Scarlett.

"My feelings for her haven't changed. I still love her." He shook his head. "No, that's not entirely true. I'm more in love with her now than I was in high school."

"I know, son." She patted his leg. "Your face lights up when you say her name. How does she feel about you?"

"She's holding back. Not that I blame her. I really hurt her when I broke up with her. And the years of believing I sent the NDA added to her pain." He scrubbed his hand over his mouth. "I'm trying to win back her trust."

"Stay faithful and pray about your relationship. If it's God's will, He'll take care of the rest."

"Does Dad know?" His gut churned.

She pursed her lips and nodded. "I told him what I suspected."

His morally upright father was sure to have a few choice words about Jake's behavior. Jake swallowed around the lump in his throat. "How'd he take it?"

"Not as well as I did." She gave him a sad smile. "I told him to get some sleep and we'd discuss it in the morning."

"Thanks, Mom."

She tilted her head to the side. "They didn't come back with you, so where are they? I thought I heard a car earlier."

"Levi drove her back so she could pick her car up and go to their house in Fairview tonight. Scarlett knew you'd be able to help me out in the morning and wanted to give us a chance to talk and you some time to absorb this. She adores you guys."

"As we do her. She's had a special place in my heart ever since she rode her horse through my garden." A twinkle lit her eyes.

He laughed. "I forgot about that."

"No, you didn't." Mom stood and rested a hand on his shoulder before picking up the towel-encased ice pack from the coffee table and leaving the room.

Jake leaned back in his chair. No, he hadn't forgotten that day when Mom's scream had woken three-year-old Jordyn from her nap.

"Go see what's wrong, Jake." Dad lifted the baby from the couch where she'd fallen asleep watching a movie and held her against his chest while whispering words of comfort to calm her.

Jake abandoned his racetrack and sprinted outside to where Mom stood on the porch. Her mouth gaped open as she stared at her garden. He glanced at the plot of land, back to Mom, then again to the garden. His eyes bugged out. All of Mom's plants were trampled. The ruby red tomatoes squashed into the ground like giant bugs on a windshield. The bean stalks strewn across the dirt instead of stretching to toward the sun.

"What happened?" Had a tornado hit? He leaned his head back and looked up at the cloudless sky.

"That girl ruined my garden!" Her short curls flew in the breeze as she shook her head and slapped a pair of gloves against her jeans.

"What girl?" Jake stepped off the porch and turned in a circle, searching every direction for someone.

Mom's hands rested on her hips. "The one with the horse. I knew that family would be trouble."

Ah, the new neighbors, but something else was more important. "She was on a horse?" Someone to ride with instead of roaming the boring trails alone like he usually did.

"A white one." Mom peered down at him. "I know what you're thinking, Jacob, and you will not go riding with someone who has no respect for my garden."

Jake's shoulders hunched. "Was she any good?"

Mom's laughter took him by surprise. "Yes, I'd say she's a natural."

A streak of white to the east caught the edge of Jake's vision, and he turned in time to see a horse jump the fence dividing the two properties.

"Mom." He pointed. "She's coming back."

"Good. I have a few things to say to her." She picked up the broom next to the front door.

His backside knew those bristles far too well. He took two steps away. Would Mom swat a girl she didn't even know?

A burst of laughter sounded from inside the house.

"Alan Turnquist, are you eavesdropping?" Mom turned and strode inside, leaving Jake alone in the yard.

He stared as the horse neared. Would she traipse through the garden again? When they were a few yards away, he realized the girl was his age—or close to it. It would be nice to have a friend to hang out with and go riding.

The girl pulled the horse to a stop before she reached the plants and dismounted. Her red-blonde hair flew in every different direction. She looked wild. Exciting. Adventuresome.

"Hi." She gave a little wave and bit her bottom lip.

"You ruined my mom's garden." He pointed at the churned-up dirt.

She looked down at the plants and wiped at her cheek.

He squinted at her. Was she crying?

"I didn't mean to. The horse is new, and while I know I jumped your fence and was racing through property that isn't mine, I didn't see the garden in time." Her breath caught. "I just wanted to meet all of my neighbors today."

"Couldn't turn...?" How fast was she going? Did she like to race? He eyed her horse. Would she beat Cash?

"I'm sorry." She sniffled.

"Oh, honey." Mom scurried out of the house and wrapped the girl in a hug. "It's okay. I can get more tomato plants."

Jake stared at his mom. She'd just been ranting about the garden, ready to excommunicate the neighbors or something. He didn't really know what that word meant but heard someone at church use it when they were talking about someone who no longer came.

"I'll tell you a secret, Jake." Dad squatted beside him. "You will never understand women. No matter how long you live, they will always confound you." He squeezed Jake's shoulder. "Best learn that truth now."

"What's your name, honey?" Mom swept the girl's hair back from her face.

"S-Sc-Scarlett S-sykes."

The prettiest name he'd ever heard.

From that moment on, Jake and Scarlett had been inseparable —best friends until they were more.

He scrubbed his face with his hand, wiping away the last of the memory. Perhaps his mom was right. Not only had he not forgotten that day, he might have fallen a little in love with her then.

Twenty-Three

Thursday afternoon, Scarlett opened the back car door and waited for Harmony. She leaned inside and pulled the box of photo albums from the backseat, then glanced at the house. She couldn't believe she was back here so soon.

Jake had called after breakfast to give her an update on both dogs and assure her he'd talked to his parents, so she had no reason to stay away.

They now knew everything and, according to Jake, weren't upset. How could that be? Shelly Turnquist had a temper that had become legendary in Fiddler Creek. And that was before someone had kept a secret like a granddaughter from her. How could she forgive Scarlett so easily?

"Hey." Jake approached with a tentative smile. "What do you have there?"

"Pictures. Mom thought you would like to see them." Harmony shifted from one foot to the other.

Scarlett glanced at her and set the box on the ground. "Go ahead and ask him."

Jake raised an eyebrow.

"When's Trigger coming home?" The girl leaned against Scarlett's side.

Jake squatted and put his left hand on Harmony's shoulder. "He'll be healed enough to come home in a few days, but he's going to have to stay calm, so no playing with him and Max, okay?"

"Okay." She looked up at Scarlett. "Can I go see Max now?"

"Yes, you may. He's in his crate."

As she raced to the house, Jake stood. His eyes remained fixed on Scarlett, searching, peering into her soul. Heating her insides more than the sun warmed her shoulders.

The tip of his boot nudged the box, breaking the spell. "We *would* like to see these."

She bit her lip. Would these soothe any ruffled feelings or cause more pain?

He moved closer, stealing all the oxygen from her. How did he manage that when they stood outside in the fresh air? "I missed you."

You just saw me last night and let me cry all over your shirt. "Jake..."

"Scarlett Sykes!" a young woman squealed as she rushed toward them.

Jake groaned. "Jordyn's here, and she doesn't know yet." He stepped aside. "They sprang the surprise on me this morning after I'd already called you." He glanced at his sister. "We can discuss sleeping arrangements later."

"Harmony and I can double up." She glanced at Jake's sister and forced a smile onto her lips. The girl from her memories had morphed into a beautiful young woman with curly long hair the same chocolate shade as Jake's.

Jordyn squeezed her in a tight embrace. "It's been ages. You're as gorgeous as I remember." She fingered Scarlett's hair. "I've always been envious of this color."

"What?" Scarlett gaped at her for a second before turning her gaze to Jake. But he wasn't there. "Where'd Jake go?"

"Who knows?" She shrugged. "What have you been up to?"

"Uh..." What was he thinking leaving her alone with his sister?

"Hey, Jordyn." Jake walked toward them from the direction of the house with Harmony skipping along beside him holding the puppy's leash.

Scarlett's heart pounded as she shook her head at Jake.

"This is Harmony." He laid a palm on their daughter's head until she ducked out from under it.

"Oh, she's adorable." Jordyn glanced at Scarlett. "She looks just like you."

"Thank you." She rolled her eyes at Jake. They really needed to have a conversation about sharing his plans with her *before* they happened. "She definitely has some of her daddy in her, though."

The younger woman shrugged. "I'd have to see them next to each other to tell."

Scarlett pinched her lips together to keep from laughing at the oblivious comment as Jake coughed into his fist.

"Are you kids going to stand outside all day?" Shelly Turnquist hollered from the back side of the house.

Jordyn shrugged and ran ahead. "Better get. You know how Mom can be."

"You could have given me some warning about that." She scowled at him.

His forehead wrinkled. "I tried to ease her into it. We'll have to lay out the facts. Take the blunt approach."

The puppy yipped, and Scarlett sighed. He was right. They could stand out here arguing or go inside and face the music.

She bent to pick the box up again and grew lightheaded as her heart thrummed against her chest.

"Breathe, Scarlett." Jake drew alongside her. "Everything is going to be okay. I'm right here. Every step of the way."

As if to illustrate his words, Jake kept pace with her on his right and Harmony on his left as they walked to the back door.

As soon as Scarlett set the box on the kitchen table, Shelly wrapped her arms around her. "Scarlett, honey, it's wonderful to see you." She stepped back. "How are you? Jake told me about what happened in high school, but what are you doing now?"

"Give her some space, Mom." Jake laughed. "Scarlett brought some photo albums. Why don't you get settled in the family room while I talk to Jordyn."

Scarlett tried to catch his eye, but he shifted his focus to his sister and tugged her toward the living room. Hadn't he just promised to stay by her side? She held in a sigh. They couldn't blindside Jordyn with the photos.

Harmony led the way down the hall and plopped down in the center of the sofa. "Can I hold the book?"

"Sure." Scarlett handed her the oldest one first and sat on her left while Shelly took the other side. "But make sure everyone is ready before you turn the page."

"This is before I was born." She pointed at a photo of Scarlett wearing black flip flops and a turquoise maternity dress, taken three weeks before Harmony's birth. The girl ran a finger over the plastic, then tapped the next picture of her as a baby wrapped in a blanket cradled in her grandfather's arms.

"And here's me and Nana and Papa."

Shelly placed a hand on Scarlett's shoulder and squeezed. Their eyes met over Harmony's head, and without words, Jake's mom told Scarlett how sorry she was for their loss.

"My first birthday." Harmony turned the page and pointed at a photo of her in a highchair, grinning at her grandparents with frosting coating the bottom half of her face in a vanilla bean beard.

Jake and Jordyn joined them, and Scarlett stood.

"Where are you going, Mom?" Harmony stopped in the middle of another explanation.

"To the chair. Jake and Jordyn haven't seen any of these yet, so they can sit by you."

"Both of them won't fit." Her daughter was a smart one.

Jake chuckled. "We will if you sit on my lap, and Jordyn sits beside us."

"Okay." Harmony handed Shelly the album and hopped up.

As Jordyn passed, she gave Scarlett another quick hug and whispered, "Aunt Jordyn sounds great, doesn't it?"

It did. She nodded. But someone was missing here. "Where's Alan?"

Shelly and Jake exchanged a glance. Apparently, all was not as well as he'd indicated during their morning phone call.

"He went over to check on the horses." Jake gave her a half smile, then leaned to look over Harmony's shoulder. "How old are you here?"

Harmony chattered, happy to have an audience to share her albums with.

Had Alan gone next door to think or to cool off? Maybe take out some aggression with some physical labor?

"Don't worry about him. He'll come around." Shelly rose. "I'm parched. Would anyone else like something to drink?"

"I would." Jordyn raised her hand.

"Me too," Harmony said.

Jake nodded. "Guess I'll have something, too."

"I can't carry all of those." Shelly held out a hand. "Scarlett, would you mind helping me? Harmony, why don't you show Jake and Jordyn the pictures I already saw." She shook her finger at the girl but tempered it with a smile. "But don't look at any new ones without me."

"I won't." Her daughter flipped to the beginning of the album and started over.

Jake winked at Scarlett and mouthed *go*.

The second they reached the kitchen, Shelly scooped her into the warmest, most encompassing and compassionate hug she'd received in years.

"I forgive you, Scarlett. You don't owe me an explanation or an apology. Let's get that in the open right now."

Scarlett held on for a few seconds longer. After her own mother, Jake's mom had once been the next person she turned to for advice.

"No matter what happens between you and Jake..." Shelly released the embrace but kept her hands on Scarlett's shoulders. "You are the mother of my first grandchild. You can come to me for advice, to vent, or if you need a babysitter."

Scarlett stifled a giggle. "A sitter who lives ninety minutes away?"

"Okay, that one may be difficult, but I'm a phone call away if you need someone to talk to. Always."

The assurances and invitation soothed the empty cracks last night's cryfest in the waiting room had begun to heal. "Thank you."

Shelly removed a pitcher of sweet tea from the fridge while Scarlett filled the glasses with ice.

Jake's mom filled each one, then set the almost empty pitcher on the counter. "I noticed Harmony called your parents Nana and Papa, and I don't want to take away from their memory. What should we have her call us?"

"Do you have a preference?"

"I've considered this while waiting for one of my children to give me a grandbaby." She gave her a wry smile. "What do you think of Mimi?"

"It's perfect."

Shelly was not a *grandma*.

"What about Alan?"

"I don't think he'd mind Grandpa, but we could also go with Gramps or Grampy."

Scarlett wrinkled her nose at the last one. Too much like grumpy. And it hit too close.

"Okay, not Grampy." Shelly wiped a small puddle from the counter. "But Gramps is nice."

"And easy," Scarlett agreed.

"Then it's settled."

But not everything was. She had to ask. "How'd he take the news?"

"I only had my suspicions when I first talked to him, but even after Jake explained the NDA mess..." Shelly released a long exhale and shook her head. "I imagine it was the same as Jake."

It gave her hope. Jake had been angry at first, but came around, ready to welcome Harmony and her into his home—and his life.

Twenty-Four

J ake walked into the lobby of his record label in downtown Nashville Thursday afternoon with light steps. Since his family had left the morning after the Fourth of July fireworks and Scarlett agreed to stay at his house one more week, life had been almost perfect as he spent time with his daughter and worked to get closer to Scarlett.

He strode to the reception desk and signed in.

When he turned around, Becker rose from one of the plush armchairs bordering two walls. "Jake, how's the shoulder?"

"Getting there." He adjusted his sling, and the soreness in his arm conjured memories of Harmony coaching and nagging him with the rehab exercises his doctor had given him.

"Excellent." His manager sat again and rubbed his palms together. "It's time to make some appearances."

Jake settled in a few chairs away and spun his hat in his hand. "I've got the show next Wednesday." An acoustic showcase on music's most storied stage. His girls and Cassidy were coming, too.

"It's a start, but people are forgetting about you."

He wouldn't mind if they did. Scarlett refused to let him go to the grocery store with her anymore after people asked for autographs and selfies during their second outing.

Most people left him alone when he was out and about, but once in a while, one person would ask, lending courage to others in the vicinity.

"Jake. Becker." The producer walked out from the back offices and welcomed them. "We're all set up and can't wait to hear what you've got for us."

They followed the man to a conference room where three other men and two women sat around a large table. The producer made introductions even though Jake recognized them from previous meetings and industry parties, then gave the meeting over to him.

He stood and took a deep breath for courage. "As I mentioned a few weeks ago, I'd like to take this album in a new direction." He pasted on a smile and made eye contact with everyone. "I've brought a few of my songs but also a few more that showcase the additional talent in our band."

Becker's face reddened. "I thought you'd given up on that."

"Please keep an open mind." Jake shook his head at his manager, then pulled a flash drive from his jeans pocket and held it up. "These songs are better than most of my hits." He handed the rough recordings to a spiky-haired young guy who plugged it into the console and adjusted a few knobs.

As music filled the room, Jake sat and watched the others' expressions. This could be the catalyst for his next career move. Andi's first song—one of the best in the bunch—was a great start. *Please let them consider this seriously.*

The melodies and harmonies mingled in the air while the people around the table nodded or tapped their fingers against the table in time to the rhythm. He risked a glance at Becker, who typed on his phone instead of listening.

Next, Seth's twangy baritone filled the room, and a couple of the women at the table exchanged smiles. Jake's own tenor rang out during a rousing swing-dance inspired tune. When that song faded, Mia's sweet alto voice took center stage on the folksy ballad Andi had written. The producer scribbled nonstop on the pad of paper on the table in front of him.

When the final notes of Andi's second song faded, Jake straightened in his seat. This was it.

"It's different." The producer spoke first.

Good or bad? "It is." He held his breath.

"It's a great sound." The label's VP folded his hands on top of the table and looked at the others.

"But?" He heard the unspoken hesitation.

"Fans expect Jake Turnquist." The marketing director frowned. "How will they receive a compilation album?"

The band had discussed that issue. "Then let's not call it a *Jake Turnquist* album."

Becker slammed his palm on the table. "No matter what you call it, you're going to lose sales."

Something he didn't care about but wouldn't dare admit in front of the people whose sole job was to generate income.

One of the publicists raised her hand. "The song you sang at the party for 'Favored' wasn't in what you played for us today."

"No, it's not." He clenched his fist on his knee under the table. "That song is not going on the album."

"Why not?" Jake glanced over to find a glaring Becker. "It's already gone viral online."

"I'm aware." He couldn't get the video taken down. "I shouldn't have played 'Rain' in front of an audience. It's not an option for this album."

Becker hissed out the side of his mouth. "That video is the only positive press you're getting after postponing the tour. And fans are eating it up."

His jaw locked as his face heated, but he didn't break eye contact. That song belonged to Scarlett—and now Harmony. If his manager couldn't back him up, the man would be updating his resume within an hour.

"Fine, fine." Becker rubbed a hand over his scalp. "You've got plenty here for another album."

"Thank you." He took a couple deep breaths to calm his temper.

Tell them.

The undeniable nudge had him opening his mouth. "This week, I made another decision." He took a deep breath and plunged ahead. "The fame has been more than I dreamed, but I've learned something about myself.

"I'm not happy spending months on the road. Touring and recognition from fans don't fill me up like it does some artists. My passion is in the creative process, the collaboration of writing a moving or enjoyable song." When the young kid handed the thumb drive back to Jake, he held it up in front of him. "This is a reflection of why I love music. And this album belongs to the band. If it will help with sales, add something like 'Featuring Jake Turnquist,' but I'm retiring after this album is recorded."

He sagged back in his chair as relief and peace filled him.

Becker jumped from his chair. "You need to stop and consider what you're saying, Jake. If you retire only to get bored and return in a year or two, you'll lose credibility. Not only with your fans, but with the industry."

"I've had nothing but time to think about this." He turned in his chair to face the livid man. "I won't be back in the spotlight."

The producer stood. "We'll give you until next Friday to make a final decision about fronting the band, Jake. If you still want to retire, we'll need to meet with the others and come up with a plan about the future of the band. Either way, we liked what we heard today and want the compilation album even if you decide not to go on tour with it." The man eyed Jake. "You're willing to give the others the rights to these songs?"

He rose to his feet. "Only for half of these songs. Andi wrote the others you heard."

"Good. We'll probably want to record two versions of this album. One with you singing lead vocals and another with someone else singing for future tours and appearances." He glanced at Becker. "You'll have the modified contract once Jake has confirmed his decision. If he chooses to retire, we'll discuss a new agreement for the band to tour with some of Jake's past hits if they'd like to."

All but 'Midnight Blue.' That song would be retiring with Jake.

His manager nodded. "I'll watch for it."

Jake stood and accepted handshakes and well wishes from each person as they filed out of the room. When only he and Becker remained, Jake released a genuine grin. By the end of the November, the tour would be over, and he'd be free to build a life with Scarlett and Harmony without interruptions. A week wasn't going to change his mind. In fact, he would make some phone calls to the band and his parents on his drive home.

"What's this really about, Jake?" Becker paced in front of the window as his bald head reddened. "You break a bone and come face to face with your mortality or something?"

How did his manager become so cynical? "This is something I've struggled with for a couple years now." He swiveled in his chair and stood. "Ask anyone in the band. They'll confirm it. Breaking my collarbone allowed me extra rest I haven't had in the ten years since moving here to chase music. It's given me the chance to focus on parts of my life I've neglected." Like his faith. And his future family. He smiled.

Becker scowled. "What about your contract?"

"What about it? I'm giving them a new album as promised. One that will blow anything I'd do out of the water."

"Don't come running to me when you decide hiding in the shadows isn't what you wanted after all." Becker pushed past him, leaving Jake leaning against the wall.

"I won't." The label wanted the album, and Becker would eventually cool off when he realized he'd still get royalties from the other band members as well as residual earnings from their back-list sales and downloads. Jake could go home with a clear conscience to enjoy the last two weeks before the tour started again. He'd wait until it wrapped up in November to tell Scarlett he was coming home for good.

~

S carlett stood before the bathroom mirror and held the mint green dress up in front of her. If she had this much difficulty choosing an outfit, she should have declined the invitation to the concert, but both Cassidy and Harmony were thrilled about attending the show tonight.

This wasn't even the first time she'd taken Harmony to a Jake Turnquist concert. Something he'd been shocked to learn.

"Why didn't you come say hello?"

"Oh, please, Jake. Like every fan hasn't used the 'I'm an old friend' excuse to sneak backstage."

"Scarlett, my security guys have a standing order to tell me immediately if someone named Scarlett Sykes comes to a show."

All these wasted years. If she'd let go of her disappointment over his rejection, they could have discovered the truth so much sooner. She shook her head. No sense dwelling on a past she couldn't change. She trusted God would take that time and create some good out of it.

"Scarlett?" Jake's voice carried to her, and she walked to the top of the stairs. "I'm leaving. You got your tickets?"

It was the third time he'd asked. She had double and triple checked they were tucked in her crossbody purse on her nightstand. "Yes, and Cassidy's picking us up at six, so we'll be there in plenty of time."

"Excellent." His show-stopping grin increased the flutters in her stomach. "Can't wait to find you in the audience."

She didn't have anything to say to that. "We'll see you there. Break a leg tonight." She cringed as her gaze shifted to his injured shoulder where kinetic tape offered additional support. While he'd been allowed to ditch the sling, all that strumming could cause him pain.

"I hope not." He chuckled. "Although, if it meant I could keep you gals here with me for another month, it would be worth it." He waggled his eyebrows.

"Jake." She tried to frown, but her lips wouldn't cooperate.

"Don't worry, babe. I'll be careful." A horn honked outside. "I gotta go."

Once he left, she returned to her room and grabbed her denim jacket and cowboy boots, aiming for a casual air.

"Harmony?" She knocked on the door. "Are you about ready? Aunt Cass should be here shortly."

When her daughter swung the door open, she wore jeans and a pink lacy top with the new pink cowboy boots Jake had bought her last week. "Will you braid my hair, Mom?"

"Sure." Scarlett followed her inside the room. "Pigtail braids or French?"

"I want to wear my hat."

Another gift from Jake. He'd only bought Harmony a few gifts, even though most of them exceeded Scarlett's budget.

"Let's go with two braids, then. The hat will only hide a French braid."

"Okay." She perched on the end of the bed, and Scarlett moved behind her.

Soon, Harmony would want to do this herself instead of coming to her. She was growing up too fast. Scarlett wished for a close-knit family with three or four children, but that wouldn't happen until she was happily married with someone who stuck around. She'd parented alone long enough. What would it be like to have more children with Jake? Maybe a Jake Jr.? J.J.? No, she couldn't go there. Jake had his career. One that would continue to pull him away from home. One she refused to ask him to sacrifice because she didn't want him to resent her down the road.

Scarlett had just wrapped the final rubber band around the

second pigtail when the doorbell rang. "I bet that's Aunt Cass. You ready?"

"I have to put on my hat."

"Okay." She tugged on one of the braids. "Best get to it."

Harmony picked up the pink cowboy hat from her dresser, set it on her head, and grinned. "I'm ready."

Scarlett stood. "Let's go." She grabbed her purse from her room, then led the way down the stairs and opened the door.

Cassidy hugged her tight. "When are you coming home? It's too quiet without you there."

"A week from Saturday since I agreed to stay another week until the tour starts." She laughed. "Better enjoy the quiet now."

"Aunt Cass!" Harmony threw her arms around her aunt's waist.

"Well, don't you look like the perfect cowgirl." Cass tapped the brim of the girl's hat.

"Jake got me the boots and the hat to wear tonight." She twirled in a circle. "Don't you love them?"

"They're perfect." Cassidy tweaked her nose. "So, any chance we can grab something to eat on our way to the show? I'm starving."

"If it's quick." Scarlett locked the door and shoved her keys into her purse before following Harmony and Cass down the steps to her cousin's minivan.

After a meal at a local deli and a drive that took longer than anticipated, the three of them arrived at the venue and found their seats just before the lights dimmed, and the emcee announced the first act.

Scarlett glanced at the order of artists in the program. "Looks like Jake's on second to last."

"At least we'll hear some great music tonight." Cassidy leaned over the arm rest. "How's everything going?"

"Fine." No need to dive into her swirling emotions that refused to settle. Ever since they started spending time together after Harmony went to bed, their friendship from high school had matured into something she was hesitant to define.

"Are you sure you want to move home next weekend?"

No. Scarlett glanced at Harmony in the seat on the other side of her and leaned closer to her cousin. "Does it matter? He's leaving on tour in a week and a half."

"Yes, but I have great vision and see the way your face lights up when either of you talk about him."

"He's married to his music, which doesn't allow time for a family. Not the kind I want, anyway."

"We'll see." The lights dimmed, and a group gaining in popularity took the stage.

Scarlett sat back, determined to stop dwelling on Jake and enjoy the evening. As each group played three or four songs before switching and bringing Jake's set closer, the more her nerves jittered. Did he get anxious backstage or just want to get the performance over like Levi had suggested?

Before she could start to hope again, Jake led the others onstage, his guitar already strapped across his shoulder. Seth tucked the fiddle under his chin as Andi adjusted her mic stand. Levi took a seat in the drummer's box and glanced at Mia at the piano.

Then Scarlett zeroed in on Jake, who stared back at her.

Twenty-Five

Scarlett's heart raced with anticipation as a slow grin spread across Jake's face, and he stepped to the microphone. "Good evening, Nashville. It's always an honor to play in this hallowed building. We're going to unplug tonight, and just enjoy the music."

Harmony bounced in her seat and grinned from ear to ear as she sang along with the audience as the band played three of their hits.

As Jake waited for the applause to die down, he strummed his guitar. "For years, people have asked who I wrote this next song for. Who inspired me. I've never shared that information. Until tonight."

Several gasps and murmurs came from the audience as everything in Scarlett froze. He wouldn't. Not here.

"You see, I fell in love with a girl my sophomore year of high school." He leaned into the microphone and chuckled as his gaze swept over the packed venue. "Well, probably earlier than that, but my head didn't catch up until then."

The audience laughed along with him. Cass giggled as Scarlett latched on to the arm rests on either side of her.

"The good Lord brought that girl back into my life a couple

months ago, and she's sitting out there with you tonight. She's given me the best gift. A daughter."

A collective gasp rolled through the auditorium, and Scarlett's vision darkened at the edges. Did he think she liked being blind-sided like this? The carefully crafted press release they'd worked so hard on was now nothing more than scratch paper.

He smiled wide in her direction. "Scarlett Sykes, this one's for you."

She forced herself to breathe and act normal as he sang the lyrics she'd always hoped were for her. If she got up and climbed over people in the middle of the song, she'd draw attention to herself, and everyone would know she was the woman he'd written it for. Besides, she wouldn't get far without a car. She didn't dare draw more attention to herself or Harmony.

The music continued, and Jake's voice carried around the room, the crowd joining in on the final chorus. But this time he changed the words. "From where I stand, there's no better view as I count the stars with you. The days are short, the hours too few because I'm in love with my midnight blue."

Scarlett wanted to scream or cry. Or throw something when he looked her direction again. As much as her heart longed to hear his declaration of love, didn't he understand what he'd done? No one would leave them alone now. Instead of quietly issuing the press release as planned, he'd gone and made a public spectacle of them instead. Her peaceful, quiet existence was about to become nonexistent. And Harmony would get caught up in the media storm.

She tapped Cassidy's arm as the stagehands set up for the next act. "I'm going to get some air."

Cass's forehead creased, and she glanced at Harmony. "Want us to come, too?"

"No, you two stay and enjoy the rest of the show." She stood, slung her purse over her shoulder, and patted the side. "I've got my phone if you need to get ahold of me."

When she exited the auditorium, several people descended on

her. One held up his phone. Was he taking her picture? Or worse, recording her?

"Are you Scarlett Sykes?"

She ducked her head and tried to push past them, but they followed her, shooting question after question at her. She heard the click of a camera phone and raised her hand to block her face as she moved down the stairs to the sidewalk.

"How long have you known Jake Turnquist?"

"How old is your daughter? What's her name?"

"When did you get back together?"

"Are you living with him?"

The arrangement she had with Jake took on an unsavory air. If they knew the reason she was staying with him, people would assume more about the situation. She and Harmony would be leaving his house tomorrow as soon as she got them packed up. With everything they had accumulated or moved over the past few weeks, she would already have to make multiple trips. She had to beat the inevitable gauntlet of vehicles camped outside his house to follow her home. The press would set up their long-range camera lenses in only a matter of time.

She held her arms over her head and huddled next to a turnstile, panic building at the crush of people trapping her.

"Hey!" a male voice cut in. "Back off, guys." A warm arm wrapped around her shoulders. "Are you okay?"

She glanced up, and the pressure inside released. She shook her head.

Levi led her through the mass of bodies and down the sidewalk. "I had no idea he was doing that, or I would've warned you."

"Don't apologize. This was all him." She glanced over her shoulder at the people aiming their cell phone cameras now capturing her and Levi. "Where is he?" Part of her—the half that wasn't quaking in fear and refusing to utter his name—wanted to rail at him.

"Doing an interview Becker lined up." He grumbled as he

knocked on a door at the side of the venue. It swung open, and they stepped inside.

Scarlett leaned against Levi as her adrenaline crashed. "Who's Becker again?"

"Our manager. I'm surprised you haven't met him yet. He tends to micromanage Jake's life." He gave an accompanying snort of disgust as they continued down a hallway, then turned right.

"Oh, I might have at the party Cassidy catered. Big guy? Bald? Bossy?"

"Yep, that's him." He ducked his head, and his eyes searched her face. "You sure you're okay?"

"No, but I'll manage." She hoped so, anyway. "Why'd he have to make the announcement in such a public way instead of how we'd planned?"

Levi sighed. "I doubt the press release crossed his mind."

"He gave us backstage passes, but will you tell him we left with Cass instead?" Her hands shook as she dug her phone from her purse and texted her cousin. She had to find a way to get to the car without running the gauntlet Levi had just rescued her from.

"You're leaving, aren't you?" He turned down another hallway.

"He didn't give me much choice. What are people going to say when they find out we've been in his house for the last month?" She frowned and stopped walking. "Where are we going?"

"We're here." Levi waved a hand at an elevator. "This goes to a private level of the parking garage. I'll text Cassidy the entry code so she can meet you there." He pressed a keycard into her hand and held on. "Talk to Jake before you go. Don't just disappear on us."

"I'm not leaving Fairview, Levi. Harmony has friends here, and I can't uproot her again. But I can't be around Jake right now. I'll talk to him, but Harmony's privacy and safety are my first priority."

"I understand that." Levi pulled her in for a quick hug. "Just don't shut him out because he made a mistake in the heat of the moment."

A mistake that held huge repercussions for her and Harmony.

$\sim$

J ake had finally finished with his interview. Now, he could find Scarlett and tell her he loved her in person. Face-to-face.

He snatched his guitar case from the floor and opened the door of the green room.

"What in the world were you thinking?" Levi leaned against the far wall with his arms folded and a scowl marring his face.

"What are you talking about?"

"You *know* what the fans and press are like, so why would you subject Scarlett to their scrutiny with that half-baked declaration? I just rescued her from a mob outside."

The hair on the back of Jake's neck stood up. "Is she okay? Was Harmony with her? Where are they now?"

Levi stood tall. "She's fine now. No, Harmony wasn't with her. And she left with Cassidy after I got them both to the private garage."

What had he done? Jake placed his palm on the wall, wanting to kick himself. Instead of being strategic about it, he'd let his emotions overrule his common sense and dropped her right in the hands of the fans and media. He had to get to her. To explain himself. To ensure he hadn't lost her.

"Come on." Levi took the case from his hands. "I'll drive you home and give you the whole story."

Minutes later, Jake leaned forward in the passenger seat willing the SUV to go faster. His cell phone vibrated, and he declined another call in the constant barrage.

What an idiot he was. If Levi hadn't been there to rescue Scarlett and make sure she escaped... He didn't want to consider what might have happened.

"Why do I keep running ahead of God?" He glanced at Levi staring straight ahead, thankfully giving him the space to work out the answer.

He hadn't felt at peace about his announcement. Hadn't prayed about it. Instead, just the sight of her in the audience cleared the path from his heart to his mouth. He should have taken the time to consider the repercussions. Wasn't that what got him here to begin with? Having a child before marriage. Choosing his career over the woman who inspired him? *Forgive me for taking my eyes off You, Lord. If it's Your will, help me clean up the mess I made tonight.*

As soon as the headlights illuminated Scarlett's sedan still parked beside his house, Jake loosened his iron hold on the door grip. He'd made a vital error in judgement tonight. And was sure she'd be packed and gone before he and Levi made it back from the north side of Nashville.

Once inside, he headed straight upstairs, saw the light through the crack at the bottom of the door of her bedroom and knocked. "Can we talk?"

Scarlett cracked open the door, her cell pressed to her shoulder. "I'm on the phone. I'll meet you in the kitchen."

The firm snick of the door closing sounded before he uttered a response. His shoulders fell as he returned downstairs. How had he screwed this up so badly? And who was she on the phone with this late? Had she heard him return and called Levi? Could he blame her? The guy had been the hero who rescued her while Jake took on the role of her adversary.

He went to the kitchen and started a pot of coffee before pacing the floor. No way was he getting any sleep tonight.

Scarlett entered the room and stopped on the other side of the island with a rigid stance and her arms crossed in front of her. "We're going home tomorrow."

"I know I screwed up." He took a slow step toward her and held his hand out as though approaching a skittish horse. "But can't we talk about this?"

"No, Jake." She stepped away from his touch. "The time to *talk* was before you gave my full name to the press and your rabid fans. Do you have any idea how many phone calls I've fielded tonight from friends?"

He'd ignored several of those during his interview and on the drive home. His hand fell to his side.

"And those were the easy ones. I haven't been coached on how to handle the media or answer their questions. I never wanted the attention, and you put us right in the center of it without any warning."

He slumped onto a stool. "I love you, Scarlett. I wanted to shout it from the rooftop and tell the world."

Her dark blue eyes turned to almost black with her glower. "What you did tonight was not an act of love. If you truly loved me, you would put my wishes first or at least protect our daughter."

Her words gut punched him, more painful than the injury to his collarbone. To think of Scarlett as Levi described finding her. Scared. Paralyzed. Surrounded by strangers pressing in on her. He folded in on himself, wishing he hadn't obliterated his second chance with Scarlett.

"That wasn't fair to your daughter either. To be outed so publicly." She looked at the ceiling as if she could see the girl. "She loves you, but she's not prepared for what she'll face when she goes back to school. The attention? The cameras? The questions about her parents? The nasty comments some will say?"

If he wasn't already sitting, that truth would have brought him to his knees. He blinked back the moisture filling his eyes. Had he lost them both with his impulsive announcement?

"I understand you need distance, but please don't cut me off from Harmony. Can we please work something out?"

"Let's discuss it in the morning after I've gotten some rest." A flash of indecision crossed her face before it went blank. She uncrossed her arms and spun away from him. "Goodbye, Jake."

As her footsteps sounded on the stairs, he dropped his chin to his chest and welcomed the dull pain in his overused shoulder. A reminder he was still alive despite the numbness surrounding his heart. He turned around and folded his arms on the counter and rested his forehead on them as the wreckage of his relationship with Scarlett pressed down on him.

Lord, I made a mess of everything. Will I ever learn to wait on You? Give me the words and wisdom of how to fix this. Scarlett's upset, and I don't blame her, but I can't lose her. My heart won't survive giving her up again.

His cell phone buzzed. He glanced at the screen to see Becker's name. Jake wouldn't put it past the man to show up here in the middle of the night if he didn't answer the call, and he didn't have the capacity to deal with him face-to-face.

He sighed. "Hello?"

"Is she why you want to quit the band?"

"Not a good time, Becker." He stood and trudged up the stairs while rubbing the heel of his palm over his throbbing heart. Once in his room, he shut the door, staggered to the bed, and dropped onto it. He just wanted oblivion from the pain of losing the woman he loved and the daughter he was just getting to know.

"I warned you to keep your head in the music and not get distracted. You never listen—"

Jake hung up, turned off the phone, and tossed it on the nightstand. He didn't need a lecture from the man who had run his life for too long.

Twenty-Six

⤳

Scarlett stifled a yawn as she turned onto Jake's driveway Thursday morning. She'd woken up before the sun rose, and unable to fall back asleep, had already loaded and emptied a carful of her and Harmony's belongings at home. After a long hug from Cassidy, Scarlett had reassured her cousin her decision to return to Fairview was the right one and driven back to Jake's place.

Her heart raced at the sight of a black sports car in the spot where she usually parked. Had a reporter dared to trespass? Could she make it past them without getting accosted? She removed her keys from the ignition and grabbed her purse from the passenger seat, ready to make a run for the back door.

As soon as Scarlett slid out of her car, a bald man with broad shoulders exited the other vehicle. The tension in her muscles eased upon recognition of Jake's manager.

He stalked toward her and stabbed a finger in the air. "I knew you were going to be trouble the moment I saw you."

The vehemence in his voice and the sneer on his face made her insides quake. She'd only met him briefly one time, but Levi's obvious dislike in the handful of words he'd said last night set off alarm bells in her mind. She eyed the distance to the safety of the house.

"I warned Jake not to get involved with the help." He smoothed a burgundy tie over his light blue dress shirt with his fingers and stepped closer, cutting off her escape. "Now he's got it in his head he can retire and be happy writing in the shadows."

Scarlett blinked several times. Jake never said anything about retiring. Was the man delusional? "I don't know anything about that."

When she tried to skirt around him, the man grabbed her wrist. "This is your fault. So now you're going to convince him not to leave."

"It's Jake's decision." She tried to pull her arm away, but he held firm. Shivers raced down her spine. "You're hurting me."

He pressed closer and leaned his head down until his hot breath warmed her cheek. "You can change his mind. I knew I should have offered you more money."

Money? Other than paying Cass for the catering job, no one had paid... His grip tightened enough that she'd have bruises. "Ow!" She blinked back tears at his now vise-like hold.

"Let her go... Now!"

Scarlett shifted to see Jake rushing toward them with fury written all over his face.

"Why are you here, Becker?" He had almost reached them. "To harass Scarlett? Try to convince her to change my mind?"

The guy released her arm, and she stepped back. As she rubbed her wrist, she glanced at Jake's manager. An amiable smile replaced the cold hatred from moments before as he turned toward Jake. "Just wanted to talk to you. We need to make a plan after your shenanigans last night."

Jake ignored him and came straight to her. With a gentle touch, he lifted the arm Scarlett cradled to her body. "You okay?"

A bracelet of angry crimson colored her skin.

"You hurt her." He rounded on his manager. "That's not how you treat a lady. Or any human being."

"Sorry." He shoved his hands in his pockets and looked over their heads.

"Wait." With the pain and fear of being trapped no longer paralyzing her, Scarlett removed her arm from Jake's tender hold, raised her chin, and stiffened her spine. "What did you mean about the money?"

"What?" He reared back with wide eyes and his hand to his heart. "I didn't say anything about money."

"Yes, you did." She would not cower from this bully. "Right before Jake came outside, you said, 'I knew I should have offered you more money.'"

"It was you!" Jake's hands balled into fists. "You're the one who kept me from my daughter with that vile NDA and payoff. Not to mention you're the one who assigned the roadies and interns to handle all my mail and phone calls those first few years while I focused on my music."

Was that what happened? Why she'd never heard from him? Could never get a hold of him? She took another step back and leaned against the side of her car as her knees shook.

"Was that all to keep me away from Scarlett? From learning about the baby? Or did you interfere more? What else haven't you told me... or lied about?"

Scarlett looked between Jake and Becker. How much had the man manipulated a young Jake—a kid, really—at the start of his career? Did Becker only care about the bottom line? What Jake could do for him and not the person behind the musician? Her heart hurt for Jake. He'd trusted the man. Believed Becker had his best interests in mind when making decisions for him and the band.

He jabbed a finger toward Jake's chest as the man's entire head grew as red as a strawberry. "I did you a favor. Your career would have tanked with a woman and a kid distracting you." He waved a hand toward Scarlett, then at himself. "Instead, I built an empire around you. One you're now going to just throw away without any consideration of how it will affect everyone."

"You mean how it will affect *you*." Jake stepped closer. "Whether or not you like it, what happens with my music is up to me. I've spent weeks, months even, doing nothing but studying this from every angle. I talked with the band, prayed, and sought counsel. This is *my* life."

Scarlett bit her lip. Was Jake really considering giving up his successful music career? Had life in the spotlight truly lost its shine? Did she dare hope she wouldn't take second place anymore like Levi had implied?

"I'm not some clueless kid who needs to be led around by the nose any longer." Jake widened his stance and straightened his shoulders. "You're fired."

"Y-you can't do that." Spittle flew from the man's mouth as he staggered back.

"I just did. And I'll be talking with my lawyer about you forging my name on legal documents." Jake pointed a finger toward the sports car. "Now, get off my property."

Becker inched toward his car while holding his palms out. "You have no idea what a mistake you're making."

A lump formed in Scarlett's throat. Becker had made his choices, but a flutter of guilt rose inside her chest for her part in ending his career.

"The way I see it, this decision is long overdue." Jake moved beside her and circled an arm around her shoulders. "One I should have made years ago."

She leaned into his warmth and protection.

"The others won't go for it." Becker dropped his hands to his sides and puffed out his chest. "They need me."

"No, they don't." He huffed a humorless laugh. "They've wanted me to get rid of you for years. When they hear about this, they'll throw a party."

Becker's lip curled into a sneer as he waved a hand at her. "You're really going to give up everything for this hussy?"

Scarlett gasped and glanced toward the house to make sure Harmony hadn't wandered outside.

Jake stiffened, then released Scarlett. He marched three steps, drew back his arm, and punched Becker in the nose. The other man fell to the ground as Jake stood over him.

"Jake, stop." Scarlett rushed to stand in front of him to prevent him from re-injuring his shoulder. "He's not worth it."

His chest heaved as he stared at the man on the ground. "If you say one word about Scarlett or my daughter to anyone, I'll sue you for libel. After everything you just confessed, I'll have an excellent case."

She turned her head to see Becker swipe a hand under his nose to catch the dripping blood.

His eyes narrowed on Jake. "You assaulted me. How's that going to look?"

"Do you want to make that public? Because if you do, I'm more than willing to explain everything leading up to this moment. You'll lose all credibility in the industry." Jake slid his hand down her arm and took hers. "Come on, babe. We're done here."

When they were inside the safety of the kitchen, he pulled her into his arms and held her tight. "Are you okay? Do you need something for your wrist?"

"No. It's just a little sore."

She leaned into his strength as the stress of the morning faded away. This was where she belonged. If only he weren't married to his music... wait. She lifted her head. "Are you really retiring?"

"I am." He kissed the top of her forehead. "Only a handful of people know about it right now. The band, the label, Mom and Dad. Becker." His jaw clenched at the name. "I need to call the record label this morning and ask them to hold off on sending the contract until the band hires a new manager. I'm done with the grind of performing."

Levi had told her almost the same thing, but would Jake miss the notoriety when he walked away? Or could he be content living a quiet life?

"I'll keep writing, but after I wrap up this tour and record one more album at the studio in Nashville, I'm stepping down from the stage."

Just last night, she'd sat in an auditorium filled with people clapping and singing along with him. He had a gift. "You can't quit. You're a fantastic singer." She studied his face for any remorse. "How can you give it up?"

"Easy." He ran a knuckle down her cheek. "There's something I want more than headlining every night."

Her heart stuttered. Warmth radiated from the spot where his skin touched hers and ignited dormant dreams. "Wh-what?"

"You and Harmony. A family."

Last night, he'd betrayed her trust when he put her on display. This morning, he'd stepped in and rescued her like she'd always wished he would. Her emotions were all over the place, and she had to get them under control. Consider all sides of how pursuing a relationship with Jake would affect her and Harmony. She'd made one rash decision in the moment that had changed the course of her life with a baby and didn't want to make another.

She ducked her head. "I can't, Jake."

Footsteps on the stairs forced her to create space between them. Harmony could not catch them together like this. She'd already had too many questions on the drive back to Franklin the night before. Scarlett had to be sure of her heart before giving the girl anymore hope of her parents getting back together.

"What can't you do, Scarlett?" Jake's eyes pleaded with her. "Love me? Because I have enough for both of us."

Part of her wanted to give in, to tell him she was falling in love with him all over again. But she'd learned words were cheap. Easily spoken but not always followed through. Since he hadn't publicly announced his retirement yet, she couldn't be absolutely sure he wouldn't change his mind after going out on tour again.

"Mom!" Harmony rushed their way in her pajama shorts and a pink T-shirt, her hair a matted mess from her braids unraveling during the night. "You promised I could ride horses today."

Her heart sank. How could she have forgotten? They'd only

gone to the stables once since Harmony's grounding ended, and this would be their last opportunity to ride for the foreseeable future. But she couldn't squeeze one in today between packing and moving back to Fairview. "Harmony—"

"How about I take you?" Jake stepped away from Scarlett and ruffled Harmony's hair. "Your mom has a lot to do." He glanced at her with pain in his eyes.

From her rejection or the overuse of his shoulder? "How does your shoulder feel?" He'd taxed himself last night and again outside when he'd hit Becker. "Are you okay to ride?" And watch out for Harmony?

"Almost as good as new." He rolled his right shoulder but failed to hide a wince. "I'll take some pain killers, and we'll take it easy when we go."

She had to trust Jake's word if they had any chance of moving forward. "Fine."

"Yay!" Harmony jumped up and down. "I'll go get my boots."

"Breakfast first and then you can get ready." She retrieved a box of cereal from the pantry, pulled milk from the fridge, grabbed a bowl from the cupboard, and set them in front of a stool on the island. "And we need to fix your hair."

"Mom."

She raised an eyebrow at the whine. "Do you want to go riding or not?"

"Yeah." Harmony's bottom lip pushed forward.

"Then you'll do as I say." An echo of similar words her mom had said to a young Scarlett teased the edges of her memory.

Jake cleared his throat. "I'm going to make some eggs. Anyone else want some?"

Harmony scrunched her nose in answer.

"I already ate. But if you make toast, Harmony might like a piece." She poured milk over the girl's cereal and handed her a spoon. "I'll leave you two to it while I get some work done." She left the kitchen but wasn't as eager to escape Jake's house and presence as she had been a few hours ago.

Twenty-Seven

ake watched Scarlett leave. What was she afraid of? Why
wouldn't she open up to him? He shook his head. He'd only
make himself insane trying to guess what was going through
her head. He'd just have to show her how serious he was about
retiring. Every. Single. Day.

"Would you like some toast?" He shifted his gaze to Harmony
as she stuck a spoonful of cereal in her mouth.

She nodded until she swallowed. "Yes, please."

He chuckled. "How many pieces?"

"Two." She held up two fingers. "With butter and strawberry
jam."

"Coming right up." He walked into the pantry for the loaf of
bread.

"Thanks, Dad."

His step stuttered, and his spirits lifted. Every time she called
him that, his heart puddled. It was his favorite word. One he'd
never tire of hearing.

He popped two pieces of bread in the toaster and set a pan on
the stove to heat. "Any plans after we go riding?"

Harmony sighed as though the weight of the world rested in

her hands. "Last night before bed, Mom said we're going home today."

"Aren't you excited to go back? You'll get to see your friends again." He forced a smile into his voice. He sure wasn't thrilled about them leaving, but he was also the cause of the sudden departure.

"Yeah." Harmony rested her head on one hand while chasing the chocolate puffs around her bowl with the spoon in her other. "But I like it here. There's lots more room, and Mom isn't gone all the time. When we leave here, she has to go back to work."

"Does your mom like working at the restaurant?" Jake should feel guilty about using their daughter to pry, but how else was he supposed to get information when Scarlett closed up tighter than a safe?

"Nuh-uh." She frowned at her bowl. "She always tells Aunt Cass she should find something else."

"Maybe you can come over a couple days before I leave on tour."

"I like it better when all of us are here."

"Me too, sweetheart." He wanted all of them together but needed to show Scarlett that he loved her enough to give her the space she asked for. The toaster popped up the bread, and Jake turned to retrieve it, grateful for a moment to mask his emotions.

Harmony jabbered about the pony she'd ridden last week as they ate and moved on to Max and the new trick she was teaching him while they transferred their dishes to the sink. The girl could talk an ear off a cornstalk, but he cherished every second.

Jake put the butter and jam in the fridge. "Okay, Harmony, you go get dressed, and I'll do the dishes."

"Thanks, Dad." She threw her arms around his waist. "I love you."

And he had three new favorite words to add to his collection. They were more rewarding than a standing ovation or a call for an encore. He cleared his throat and whispered them back. He tugged a lock of her hair as she released her hold around him. "You best skedaddle so we can get going."

As soon as he finished the dishes, he went in search of Scarlett and found her in her room with a half-full suitcase opened on the bed. "Harmony's getting ready."

She spun around, holding a light blue shirt against her chest. "I heard her come up. Thanks for taking her riding."

"My pleasure. It's time I got back on Hercules." Jake leaned against the doorframe, and his resolve not to beg her to stay crumbled like a two-week old cookie. "Don't go. Stay here like we originally planned. For Harmony?"

"It's only another week." She set the shirt in the suitcase. "It will be just as hard for her to leave then as it is now."

"Do you really want to go back? To Cassidy's? To your job?"

"Stop it." She pivoted to the dresser and slammed the drawer shut before yanking open the one below it. "I have a life. We can't rely on you to take care of us forever."

"Why not?" He stepped farther into the room. "I have the means to provide for both of you."

Scarlett shook her head but didn't turn to look at him. "This isn't about money."

"Then what's it about?"

"I don't want to talk about it." Her shoulders fell.

"If you could have anything, what would it be, Scarlett?" Because he would give it to her no matter the cost. "What would your life look like if money wasn't a factor and all your dreams came true?"

"But it is a factor. Why bother daydreaming about something that is never going to happen?"

"Marry me." The words popped out of his mouth without a second thought, but he didn't regret them.

"What?" She spun around and glanced over his shoulder at the door before meeting his gaze.

"Marry me, and my money is yours."

Her lips pressed together, and she crossed her arms. "Jake, I'm not going to marry you for financial security."

"Then marry me because I love you. Because I want you and Harmony with me always. Because I want to make your dreams come true and have another child with you, more if God blesses us." His heart raced as he inched closer and waited for her answer.

"You can't be serious." She took a step toward him, and her eyes searched his as if trying to see into his heart.

He tucked a strand of her hair behind her ear. "I never stopped loving you."

"And how did you show that? By breaking up with me? Or by not contacting me a single time during the past ten years?"

"Is this what you're doing? Keeping record of all my mistakes or errors in judgement? You don't know how many times I picked up the phone to call you. You didn't reach out either."

Why did she keep rehashing the past? He thought they were over their regrets and mistakes. He held up a hand to halt her argument. "Yes, I *now* know why, but from my perspective, you gave up on me, too."

"You left me, Jake. After you promised me forever, you threw me aside for your music."

"Scarlett." Her name came out in a strangled groan as he raked his hands through his hair. How could he explain everything behind that heartbreaking decision without betraying her parents? "I didn't throw you aside. It involved more than just me."

"How?" Her lips pressed into a firm line, and her forehead creased.

He massaged the back of his neck with his hand. For better or for worse, they could have no more secrets between them. He sighed. "The week before I broke up with you, our parents— yours and mine—sat me down and asked me to end our relationship."

She stared at him, disbelief written all over her face.

"Your dad thought it would be easier for you to accept the

upcoming move if you didn't have any ties to me." He struggled to maintain eye contact so she could read the truth in his eyes. "My parents wanted me to be free to pursue my music since the band had garnered some local interest. Everything in me rebelled against it, but they were right. We both had dreams to chase. Some people from Nashville had shown interest in the band, and by the first of December, I was moving to Nashville with my first record contract."

"My dream was you, Jake." She held his gaze. "That's all I ever wanted."

"What about college? Becoming a nurse?"

She huffed with exasperation. "You see how well that worked out."

"Do you still want to be one? My offer from before stands. I'll pay for your schooling."

"That dream died when Harmony was born. I don't want to work long shifts or overnight, and a nursing career would require both."

"Okay, if not that, what's your dream? What would you become if nothing held you back?"

"I don't know." Her gaze darted to something near the floor behind him. "I've been so focused on Harmony's future that I haven't given much thought to mine." She returned to the dresser and took out a stack of folded shirts.

Jake's leaden heart sunk lower in his chest. Had she really stopped dreaming for herself? Because of his rejection? Could he light that spark in her again?

He turned to leave and glanced at the boots sitting on the floor next to the door. The ones Scarlett had looked at when talking about her dreams.

If he could find a way, he would do everything in his power to give her a life beyond her imagination.

Twenty-Eight

S carlett sat through the sermon the Sunday morning after she and Harmony had moved back in with Cassidy without hearing a word of it. Instead, the questions Jake had asked still looped through her mind. If she had the freedom to do anything with her life, what would it be? Was her identity so wrapped up in Harmony that she didn't have any dreams for herself? What would she do in ten years when her daughter was off living her own life? Wasn't Scarlett a daughter of God? Shouldn't her identity rest there?

And the even harder questions, the ones she didn't want to acknowledge. Including his proposal. She inwardly sighed. She didn't want to think about that right now.

Had she really kept accounts of Jake's wrongdoings? Added them up until the bad outweighed the good?

Cass nudged her as the congregation stood and the pastor gave the benediction. As Scarlett gathered her belongings, her cousin leaned nearer. "You're distracted this morning and have been ever since you moved back. What's on your mind?"

She glanced around the rows of seats in front of and behind them. Everyone was absorbed in their own conversations. "Jake said some things before we left. I don't know who I am anymore. I used to have my entire life planned out. Graduate high school, go to college and become a nurse, get married, start a family, and so on. Then, Harmony came along, and my world became all about taking care of her. And I've lost myself along the way." She wouldn't mention the rest because it made her feel petty and judgmental.

"You can always go to school and become a nurse. I don't know why you haven't done it already."

She shook her head. "I'm not interested in that anymore." She shrugged, stumped as to what *would* interest her instead. "I'm not sure what I *do* want, but I'm not happy waitressing."

Cassidy sat back down on the cushioned chair and gestured for Scarlett to follow suit. "Since you were seven, your happiest moments involved Jake or horses. If Jake's out of the equation..." She raised an eyebrow. "You're left with the horses. What about something at a ranch? You'd love it, and I want nothing more than for you to find joy. I heard a little of the old Scarlett whenever we talked, especially after you'd taken Harmony riding."

"It's a relief to know he never rejected Harmony. And now she has a dad who will take good care of her."

"Don't do that." Cassidy squeezed Scarlett's knee. "This isn't about Harmony. It's about you and Jake. He told the world he loved you, and the next thing I know, you're packing up and moving home. Despite the way it ended, spending time with him was good for you. What happened, Scar? What are you afraid of?"

She stared at her clasped hands to avoid her cousin's too-knowing gaze. "I can't love Jake again." But deep down, she already did. "What if he chooses something else over me?" Although, from what he'd said Thursday, that wasn't entirely his decision, and she wasn't giving him the benefit of the doubt. She didn't like the direction of those thoughts, so she stood instead. "I need to get Harmony from Sunday school before she thinks I left without her."

"You need to forgive Jake. For everything. Stop holding his mistakes against him and believe he wants the best for you."

Scarlett winced. That was twice in the past few days someone had called her on her sin.

"I'm praying for you." Cassidy gathered her Bible, notebook, and keys. "God has big plans for your life—with or without Jake Turnquist." She gave her a brief hug. "I love you."

"You too, Cass." She returned the hug. "I would have lost my sanity long ago if not for you."

After lunch, Scarlett sent Harmony outside to play with Max. Once satisfied she'd be entertained a while, Scarlett sat on the couch and scrolled through her contacts until she found the right one and hit the call button.

"Hello?"

She braced herself for whatever Jake's dad might say to her. "Alan? This is Scarlett. Sykes. Is Shelly available?"

"Sure, Scarlett." A few seconds of silence passed. "Before I get her, I need to apologize. I reacted poorly during our visit."

He'd been quiet over the long weekend they had visited Jake, but Scarlett had also stayed on the outskirts, allowing them time to get to know Harmony.

"It's okay. I kept you from your granddaughter."

"Maybe, but Jake explained the situation. You were young and scared about your future. I can't blame you for taking the money and signing those papers. Besides, your parents also shoulder some of the responsibility." He sighed as a rustling sounded in the background. "They could have at least told us you had a child. I thought we were friends."

"You were. However, they cut ties with you for my benefit when they saw how hard I took the breakup. Then, months later when those papers came, it was like being rejected a second time, but worse because there was an innocent person involved." Her parents had begged her to tell the Turnquists, but she'd wanted to distance herself from anything relating to Jake. "I guess Mom and Dad continued to protect me by cutting all traces of him out of our lives... especially after I signed that NDA."

He sniffed, and his voice had a nasal quality when he spoke again. "Scarlett, you are such a strong young lady. I'm grateful you chose to raise Harmony as a single mother instead of giving her up for adoption. You and that little girl are in our prayers, and if you ever need anything, don't hesitate to call us."

Now she fought tears. "I won't. Thank you."

"You're welcome. Here's Shelly."

"Scarlett?" Jake's mom's concern carried across the miles. "Is something wrong?"

"Not really." Not physically, anyway. She pulled herself together. "Can I ask you a question?"

"Of course, dear."

With no easy way to ask, she took a deep breath and plunged ahead. "Did you and my parents ask Jake to break up with me before my family moved away?"

Shelly sighed, and Scarlett imagined her sinking onto a chair at her kitchen table.

"You have to understand, Scarlett. You were both so young. We worried you'd regret not following your dreams and grow resentful of each other. When your mom and dad decided to move to Georgia, we sat Jake down and explained our concerns. His band had some interest from people in Nashville, but he was going to turn them down and ask you to marry him."

He had planned to turn down all Nashville had to offer... for her? Would she have let him? Scarlett's mouth opened and closed and opened again without any sound escaping.

"We shouldn't have interfered," Shelly continued. "Your mom and I talked every few days between the breakup and when Jake moved away. We saw how miserable you were without each other. We should have let the two of you decide if you wanted a long-distance relationship."

"Why didn't she tell me any of this?"

"I wish I had an answer. With the chaos of moving Jake and

the others to Nashville, time flew by before I realized we'd lost touch. I assumed you all were settling into your new lives, too." She paused. "After hearing your side of the story and how you thought he was ignoring your attempts to reach out, I assume your mom thought it would be easier just to move forward. More so after you received that NDA."

Easy? Nothing had been easy about her pregnancy or the postpartum depression after she'd given birth. Scarlett had to fight the darkness every day for three months. "It was never easy, Shelly."

"No, I imagine not, and I'm sorry we took those years from you and Jake." She sniffed. "If there was a way to give them back to you, I would."

But it wasn't possible, and now Scarlett didn't know how to move forward with Jake.

"Can I say one more thing?" Shelly asked.

She sank back into the couch cushions and hugged her midsection with her free arm. "Okay."

"I saw the way my son watched you when we were there. But I also noticed you distancing yourself. He loves you." A smile sounded in her voice. "That boy was smitten the day you rode that horse through my garden. Please don't let what we did in the past affect your relationship with Jake now."

Scarlett gulped as hope rose in her throat. "I don't know if I can—"

"Don't let your past steal your future or keep you from love. Yes, it's hard. And terrifying. And a lot of work. There are days I'd rather kick Alan out of the house than listen to him one more second, but at the end of the day, there's nothing as wonderful as the man you love telling you he loves you back. Give Jake a chance to prove himself, and his love, to you."

"I'll pray about it." Which she'd done too many times to count since she left Jake's, but it was all she could commit to for the time being.

"As will we. Thank you for calling. It feels good to get that out in the open."

But she now had more to work through. After promising to keep in touch, she ended the call. She stood and checked on Harmony once more before heading to her room where she locked the door and fell on her knees before the Throne.

Twenty-Nine

"Hey, Tom." Sunday afternoon, Jake approached the old wrangler as he brushed down a dappled gray mare near the open barn door.

The man looked up from his chore. "Weren't you just here?" He glanced behind Jake. "And why didn't you bring that cute little girl back with you?"

Jake swallowed. He would have loved to bring Harmony back again. She had taken to the horses just like her mom had at that age, and he could use a shot of her pure enthusiasm today. "Wanted to come see the new residents you mentioned would arrive this weekend." And he couldn't stand his silent house another minute. He hadn't realized how much life Scarlett and Harmony brought to it until they were gone.

"You lookin' to buy or just gawk?" Tom set aside the brush and took the quarter horse's lead with a chuckle. "Either way, you're welcome to come on in. Got four beauties."

Jake followed the older man into the barn and walked to Athena's stall to greet her while Tom settled the mare in a stall. He glanced around at the other occupants. "You're going to have to build another barn if you keep taking in animals."

"Nah, these will sell quick." His eyes crinkled at Jake.

"Besides, I'd quit boarding horses for spoiled musicians before I stop buying animals."

Jake chuckled. "If it comes to that, I'll build you that extra barn myself."

Athena nudged his chest as though agreeing with the plan.

"I'll hold you to it, Jake Turnquist." When his cackling died down, he strode to Jake. "Say, do you know if that pretty lady friend of yours with the little girl might be interested in a job?"

"What kind of job?" Was a job cleaning stalls any step up from waitressing? Would it even pay enough to support them? If only she'd let him help. He frowned. Oh, why had he begun a marriage proposal talking about money? Yes, he would share everything he had with her, but he loved Scarlett and that's what mattered most.

"Not whatever you're thinking, judging by that scowl on your face." Tom stopped in front of an empty stall and rested a boot on the bottom edge of the gated door. "I'm busy enough keeping up with all of them and having help with the exercising would be nice. Plus I'm considering offering trail rides and lessons but would need to get help for that, too. Your friend rides like she was born in a saddle." He shrugged. "It's probably too much to hope for, but I thought I'd ask."

Ride whenever she wanted? Teach people? Scarlett would be in heaven. A smile grew on his face, then faded.

Without him. The fact burned, but envy had no place here. She deserved as much happiness as she could hold and then some, but man, did he want a slice of that.

"She might be interested. I'll ask her. Could she bring her daughter sometimes?"

"I don't see why not. I'll even give her a deal on some horses if she wants her own. From what I saw the other day when you took her out, the girl seems to take to the animals like her mom. I might even hire her in a few more years." He straightened. "The new stock you're looking for is through the barn and out the back doors."

Jake scratched his Palomino's nose before he followed the man, pondering how to convince Scarlett to accept the job. Not only would she love it, she and Harmony would be close to his house almost daily. He stepped outside into the sunshine and halted when he spied the pure white mare with soft brown eyes watching him.

"Snow."

"Her name is Marshmallow." Tom gave an exaggerated shudder.

Jake bit back a grin as he imagined Scarlett's reaction to that name.

"Snow fits her better." Tom scratched his head. "Someone save us from people letting children name pets."

"Hey, my daughter named her dog Max. That's not bad."

The wrangler stared at Jake. "You have a daughter?"

Oops, that had slipped out. Oh well, everyone who had attended his last show or checked the internet knew about her existence. He cringed at the few photos he'd found of Scarlett when searching his name on social media. None of Harmony had shown up yet. "Yep. You've met her. Harmony?"

Tom's eyes narrowed. "That's Scarlett's daughter's name."

"One and the same." His chest puffed with pride.

"Well, I never..."

Me neither, Tom. Never realized how much I needed a family.

Jake inclined his head toward the thoroughbred. "How much you asking for her?"

"What are you going to do with another horse?" He slapped his dusty hat against his dirty jeans. "You already ignore the two you have."

"I'm working on that. That's another reason I came over today. Didn't want Athena to get jealous after I rode Hercules. But Marshmallow..." His tongue tripped over the name. "...isn't for me."

A slow grin spread on the man's face, creasing the lines near his eyes. "You plan to buy her for Scarlett, don't you? I knew there was more going on between you two."

"As much as I'd like that to be true, she's not ready for that. But yes, the horse is for her. When she was a girl, she had a mare who looked almost exactly like this one. Her parents had to sell their ranch, and the animals were included. I'd like to give a piece of her childhood back."

"Aw, if that's not the sweetest thing I've ever heard." The voice held more sugar than the jam Harmony had slathered on her toast. And it didn't belong to Tom.

Jake spun around to find Tom's wife swiping at her eyes with a watery smile.

"I knew there was someone special in your life from your songs, Jake Turnquist, but this is so much better than your music."

Mary Beth could be a busybody, so he may as well set her straight from the get-go. "Until she showed back up in my life, I'd almost forgotten how much I loved her." He took two steps to Mary Beth's side and rested his arm across her shoulders. "What do you think? Can I win her back? Prove my love after all these years?"

"If anyone can do it, you can." She patted his hand. "And if you need anything, you just let me know."

"Mary Beth, you stay out of it." Tom gave her the side-eye. "If it's meant to be, God will make it happen without your meddlin'."

God, it's okay with me if You want to use Mary Beth's meddling to help my cause.

He removed his arm from around the woman and turned back to Tom. "Let's get down to business."

Once the details were worked out and Jake was on the trail soaking in the afternoon sun, he began to formulate a plan to bring Scarlett back.

∾

Scarlett needed this Sunday evening girls' night to pull her off the merry-go-round of Jake memories. The microwave beeped, and she pulled the popcorn bag from the appliance. She opened the bag, poured it into a large bowl, and added some candy-coated chocolate.

"The nail salon is open whenever you're ready." Cassidy walked into the kitchen with an empty glass in her hand.

Scarlett's phone rang, and she wiped her hands on the dish-towel beside the sink before glancing at the screen and picking it up from the counter. Her heartbeat sped up as she showed Cassidy the screen.

"Answer it." She set her glass down and nudged her side. "Harmony and I will work on our manicures while you talk." She strode to the living room and asked the girl what color she wanted.

"Hi, Jake. What's up?" Scarlett kept her voice light, half hoping he'd ask her to come back while steeling herself to decline. Even though she was closer to her decision, he was leaving in six days.

"What's your schedule like this week? Can you bring Harmony over to go riding one afternoon before I head out on the tour? I didn't want to ask her without clearing it with you first."

"I appreciate that." A twinge of disappointment pinched her gut when he didn't ask about her. She forced a smile into her voice. "I can bring her on Wednesday. Or Cass could probably drop her off another day if that doesn't work."

"Yep." Cassidy's answer from the other room confirmed she had an ear on the conversation.

Scarlett chuckled. She had to love the woman even when she meddled.

"Wednesday's great. Why don't you come, too?"

Was this more than an afternoon excursion? Another proposal? Something else? She held back a sigh. Why did she read ulterior motives into Jake's invitation, and why did she wish them to be true?

She opened the fridge and took out a pitcher of water. "Sounds like fun. I'll plan on it."

"Great. Plan on me taking you both to dinner afterward, too."

She opened a cupboard for the glasses but paused at the hope in his voice. "Jake—"

"It's the least I can do, Scar. You've fed me more times than I can count while you were here. Let me return the favor. Besides, I miss my daughter."

Guilt pricked at her for taking Harmony away again. "Okay, we can do dinner." She set three glasses on a tray.

"Speaking of riding." He blew out a breath. "I took Athena out today, and Tom asked if you'd be interested in working for him. He's looking to hire someone to exercise the horses and maybe give lessons."

Her breath caught in her throat. A job with horses? Almost like Cass had suggested just this morning? Was this an answer to her prayer for finding a new dream?

"Anyway, think about it. It sounded like something you'll enjoy. You can discuss salary and hours with him when you come out on Wednesday." Jake paused. "Speaking of payment, I have a check for your time last week. I was going to mail it, but since you're coming this way, I'll give it to you then."

"That's fine." Scarlett worked to keep the tremor out of her voice and her hands steady as she poured water into the glasses.

He'd gone from a potential date to business in the space of a few sentences.

"Is Harmony around? I'd like to talk to her."

"Sure. Cass is doing her nails, so I might have to put you on speaker." With her jumbled thoughts, she went to the living room. "Jake's on the phone."

Harmony looked from her half-painted fingers to the phone and back.

Scarlett stifled a smile at her obvious internal debate. She touched the phone screen and switched the call to speaker before setting it down on the coffee table next to her daughter's arm.

The girl leaned her head and shoulders toward it. "Hi, Dad."

"Hi, Harmony. How was your day?"

"It was good. We went to church, then came home for lunch. I played with Max, and now Mom made popcorn with candy in it."

At the reminder, Scarlett detoured to the kitchen, added the bowl of sweet and salty popcorn to the tray with the water glasses, and carried it all to the living room.

"We're going to watch a princess movie." Harmony's eyes shone as she talked to her dad.

"Sounds like a fun night." Jake's patience with the chattering girl warmed her heart.

Scarlett set the tray at the end of the coffee table and sank to the floor beside Cass. She lowered her voice so she didn't disrupt the conversation between Harmony and her dad. "I was offered a job."

"When? From whom? Doing what?" Her cousin didn't temper her voice, and the conversation over the phone halted. "Oops. Ignore me." She laughed and returned her attention to coating Harmony's fingernails with hot pink polish.

"I don't have many details yet other than it's with Jake's neighbor exercising horses and giving riding lessons." Scarlett kept her volume at a whisper. "But I want to do this."

"Of course you do. It's perfect for you. See, God answered our prayers already."

"It doesn't usually happen that fast." Jake's voice caught her attention, and she looked at her giggling daughter. Scarlett pressed her palm against her heart. Would He answer her prayers for Jake and a family, too?

"Not always." Cass bumped shoulders with Scarlett. "But this time it did. Just accept it and enjoy."

Thirty

❦

J ake cinched Marshmallow's saddle and rechecked the time. Scarlett and Harmony should be there any minute, and he had yet to figure out how best to tell Scarlett he'd bought her this gift. An expensive one she would surely object to. He pinned his hopes on her falling so in love with the horse, she couldn't turn the gift down.

The crunch of tires on gravel reached his ears, and he led Marshmallow outside to the corral where Hercules and Harmony's pony were already tacked and grazing as they awaited their riders. Scarlett's old car came down the drive. If she'd let him, he'd buy her a new vehicle, too, but instinct told him to avoid that conversation.

At least for now.

Harmony hopped out of the car and raced toward him. "Dad!"

The white horse shied away from the bundle of energy and jerked his arm. Jake murmured to the mare and stroked her neck.

"Harmony, we've talked about this." Scarlett's loving reprimand soothed the underlying frustration in her tone. "You have to be quiet, so you don't scare the horses."

He could learn something from how she handled difficult

situations. Jake looped the thoroughbred's lead around a post and glanced at his girls.

His daughter's pace slowed. "Sorry, Mom." As soon as the girl reached him, she threw her arms around his waist. "I missed you."

Jake squeezed her shoulder. "I missed you, too, kiddo."

The pony sauntered over to the fence, and Harmony went over to pet her.

Jake's pulse tripled as Scarlett approached with her ponytail swinging behind her. She looked amazing in her well-fitting jeans and boots. "Thanks for coming today." He pulled a folded envelope with her check tucked inside from his back pocket. "Before I forget, this is for you."

"Thank you." She shoved it into her jeans pocket before her gaze shifted to the mare. The first genuine smile of the afternoon curved her quivering lips. She avoided his gaze as a slight pink hue filled her cheeks. "Oh, Jake, she's gorgeous. What's her name?"

"Uh." He did not want to ruin this moment

She rolled her eyes. "Oh, come on, it can't be that bad."

Yes, it could. "Marshmallow."

Scarlett eased in front of the horse and looked in her velvet brown eyes. "You poor thing. We can do better than fluffed air, can't we? How about I call you Stardust? Maybe your new owner will give you a name worthy of your beauty."

The horse nickered as if giving her agreement, but Jake couldn't take his eyes off Scarlett. If only she'd look at him the way she did the horse.

Jake cleared his throat, not quite ready to reveal his surprise. "Tom already has a buyer."

"Oh, that's good." Her tone didn't carry an ounce of excitement. She glanced at Harmony still engaged with the pony, then around the corral. "Where is Tom this afternoon?"

"He went to town but said he'll be back before we're finished. He said you called him?"

"I did." She glanced at him. "I wanted a few more details before I accepted the job."

Jake handed Scarlett the thoroughbred's reins and walked to his left to help Harmony over the fence. "And have you? Accepted?" He managed to keep his voice neutral as he looked back at her.

"Not yet. Been praying about it and talking to Cassidy." She inclined her head toward the girl but failed to hide the sparkle in her eyes. Obviously, this wasn't a conversation she wanted to have in front of their daughter.

"I've got more good news for you. You get to ride Stardust today." He winked.

"Really?" She beamed a smile at him, and all doubts about buying the horse fled as she climbed over the rails to get inside the corral.

He helped Harmony climb into the pony's saddle as Scarlett mounted the mare next to them. Once they were both settled, he clucked his tongue to call Hercules over and followed suit.

"Great. For now, let's enjoy this beautiful day." He reined his animal to one side of Harmony and Scarlett took up the other.

"When do you leave, Dad?"

"Early Saturday morning." Just a few more days. Jake vacillated between wanting to get this tour over and done with and spending the time with his girls. "Maybe you could stay with me a night before I leave?" He glanced at Scarlett.

"Can I, Mom?" The girl twisted the other way.

"Sure." She looked at him over Harmony's head. "I packed an overnight bag for her if tonight works. I know you're running out of time."

He swallowed. She'd thought of his schedule and came prepared. "Tonight's perfect. I'll bring her back to your place around lunch time tomorrow."

"Are you sure?"

He watched the breeze tousle the wisps of hair that had escaped her ponytail. His fingers itched to smooth them from her cheeks. "Positive."

"How long will you be gone?" Awkward silences didn't have a prayer of hanging around with Harmony.

"Until right before Thanksgiving." Four long months. A hollowness opened in his chest. "I'll call you every night."

"*Not* after your shows." Scarlett raised an eyebrow his way, then faced forward.

"No, that's after her bedtime. I'll call before. How's that?" He winked at Harmony.

"Great." Harmony pumped her fist before returning it to the reins. "You can tell me what city you're in. We never go anywhere."

He glanced at the girl. "I *could* fly you out to a show."

"Yeah!"

"Absolutely not." Scarlett's head whipped toward him. "She's not flying anywhere alone."

He reached down for the pony's reins, then pulled her and Hercules to a stop. "I'd fly both of you out, Scarlett. I didn't think Harmony would come by herself."

"Oh." She halted the mare as she blushed and glanced away. "We can talk about it later."

He nudged Harmony with his leg. "Want to race to that tree?" He pointed a short distance in front of them.

Harmony grinned. "Okay." She leaned forward in her saddle. "Ready. Set. Go!"

Jake watched her take off, her hair flying behind her, then followed close behind. If only he could outrun his propensity to aggravate the woman he loved.

~

Scarlett reined the beautiful horse to a stop inside the corral as Jake closed the gate behind them. Stardust was a much more appropriate name for the regal animal, and she hoped whoever her new owner was appreciated her.

"Good afternoon, ladies. Jake." Tom walked out of the barn

and tipped his hat as he smiled her way. "You available to talk for a few minutes, Scarlett?"

She dismounted and looped the mare's reins over the horn of the saddle before glancing up at Jake.

"Go ahead." He patted Hercules's neck and swung his leg over the back. Once his feet hit the ground, he held out his free hand for Harmony to hold onto as she climbed down from the pony. "We can take care of these three."

"Thanks." She followed Tom inside the farmhouse.

A woman with gray curls stood in the kitchen. "You must be Scarlett. Tom's hoping you'll come work for us. How do you like your new horse?"

"Mary Beth." Tom shook his head and glanced over his shoulder at her. "Forgive my wife, Scarlett. She doesn't know when to butt out."

"It's a pleasure to meet you." What new horse?

Tom led her to a small office and cleared off a chair. Over the next thirty minutes, she and her new boss came to an agreement about her pay, hours, and responsibilities.

They shook hands, and Tom rose with a grin on his wrinkled face. "I hope you ease that poor horse's humiliation with a new name."

"What horse?" Scarlett was more confused than ever.

"The one you were riding." He jutted his chin in the general direction of the barn. "Jake bought her."

Jake? Her heart warmed. He'd done it for her, but why not just tell her *he* was the buyer?

She said a quick goodbye to Mary Beth, who promised cookies when she came to work, and left the house. As she strode toward the barn, she caught sight of Jake and Harmony sitting on the tailgate of the truck. The girl's legs swung in the air beneath her as she took a swig from a water bottle. The sight of them side by side brought a smile to her face.

Jake glanced up, and she tilted her head toward the front of the truck. "Can I talk to you for a minute?"

"Sure." He tugged Harmony's braid. "Stay out of trouble."

The girl leaned away from him and hopped down. "Okay."

"You can go watch the horses." Scarlett waved toward the nearest corral where a blue roan and brown and white paint dozed in the shade of the barn. "But stay outside the fence."

Once certain Harmony was occupied, Scarlett turned on Jake. "Why didn't you tell me you bought Marshmallow?"

"Tom has a big mouth." He grumbled under his breath before meeting her gaze. "When I saw the horse on Sunday, she reminded me of—"

"Snow."

"Yeah." He stared deep into her eyes. "And I didn't want anyone but you to have her."

"Jake, it's too much." Her chest was about to explode with happiness. She wouldn't have to say goodbye to that beautiful animal like she did Snow. "I'll pay you back."

"Scarlett." His husky tone warmed her insides as much as the sun had her skin an hour ago. "The horse is a gift. Please don't insult me by refusing her."

He ran a hand down her arm and goose bumps followed in its wake as she read the truth in his eyes. He loved her and would stand by her.

Swallowing around the lump in her throat, she nodded, certain every feeling she had for him reflected on her face. "Thank you. She's beautiful."

He stepped close and dipped his head. "You're welcome." His lips met hers, and his hand tangled in the back of her hair.

She clung to his shirt, holding on as his kiss swept her away. When he eased back, she clutched her fists tighter and stood on her tiptoes for more. This time, she didn't push him away. This time, she held on with both hands and her whole heart.

He smiled against her mouth. "So, you like me a little?"

"Maybe." She finally backed away, allowing her senses to clear of Jake.

"Do you think you could get someone to watch Harmony Friday night? I want to take you on a proper date before I leave."

"I have to work, and you're leaving early the next day. Don't you want to get one last full night's sleep?"

"I've had more than a month of those." He pointed at his right shoulder. "I'd rather spend the time with you."

Her stomach fluttered at his earnestness. "I'll find someone to cover for me at work." She already knew of someone asking to trade shifts.

"Excellent. You're all mine Friday night. Wear something nice." He entwined his fingers with hers. "Did Tom answer your questions about the job?"

"He did." Effervescent excitement and anticipation bubbled inside her. "I'll start in two weeks." She'd give her notice to Rachel tomorrow.

"That's fantastic." Jake lifted her off her feet and spun her in a circle. "You're welcome to use my house anytime you'd like while I'm gone Actually, you could stay there instead of driving back and forth."

"I don't know, Jake." The hubbub about 'Midnight Blue's' inspiration had already died down but might start up again if she moved into his house while he was away.

"It's on the table. No pressure, just an offer." He smiled his lazy, lopsided grin. "And you already have a key."

Her cheeks heated. She'd forgotten to return it, but based on his twinkling eyes—which held the same boyish gleam he'd always teased her with—he would refuse taking it back now. Best move on from the subject.

"We've left Harmony alone long enough. Let's go see what kind of trouble she's gotten herself into."

Thirty-One

F riday evening, Jake parked in front of Scarlett's house, more nervous than he'd been the night of their homecoming dance. Tonight needed to be perfect. A pleasant memory for Scarlett to hold close while he was on the road for the last time.

Okay, Lord, I'm going to need Your help tonight. Let me honor Scarlett and treasure her like You do. Bless our time together, and please, keep the fans away.

Before he got out of the truck, she came out the door wearing a black lace dress. She'd curled her hair and put on a little makeup.

Jake hopped out of his seat and rushed to open the passenger door. "You are beautiful." In jeans or a dress, morning or night, makeup or not, she was always gorgeous to him.

She smiled, and he lost himself in her midnight blue eyes.

When he settled behind the steering wheel again, he glanced over. "Thanks for coming tonight."

"My pleasure. Where are we going?" She rubbed her thumb along the back of her opposite hand like she used to do in high school to calm her nerves before a presentation.

"Patience, Scarlett." He reached over, took her hand, and brought it to the arm rest between them. "It's a surprise."

"Oh, you mean like that time we tried sushi and ended up at the burger joint?" She giggled.

He shook his head. "I thought I was so grown up, driving my dad's truck and taking a pretty girl to the fanciest place in town."

"You used to ask what I wanted to do. What I wanted to eat. Where I wanted to go. I was impressed when you made all of the plans without asking my opinion about a single detail." It was a side of Jake she hadn't seen. Some of his surprises were good ones. "And then, when you pulled up to the restaurant, I was floored."

He made a face. "I still can't stand the stuff. Why did I ever think raw fish would impress you?"

"Because you were sweet and knew I wanted to try it." She squeezed his hand. "That was a good night."

Despite their disgust with their first bites of sushi, their first date had been magical. He glanced at her as she turned to smile at him.

"Are we headed to the drive-thru?" The girl from high school was back.

His shoulders relaxed, and his nerves settled as he pulled up to the valet stand in front of a trendy restaurant in downtown Nashville.

Scarlett looked at him with wide eyes. "Here? I've always wanted to try this place."

"Here." He got out of the truck and walked around to the other side, offered his elbow, and leaned down. "Cassidy hinted this place would impress you."

"You called her?" Her gaze lifted to his face.

"Uh..." He nodded at the man who held the door open for them.

She burst out laughing. "She called you, didn't she? Did you get a lecture, too?"

His eyebrows pinched together. "No, she just said you'd mentioned this place a few times and if I could get a reservation, it would make your night even better."

"Oh." Her cheeks grew pinker, and he resisted rubbing his thumb across one as she looked away.

"What kind of lecture?" Her embarrassment made him more curious.

"Never mind." She stepped up to the hostess stand.

Jake lowered his voice. "I have reservations for two for Jake—"

"Turnquist." The young brunette grinned. "We had a wager going on whether it was really you or someone trying to pull a fast one."

Scarlett squeezed his elbow and leaned forward. "I hope you won."

"I did." The co-ed's eyes widened before she grabbed two menus.

Had she recognized Scarlett from the media this past week?

"Right this way." She gave them a polite smile, then led them to a table in the back corner, just as he had requested. "Luke will be with you shortly."

"Thank you." Jake breathed a sigh of relief as he held a chair out for Scarlett.

Scarlett glanced around the dining room. "I guess being famous has its perks."

"It does, but I only flaunt my celebrity status for special occasions." He sat across from her and winked. "And this qualifies. Now, what were we talking about?" He held his chin between his fingers as though pondering a deep question, then snapped his fingers. "I remember. What lecture was Cassidy supposed to give me?"

Scarlett blushed some more and ducked behind her menu. "The one that goes something like 'you hurt her, I'll hurt you.'"

When the waiter walked away with their drink orders, Jake reached across the table and tugged her menu down a smidge. "You know Cass isn't the only one who has said those words to me right?"

"So she did give you the lecture?" She raised one eyebrow in challenge.

"Not when she called, but yes, she's warned me." He maintained eye contact. "As have Levi, my parents, and Mia. You've got people in your corner, Scarlett. You are loved."

Her eyes glistened, and she swiped a finger beneath one.

Time to lighten things up again. "Tell me more about your new job." He'd gone riding this morning and wasn't sure who was more excited about the hire, Tom or his matchmaking wife. "Tom's thrilled to have you onboard."

Her face lit up. "I can't wait to get started. He's letting me plan all of the lessons and rides. Plus, he said Harmony's welcome to come with me whenever she'd like. It's the next best thing to living on the farm again."

"My offer to use the house still stands." He would rest easier on the road if he knew she was tucked away at his place. "It would save you some driving time and gas money."

She set her menu on the table and laid her hand over the top of it. "Except Harmony is starting school around then, and that's in Fairview."

If he had his way, their daughter would have to find a new school and friends in Franklin. "Either way, I'm glad it worked out with Tom. You deserve a job that makes you happy."

Her blue eyes sparkled in the candlelight as she smiled at him. "Thanks for passing the message along."

"My pleasure." He laid his hand over hers. "No matter what happens between us, I wish you nothing but joy." But he'd give anything for it to include him.

She blinked back tears as their server returned.

They talked and laughed throughout dinner, sharing memories from when they were kids and swapping funny stories about the band and some of her customers. They were comparing favorite movies when the waiter gathered their empty plates.

Jake caught the man's eye. "Could we look at the dessert menu?"

Scarlett puffed out her cheeks. "I can't eat another bite."

"We'll share something. You can't pass up dessert here." He was full, too, but didn't want the night to end.

"You choose whatever you want." She took a sip of her water.

All he wanted was sitting across from him, but he was leaving in the morning and couldn't rush her. He skimmed the list of desserts and grinned.

Their server returned. "Did you make a decision?"

"We'll share a strawberry shortcake."

She grinned. "I might find room after all."

He held her gaze. "You'd be surprised how much I remember about you."

She rested her chin on her hand and studied him. "Are you ready for the tour?"

He glanced around the room to ensure no one was paying attention to them. "Truth?" How much should he say? Should he lay it all out there?

"Please." She leaned forward. "Even if it hurts."

"Not at all." He ran a hand through his hair. "I've never been a fan of the travel—long hours on the road, sleeping on the bus. But I'm dreading this one more than usual."

"Why?"

He gazed into her eyes. "Because I'm leaving you and Harmony behind, and even though I know this is my last tour, I still wish you could come with me."

"It's not practical, Jake." She looked away, but not before he caught a glimpse of longing in her eyes. "Besides, you'll be so busy, you won't even notice our absence."

"Oh, I'll notice." Like he had for the past week. "I miss you both every minute you're not with me."

She sighed and reached her hand across the table. "We'll miss you, too."

He took it and held on. "What do you think about me flying you out to a show?"

"I don't know. It would have to fit into our schedules. I don't want to ask Tom for time off right away, and Harmony shouldn't miss any days at the start of the school year. Maybe if you're within driving distance on a weekend, we could meet you."

She took her phone from her purse and set it on the table before she began tapping on the screen.

He leaned forward to see what she was doing, and his heart soared to see her pull up the band's website and scroll through the list of tour dates with her free hand.

He already had an idea of what might work. He pointed at the Atlanta show. "Mom and Dad are driving to his one. It's on Saturday of Labor Day weekend. I'm sure you could ride down with them."

She nodded. "That might work."

Going six weeks without her would be a challenge, but it was better than four months. He'd put his trust in God's ability to work everything out. "Think about it."

She leaned back in her seat as the waiter set their dessert in front of her. Jake reluctantly released her hand as she picked up the second fork.

After fighting over the last strawberry on the plate, he escorted her from the restaurant. Once parked in her driveway, he grasped her hand before she scooted from the truck. "I had a great time tonight."

"So did I." She leaned in, and her lips brushed his cheek with a feather-light touch. "Thank you."

He tugged her closer and gave her a proper kiss, one that left them both breathless. "I love you, Scarlett Sykes."

She stared into his eyes and opened her mouth. She swallowed hard before slipping out of his truck and into her house without another word.

It wasn't the response he'd hoped for, but while the tour was an obstacle, Jake had never been a quitter.

Thirty-Two

They passed another sign for Atlanta, and the butterflies in Scarlett's stomach beat their wings. She was grateful Alan was driving because she couldn't deal with the Saturday afternoon holiday traffic on top of her excitement.

In a few short hours, she'd see Jake. Could she follow through with her plan? She rubbed her stomach and glanced at Harmony as she giggled with Olivia, who Jake had insisted come along.

Over the past six weeks, he'd called every day to tell their daughter about the current city or a funny story from the band on the bus. And every time, Harmony would then hand her the phone before running off to play with Max. They'd talked for hours over the past weeks. About how thrilled the band was with their new manager. And how Levi and Andi were adjusting to the dynamic of working with the man while Jake counted down the days to his retirement. He asked about her riding students and the fall trail rides. She told him about Harmony's successes and mishaps training Max and how the girl's friends at school treated her.

No matter how long their conversations, Jake said he loved her at the end of every phone call.

Oh, how she struggled not to say it back.

She bit her lip and peered out the window. She'd admitted it to herself the day he'd given her Stardust but had been too nervous to say it the night of their date.

And now all she wanted was to look into his eyes so he could see her sincerity when she said those three precious words that were as honest now as they were ten years ago.

She rubbed her thumb over the back of her hand.

"Mom, are you nervous?" Harmony's loud question reverberated around the now-silent car.

Shelly twisted from the front seat and smiled at Scarlett before turning her attention to the girls. "It's been a while since we've all seen Jake so we're looking forward to spending some time with him. In fact, he's leaving passes for all of us to go backstage before *and* after the show."

"Cool!" Harmony and Olivia picked up their chatter about what songs they wanted to hear tonight.

Scarlett mouthed a *thank you* to Shelly, whose knowing grin grew wider before she resumed her role as navigator.

In addition to the concert tickets and backstage passes, Jake had reserved rooms for everyone at the same hotel where the band was staying. Even better, since they didn't have another show until Tuesday, the band planned to spend a couple days in Atlanta before driving to their next stop, which meant they had all day tomorrow and Monday morning to explore the city together.

The sooner she could declare her love, the sooner she could enjoy the time making memories with her family.

Thirty minutes later, Scarlett swiped her keycard and opened the door to the suite she and the girls would share. On a console table just inside sat a vase with a dozen red roses, and nestled within them was an envelope with her name scrawled on the front in familiar handwriting.

She rested her palm over her heart. Oh, how she loved this man. With trembling fingers, she lifted the envelope and pulled out the card.

Welcome to Atlanta. Can't wait to see you. I love you, Jake.

She smiled as joy welled in her.

"Mom, come see what Dad left us." Harmony raced over, caught her hand, and dragged her across the common area to one of the bedrooms.

Every single Jake Turnquist item a person could possibly purchase was spread across the bed. He'd even signed some posters and a couple T-shirts for the girls.

"I'm going to wear this one." Olivia squealed as she held up a gray shirt with Jake's face plastered across the front.

Scarlett couldn't wait to see the real thing and watch his gray eyes light up as he smiled at her.

Harmony skipped to the other side of the queen-size bed and chose a light blue shirt with a pair of blue eyes screen printed on it. "This is my favorite."

Hers too.

Friends had sent her links to clips of Jake singing the revised lyrics of 'Midnight Blue' on this tour, and she felt closer to him whenever she watched the videos.

"You girls go ahead and get changed. We need to meet Shelly and Alan in thirty minutes for dinner." Scarlett crossed the suite to the other bedroom wondering which of her three outfits she should wear. A large package with a navy ribbon tied around it sat on the bed.

"Jake, what did you do now?" She smiled and did a little happy dance, then plucked the card out from under the bow and read the handwritten note.

Scarlett,

I've missed you more than I thought possible, and everything reminds me of you. I picked this up in Charleston because the color matches your eyes perfectly. I'd be honored if you'd wear it tonight. I love you with all my heart.

Forever yours,

Jake

It was too much. Her heart swelled. Why had she ever doubted?

She tossed the card aside, untied the ribbon, and lifted the lid. She gasped. A gorgeous blue dress with ruffles at the sleeves rested inside. Did she have time to run to the store and buy shoes to go with it? Could she get away with her flip-flops until then?

Someone knocked at the outer door, and Harmony yelled across the suite she'd get it. Scarlett moved to the doorway of her room to confirm all was well.

"Hi, Mimi. Dad got me and Olivia so much cool stuff. You have to come see it."

Shelly smiled down at her. "Oh, I will in a minute, but let me talk to your mom first."

"Okay." With that, Harmony darted back to her room as Scarlett entered the common room.

"Quite the energy in that one." Shelly's indulgent smile showed how much she loved having the girl around. "Serves Jake right for all the trouble he caused at that age."

Scarlett laughed. "He was a good kid, and you know it."

"I do, and I'm proud of the man he's become." She handed Scarlett a large gift bag with a grin. "He asked me to make sure you got this before we go to dinner."

"Another gift?" Scarlett already felt guilty about the lavish weekend.

As if reading her mind, Shelly lifted Scarlett's chin with a finger. "He can afford it. Let him spoil you for once."

How could she argue with that? She peeked in the bag where a brand-new pair of silver sandals greeted her. She pulled them out of the bag to show Jake's mom. "Oh, these will go perfectly with the dress he just gave me."

She whistled. "Looks like you might have big plans after the show, and I'm volunteering right now to babysit." With a grin, she waved her fingers in a shooing motion. "What are you waiting for? Go get ready while I check out the girls' loot."

"Thanks." Scarlett hurried to her room, anxious to see the finished product. Everything was a perfect fit, but when she glanced in the mirror, her hair was a mess, and a little makeup wouldn't hurt, either. She scurried into the attached bathroom.

Tonight, she would knock Jake's boots off.

~

J ake paced the floor of the green room. Had Scarlett gotten his gifts? Did she like them? Would she wear the dress? He hadn't been this nervous before a show in years.

"Did you hear me?"

Jake snatched the phone Andi waved in front of his face from her fingers.

She grabbed it back before he could read the screen. "Noah just texted the news. 'Promises' hit the top five on the charts."

She and their new manager had been working nonstop to make a smooth transition for the band when Jake announced his retirement before Thanksgiving.

"Congratulations." He couldn't wait to tell Scarlett about the success of Andi's first single from the upcoming album. Every step closer he came to November fanned the flame burning in him to focus on his family.

Seth slapped him on the back. "Give him a break, Andi. We all know he's got something—or should I say *someone*—else on his mind tonight."

"Are they coming backstage beforehand?" Mia perched on the arm of the black leather couch. "I can't wait to see Scarlett in that dress."

He couldn't either. *If* she wore it as he requested. Mia had helped him with the size when he'd found it in the shop, then insisted he buy the shoes, too. His mom was tickled when he'd explained his plan for the evening and included her when he asked her to deliver one of Scarlett's gifts.

"I haven't heard anything since Mom called to let me know they checked into the hotel without any issues." But he needed to see Scarlett. He sidestepped Levi, who blocked the path to the door, opened it, and checked the hallway. One of the security guys shook his head, and Jake sighed before returning to his friends.

"Is everything all set for tonight?" Mia raised her eyebrows.

"Yep." He'd swiped a hand through his hair, glad his hat would cover up the mess he'd made of it. With the help of his bandmates and the hotel staff, this would be a night to remember.

If all went as he prayed it would, the best night of his life.

"Where are they, Mimi?" Harmony's voice carried from the hallway, and he couldn't contain his grin.

Finally!

"Go on in," his mom said.

Harmony and her friend bounded into the room, and his little girl launched herself at him. "Dad! Thanks for all the cool stuff."

"You're welcome." When he picked her up, she looped her arms around his neck and squeezed. "How was the drive? Do you like your room?"

Her head bobbed. "It's so cool. Mimi and Gramps are going to have a movie night with us." While she ticked off everything they planned to do, Jake watched the door.

His parents entered arm-in-arm and greeted everyone.

Where was Scarlett?

He glanced at his mom, but she was busy talking with Mia and Levi. Andi kept Dad's attention while Seth signed the other wide-eyed girl's shirt. Was she not coming? Had he offended her with his gifts?

His heart plunged to his toes before he shoved the disappointment into a box and locked it up. He set Harmony down so she could make the rounds.

At least his daughter had come...

A hush descended on the room. Even Harmony stopped talking mid-sentence and held her hands over her mouth, her eyes gleaming. He spun around, and everything else faded away.

Scarlett was so stunning, he had to remind himself to breathe as he closed the distance between them. A few chuckles followed him, but he didn't care.

"Scarlett."

Pink spread across her cheeks, but she maintained eye contact. "Hi, Jake."

He swept her into his arms and poured every missed minute of the last month and a half into his kiss. He wanted to stay here forever. With reluctance, he finally eased away and wrapped a curl around his index finger. "I missed you."

"Me too."

"I love you."

Her eyes sparkled, and she rested her soft palm against his cheek. "I love you, too. Always have. Always will."

Thank You for bringing this woman back into my life, Lord.

Last May, he hadn't understood how much he longed for a second chance with Scarlett. God had not only redeemed their past hurts, He was making a new path—one paved with love and hope—for their future. Now, he just might get forever with his Midnight Blue.

Scarlett tapped her heels against the floor as she sat on one of the wingback chairs in the hotel lobby, waiting as Jake had asked. The show had ended almost an hour ago, and her skin still tingled from the hungry look he had given her before his new manager swept him away to sign autographs at the merchandise table.

She'd left the girls upstairs with pajamas on and tucked into bed with a movie playing on the TV. Mimi and Gramps camped out on the couch in the common room since Harmony and Olivia wouldn't last much longer after the drive and the excitement of the concert.

Jake walked through the sliding glass doors wearing black jeans and a navy button-down shirt and walked straight to Scarlett. Her heart beat double time. Had he purposely changed to match her dress? Either way, he took her breath away.

"You ready?" He held his hand out.

She slipped her palm against his and stood. Before she read his intentions, he twirled her into his arms and rested his forehead against hers. She could stay right here in his embrace and be happy.

He stepped back and laced their fingers together. "Come on. I want to show you something."

He led her to the other side of the building and through the doors to a courtyard.

The evening air cocooned her in its warmth, and landscape lights illuminated the path. Scarlett inhaled the scents of her time in Georgia and Jake's spicy aftershave.

They rounded a bend, and Scarlett gaped at the sight of a pergola wrapped in white twinkle lights and the perimeter lined with luminaries. "Wow." She'd never seen anything so magical. Had Jake done this? She snuck a peek at him.

As if sensing her gaze, he peered down and winked before steering her to one of two chairs centered under the canopy. "For you, my lady."

Despite the humidity blanketing her, goose bumps pebbled Scarlett's arms as she eased onto the seat.

He walked to a guitar, lifted the strap over his head, and walked back. "I wrote a little something for you."

She squinted when he sat across from her. That was his guitar. Who brought it here?

He sat and strummed a chord, erasing the questions circling her head.

"I once loved a girl, but I let her go." His tenor voice sent shivers up her spine. "And my life became nothing more than the status quo. Now, that girl is back in my life. A beautiful woman I hope to make my wife."

She gasped. Was this...was he...?

He winked at her but didn't miss a beat. "Her determination

and grit inspire me to be the man God intended me to be. Thank You, Lord for making a way for me to love this woman every day. I hope to make all her dreams come true and promise to love her like You do."

This was too much. She wanted to slow down time and remember every detail about this night. The love filling Jake's eyes. The earnestness in his voice. The hope filling her heart and soul.

The final note faded, and Jake set the guitar on the ground, then knelt in front of her and took both of her hands in his. "This is something I planned once before, but our lives took separate paths. God answered a prayer I didn't know to pray when He brought you back into my life. Will you marry me, Scarlett? I may not always go about it the right way, but I promise to spend the rest of my life making your dreams come true."

Oh, he certainly had done it right this time.

She blinked several times but failed to stop her tears of joy from falling. "Yes, Jake. I'll marry you."

With a whoop, he stood, and she followed. He swung her in a circle, and when her feet touched the ground again, he pulled a small box from his pocket and lifted the black velvet-lined lid. Inside sat a gold band with a single diamond teardrop.

"It's gorgeous." It fit her personality perfectly. "When did you have time to get it?"

He took the ring out and held it up. "If you want something bigger, I'll buy it for you, but I've had this one since I was seventeen."

She gasped. This was further proof God had granted them a second chance.

"If you've held onto that ring all these years, it's not going anywhere but on my finger." She held her hand out.

He chuckled as he slid the ring onto the place it belonged.

Scarlett splayed her hand over his chest and watched the diamond reflect the light as Jake's solid heartbeat thumped beneath her palm. His warm hands rested at her waist as he gazed into her eyes.

He kissed her for several minutes before they paused. Their breaths mingled as he rested his forehead against hers. "I want to get married after the tour, and I want more children. I want to experience everything this time. Holding my baby in my arms for the first time, hearing him call me daddy, watching him take his first steps."

A son who looked like Jake? Scarlett laughed, the joy bubbling out of her in waves. "As long as you get up in the middle of the night to feed *him*, too."

"You've got yourself a deal." He took her in his arms and sealed their future with another long, lingering kiss.

Acknowledgments

First and foremost, thank you to the One who has and continues to Author my life. Without You, Jesus, I am nothing.

My amazing editor, Candee Fick, was the first to see Jake and Scarlett's potential. Thank you for your diligence and patience in helping me shine and polish this story. I learned so much from you during the process, a few words of gratitude hardly seem enough.

Paige Reed and Lianne Lopes, I am so grateful God brought us together. I couldn't ask for better critique partners. Thank you for checking in on me during edits and joining me in this author life. I can't wait to celebrate your successes with you.

Finally, thank you, reader, for picking up this book. I know there are plenty of options out there and am appreciative and humbled that you chose this one.

About the Author

Suzie Waltner is a lover of fiction and is first and foremost a reader. When she's not at work or reading or writing, you can find her cheering on the Nashville Predators (hockey) or dancing an hour away in Zumba class. Until her second year of college, her life plan was to become a veterinarian. A fainting spell while watching a surgery performed on a sheep changed that plan. Now she works in the corporate world during the day while creating stories in her free time. Suzie resides in a suburb of Nashville, TN and is a member of American Christian Fiction Writers and Faith Hope and Love Christian Writers. She currently serves as the president of the Middle Tennessee ACFW chapter.

Visit her at https://suziewaltner.com

Made in United States
Orlando, FL
27 October 2023

38297138R00167